To Suzanne,
wishing you a JKU!
"read" of this book!

Happy Belated!

Klee!

ANOTHER CHRISTMAS CAROL

JOHN C. DERR

TROTWOOD PRESS

This book is dedicated to people of all ages who find themselves outside of a safe, loving, and permanent family and to the kind people of a generous spirit who welcome them into theirs.

This book is also dedicated to my family – those who have passed, those who are in the present, and those who are yet to come.

10% of the profits from this book will be donated to the Dave Thomas Foundation for Adoption.

The Dave Thomas Foundation for Adoption is the only public nonprofit charity in the United States that is focused exclusively on foster care adoption. Through its signature program, Wendy's Wonderful Kids®, the Foundation provides grants to adoption agencies to hire recruiters who use an evidence-based, child-focused recruitment model to find loving, permanent homes for children waiting in foster care.

The Foundation works closely with child welfare advocates and policymakers, provides free resources about foster care adoption and raises awareness through social media campaigns, public service announcements and events.

Visit davethomasfoundation.org, or call 1-800-ASK-DTFA to find out how you can help.

PREFACE

I have endeavored in this ghostly book to honor the spirit of Charles Dickens' original classic, which raised in me a ghost of an idea, which I hope shall not put his dear readers out of humor with themselves, with each other, with the season, or with me, that the three ghosts of Christmas did not limit their reclamation efforts to Ebenezer Scrooge on one Christmas Eve almost 180 years ago; but rather, these spirits make an annual Christmas Eve visit to the individual upon this plane who is in direst need of a good shaking down to his or her core.

May this story haunt your houses pleasantly for years to come and ward off any chance of the Christmas ghosts finding you or one of yours most deserving of their focused attention.

With you in spirit,
J.C.D.
December, 2020

STAVE 1: BERNICE'S GHOST

*B*ernice was dead. There is no doubt whatever about that. Ellie knew she was dead. Of course she did. How could it be otherwise? Even though they had never met, Ellie was one of the first to learn of Bernice's sudden demise. And although a framed picture of Bernice, presented to Ellie by Bernice's two less-than-adoring children, had had a place in Ellie's office for almost seven years, albeit a place on the farthest corner of the highest rung on a seldom-frequented bookshelf, the two women had never met.

The all but forgotten photo of Bernice, taken years prior for a corporate headshot, was currently positioned atop a collection of Charles Dickens books. Ellie, who had never cracked open even one (though Bleak House was a tempting title for her), felt that visitors to her office, observing the volumes, would leave with an improved opinion of her.

This particular picture of Bernice was the only one her children could find in which their mother sported anything even resembling a smile. If it is true that, as the song goes, "you're never fully dressed without a smile," then Bernice walked around the Earth with a persistent wardrobe malfunction.

The small, framed picture had been presented to Ellie by

Bernice's adult children and sole grandchild one stormy spring morning there in Ellie's office. They had arrived promptly and dutifully with a newspaper photographer and reporter in tow to memorialize the bestowal. Ellie was not one to go in for this type of spectacle but felt the publicity would be beneficial for business, so she consented.

Ellie made a show of receiving her guests with believable but feigned warmth and a passable display of emotion. She even promised to keep "the photo of this dear woman" on her desk where she could look at it daily and remember "this remarkable lady — saint, really — who, through her generosity of spirit, and literally, body, will remain a constant inspiration." She had not planned on saying any of that, but it came to her while in character, and she surprised herself with how earnest it sounded coming out of her mouth.

She also had not planned on holding Bernice's little, sticky granddaughter for the newspaper photograph. But when a small child is thrust into your bosom by its mother, your choices are to take her or let her drop. The decision was only made easy for Ellie by the presence of the local press in the room.

Bernice's children thought Ellie was sincere. She was not. Ellie thought Bernice's children were sincere. But they weren't either. They just wanted to be in the news and hoped the story might go viral, and they might end up on Dr. Phil or maybe even Letterman, and they would somehow be catapulted to fame and maybe, if the stars aligned, meet Katy Perry, and possibly, get their own reality show.

And when Bernice's family had left and after the photographer had finally packed away her camera and lenses and Ellie had walked her and the reporter to the reception area and asked her assistant to see them out, she returned to her office and closed the door. She was eager to get back to work, but not as eager as she was to dispense with the nonsense of the previous forty-five minutes. She picked up the frame and was not even interested enough to throw a

glance at the picture while she was surveying the office for somewhere to stow it.

If she had bothered to look at the photo, she would have seen the
face of a woman who was awkwardly and uncomfortably struggling
to raise at least one corner of her mouth into a smile. Her eyes were
pained as if she were exerting a seldom-used muscle. It looked like a
bead of sweat had just begun to form on her forehead from the strain
and had been memorialized in its infancy by the click of the camera.

Ellie had ignored her first inclination to toss the memento in the
trash. She had actually made the motion with her arm, but her
fingers got the "abort" message from her brain just before she
released it. She didn't know why, but she had some twinge way
down deep that suggested that to do so might somehow make her
appear heartless. Heartless! At that, she laughed out loud.

She decided to keep it around, but she didn't want to see it or
accidentally make eye contact with it. She placed the frame as high
up as she could reach on the bookshelf where it would not be visible
from her desk, or from the sofa or the side chair, or anywhere else
she might sit, or stand, or lay or otherwise position herself purposefully or accidentally. With that resolved, she resumed her work.

And there the photograph had sat ever since, facing off in a
random direction, perhaps bumped by a feather duster at some
point years ago or last week and never repositioned. The awkward
expression on Bernice's visage and the angle at which the frame had
come to rest made it look as if Bernice was eyeing a possible escape
from the gloomy confines of Ellie's stifling office.

Bernice was dead.

Those three words, dear reader, are by themselves unremarkable. People die every day. And very likely, at least one or two
Bernices are among them. But it is this Bernice's death that makes
this story remarkable. Bernice was dead. Not that Ellie had given it
much thought in the seven years since the transplant surgery. Nor
had it ever been a question in her mind, or anyone else's, as to
whether Bernice had or had not succumbed.

Ellie had never had any cause to invest a second of her precious time on the subject. And if she had, she would have reasoned succinctly and correctly: A heart, both literally and figuratively, cannot occupy two places at the same time. Bernice's heart was now beating in Ellie's chest. Therefore, Ellie could safely deduce that Bernice was dead, and so now, dear reader, you know why Ellie was one of the first to learn of this stranger's passing.

Now, whether Bernice was as dead as a doornail, that was not for Ellie to say or ponder, nor would she have understood the reference.

As a practical, unsentimental, and singularly-focused woman of commerce, the heart transplant was like a business transaction to Ellie. In fact, while recovering in the hospital, she frequently referred to the procedure as a heart transaction rather than transplant. Was it a slip of the tongue? Her nurses had corrected her a couple of times and then gave up, passing it off as a side effect of the medication.

To her, the dispensing of her weak and inefficient heart and the procurement of what was, by all accounts, an adequate blood pumper was no different than kicking an underperforming employee to the curb and replacing her with a proven new hire whom she was confident could do the job. "Let's get to work," were her first internal words to her new worker.

And that new employee was working away at productivity levels Ellie had never experienced before, permitting Ellie to do the same, and that's all she really cared about.

Sometimes Ellie could feel Bernice in her fingertips, sometimes in her eyes. Bernice was all over the building like an eager mail clerk. Sometimes when she had a headache, she could feel Bernice displaying her displeasure by thumping her temples.

"Easy there, Bernice," Ellie would say over her internal intercom, "You've already died once of a massive stroke. Calm yourself."

Sometimes Ellie would place two fingers on her neck and feel around until a strong and powerful pulse was moving beneath them, which Ellie measured not in beats per minute, but Bernices per minute. Feeling the swift movement of blood through her carotid artery made her feel very powerful, liberated, and greedy to make up for lost time.

Ellie was not the only one who benefited from Bernice's sudden and untimely death. Her liver went to a man in Delaware. Bernice would not have been happy about that. She hated men.

A kidney saved a young mother's life in Scranton. The front of the Christmas Day local newspaper read: "Kidney is Christmas Miracle to Mother of 5." The story got picked up by the wire services and even the CBS Evening News. Bernice was made to sound like Florence Nightingale, Joan of Arc, and Eleanor Roosevelt rolled into one.

But, first and foremost, at least to them, the two individuals who benefited most from Bernice's brain bleed were her greedy, neglected, opportunistic, bitter, unfeeling, and unremorseful children, Dicky and Diane. They came into a tidy fortune of nearly $10 million. They had no idea their mother had anything but debt. They only knew she was steadily employed and that she was the boss of a lot of people. And they knew that most of those people hated her guts, the very guts a doctor at The Cleveland Clinic put into an accounting clerk from Parma, Ohio, whose body had the good sense, but the bad fortune, to reject.

Bernice was a business owner and savvy investor. She was also a skinflint. She and her children lived like the working poor. Dicky and Diane had no reason to believe they were otherwise. So, when the details of the will were made known to them, they of course reacted as if they had won the Powerball Jackpot.

The will was read weeks after the funeral because Diane, a single mom — her boyfriend ran out to the drug store to purchase another pregnancy test just so they could be sure and never returned — living at home, working two part-time jobs, and eking out enough to feed and clothe her multi-millionaire mother's sole grandchild, while supporting her own considerable recreational drug and snack food compulsions, could not be granted time off work to get downtown to Bernice's lawyer's office during regular hours.

Dicky, serving out the last month or so of house arrest for trying to pass some bad checks, did not seek permission, nor have the inclination to attend a meeting where he expected to learn that he and his sister would inherit, at best, a three-bedroom, split-level house with a mortgage and in need of numerous repairs, and a fifteen-year old Toyota Corolla with bald tires and over 175,000 on the odometer.

The truth was, the house arrest also provided his cover for not attending his mother's funeral. In fact, there might have been a recent rash of home incarceration sentences handed down, judging by the number of mourners at the service.

Bernice was no Florence Nightingale nor Eleanor Roosevelt. And her only similarity to Joan of Arc was that plenty of people would have loved to have burned her at the stake if given the opportunity, a few sticks of kindling, some matches, and a bag of marsh-mallows.

In actuality, the generosity attributed to Bernice for her magnanimous donation of body parts and vital organs was the outcome of Dicky's deceit in tricking his mother into signing a donor registry form.

Though Bernice could lay claim to only a few gratifications, imbibing was one of them. And, during rare instances of overindul-gence, the usually impenetrable fortress that was Bernice left herself vulnerable to her son's mischievousness.

One particular evening, during an alcohol-induced rant against Dicky's slothfulness and procrastination, a wobbly and slurring Bernice demanded he "get on that compooter thish minute" and complete her driver's license renewal that she'd been asking him to do for months. While filling out the online renewal for his passed out mother, Dicky came upon the question, "Would you like to become an organ donor?"

Dicky had never been in a church, so he had never heard a choir sing. Until that very moment.

He looked around in search of the heavenly voices that were raised in "alleluias." It was as if the clouds had parted and a star appeared, its celestial light shining down on his intoxicated mother, asleep with her head on her arm and drool dripping from her mouth onto the kitchen table. He had already clicked "no" to the question, but he was now among the converted. He switched the answer to "yes."

The whole plan came together as if it were a pre-made meal straight out of God's kitchen. All he had to do was stick it in the oven. He would download the document and tell Bernice that she needed to sign the form to complete her driver's license renewal while she was still under the influence. If he hurried, which was something he had never tried before, he could have her sign it, and he could get it in the mail before she emerged from the dark cave of intoxication into the light of her natural state of complete control.

The most Dicky could have hoped for from this prank was to see his mother's reaction when her new license arrived with the organ donor information on it. He could not have known that Bernice would not live long enough to undo his handiwork. As eager as he was, he was determined not to mention it to anyone until after the grand reveal. He wanted this all to himself. Eventually, he just had to tell someone, so he shared the scheme with Diane, who asked him if he was planning on donating his organs too because "when Bernice finds out, she's going to harvest them all by herself."

Another indulgence Bernice excelled in was trashing her unfortunate ex-husband, though that term was not exactly accurate. Her husband, Howie, died during their divorce proceedings. He had suffered a heart attack right there in the courtroom in front of the judge, with Bernice and her lawyer looking on. He had been paler than usual all day, but when he clutched his left arm and slumped in his chair, his lawyer asked for a glass of water and an adjournment for the day.

Bernice, beating her lawyer to it, objected to both. The judge overruled, whereupon Howie's lawyer, Mr. Stem, took the glass of water provided by the bailiff and gulped it down. After handing the empty glass to his client, he grabbed his hat and briefcase and promptly left the courtroom.

Bernice did not accompany Howie to the hospital despite his pleas that he loved her and that he did not want to die alone in an ambulance. Bernice's only words of comfort while denying her dying husband's request were, "You won't die alone, you simpering idiot; the EMTs will be there."

While Howie lay in the hospital clinging to life for almost a week, he had just one faithful visitor, Mr. Stem who, being a lawyer, and therefore incapable of stopping himself from doing so, billed Howie's estate for the hours.

Howie died before the divorce was finalized, but Bernice referred to him as her ex-husband right up to that fateful Christmas Eve when, shortly after opening an envelope from the New York Department of Transportation containing her license with her new donor status, she suffered a massive and fatal stroke. When the paramedics arrived moments later, she was already gone and clutching the license in her hand.

Bernice had regarded Howie's death as his "getting one over on me," and nobody got one over on Bernice (with the possible exception of Dicky). He had dissolved their marriage according to their vows — 'til death do us part — before she could dissolve their union in court on her terms. She was furious.

Dicky and Diane were only five and three respectively, when their father passed away. Despite their young ages, they knew he had died of a broken heart and that their mother was the one who had knocked it off the end table.

Howie — being some twenty years older than Bernice and having been employed as a bagger at the Giant Supermarket, and having taken an unusually long time to rise to that low position in the organization, a position which was perpetually tenuous, at best, since he just could not grasp the concept that the eggs and soup cans should not go in the same bag — had thought Bernice might be his last and only chance at something resembling love. She had made the first move... gave him a questionnaire, a modified employment application, which Howie dutifully filled out and returned in the allotted forty-eight hours.

Bernice viewed Howie as someone whom she could easily control, who could look the part, who would keep a clean house if instructed to do so, and who could have a hot, edible, if not delicious, meal ready when she returned home from work. He could escort her to business functions when necessary (if he kept his mouth shut) to ward off ambitious underlings only interested in her for their own advancement.

She was wholly self-aware and critical (qualities she was conscious of and admired in herself) and knew there could be no other reason for a man to set his heart on her; she created no reason, showed no interest, gave no hint of desire, and therefore was wary of anyone offering even the slightest innuendo.

Howie would suit her purposes. It would be cheaper to marry him than to rent him and, as distasteful as the process would be, when the timing was right, she would compel him to give her a son and a daughter.

She made precise computations to determine the exact day and specific time their interaction would yield the best chance of producing the intended biological outcome. Though Bernice had performed thousands of calculations in her lifetime involving hundreds of millions of dollars, there were none with which she was more deliberate, none that she so painstakingly reviewed and double- and triple-checked than the figuring of her optimal conception window.

Bernice believed the "men who run the world" were more inclined to do business with a stable family woman with a husband and 2.3 children. She didn't want any of that, but to get ahead, she would oblige them. With Howie, she was aware that she got the husband (in the legal sense only) and the other three-tenths of a child all rolled into one.

When Howie was diagnosed with early-onset Alzheimer's, Bernice wanted no part of that, so she began divorce proceedings. The house, the bank accounts, the cars, everything was in Bernice's name only. Howie had nothing except a small account into which he deposited his paychecks from the grocery store. Bernice hired the best-rated divorce attorney in the county. Howie engaged the services of Mr. Stem, a fledgling personal injury attorney, weekend Civil War reenactor, and frequent Karaoke night participant.

Bernice was imposing, intimidating, charmless, dispassionate, humorless, unfriendly, and predisposed to extraordinary meanness. She helped no one. She supported no cause. She used people until she had squeezed all the utility of them and then discarded them like a juice box from which she had slurped the last drop, sucked the air out of, dropped on the sidewalk to be crushed underfoot, and left for someone else to pick up.

She was so solely focused on making money that there was no room for joy, no time to breathe, and no space for love. She moved through life head down, never bothering to look to her right or left, or notice the pain or joy, anguish or thrill, anxiety or calm on the faces of her fellow travelers along the road of life. Those who came into contact with her and tried to connect were summarily dispatched so she could be left alone on her icy trail, blind and deaf, walking a straight, tedious, oblivious path from her cradle to her grave. A grave she had always trusted would be much further up the road.

Suppose Bernice's heart thought (assuming hearts have minds of their own), while it was lying there face up in the Igloo cooler during the life flight to Philadelphia, that a transfer out of Bernice could only lead to its going to work in a body with much warmer blood than its previous host. In that case, it must have been a shock to its ventricles in the operating room when Ellie's blood started flowing into it. Even though the heart had been removed from the cold, vacant body of Bernice and immediately packed away in ice, it had never experienced the kind of chill it felt once placed in Ellie's chest cavity.

Bernice was born cold and maintained that same climate throughout her life. On the other hand, Ellie arrived at her low temperature over time, and her thermal reading continued to descend with each passing year.

While Bernice was uncaring and oblivious to the wants and

needs and the very lives of others, Ellie studied people like textbooks, highlighting every fact and flaw she could use to manipulate them. She could easily make people miserable and cover it up with a not-unfriendly exterior. A casual acquaintance might find it hard not to like Ellie. And as long as one did not try to get close, they might walk away unharmed.

But Ellie came on with no warning, and by the time a person realized he had crossed a line that was only visible to Ellie, he was frozen in his tracks, and there was no chance of escape.

Ellie had no friends, no family. She attended no church. She accepted no invitations, though, after decades of turning down every one that came her way, there were no more to decline. She contributed to no charities; she rooted for no sports teams — which in Philadelphia was unconscionable. She did not watch television; she read no books. She would make small talk when necessary for business, though anyone hoping to walk away from the exchange having made even the slightest inroads to any attachment left her presence decidedly unsatisfied.

She never asked a person, "How are you doing today?" Even that day, when Bernice's children were presenting her with the photo of their recently deceased mother for the sake of a local newspaper article, she never once asked Dicky and Diane, "How are you getting on?" Never asked about the child or made even a hint of a fuss. Sure, there was a look of sympathy; there were even awkward side hugs, but that was just for the press and brought about by the expectations of the moment.

The notion never crossed Ellie's mind to ask Bernice's family how they were doing because, at the heart of it, she did not care. Their answers would have no effect on her either way. The seeds of tenderness and compassion sewn in her breast in her youth had gone untended for too long. Weeds had choked out any aspiring sprout of empathy that may have hoped to break through Ellie's hardened crust.

Those who worked for her rarely saw her. On those occasions, when they passed her in a hall or near her private elevator, they would receive a slow nod and a reserved, closed-mouth smile. She had spent years practicing and perfecting the mannerism in the mirror so it would precisely convey to them: "You have been acknowledged by someone who is stations above you. Now move along and don't even think about uttering a word." Her actual thoughts were, "Get out of my sight as fast as your weak-in-the-knees legs can transport you. And if you linger, or God forbid try to make conversation with me, I will look deep into your eyes and frost your soul to such a degree that you'll be in hell a thousand years before you even start to thaw."

Her "smile" was typically returned with a nervous grin and an expression that imparted back to her, "Yeah. No. I get it," and that was followed by a hasty retreat from her proximity.

In the few instances someone had the temerity to speak to her, it was usually nothing more than a barely audible and timid, "Good morning, Ms. Printh." Ellie would acknowledge their audacity with a second slow nod and this time, an impatient smile. Then she would scurry into her private elevator and ascend directly to her fourth-floor office. There she would immediately complain to her assistant about the presumptuous employee, whom she would name, how he accosted her in the hallway. Why, she would ask, could that area not be kept clear of loafers and loiterers. Why could employees meandering about the building, far from their assigned desks, not be fired on sight!

Though Ellie was rarely seen in her own building and never engaged anyone except her assistant, she knew the names and faces and practically every detail of every one of her 107 employees.

"Ellie sightings," as they were called, were major events throughout the company and typically resulted in the person who had had the encounter becoming instantly famous and spending the rest of the day retelling the particulars to co-workers. The claims often were met at first with the same skepticism one might assign to a Big Foot spotting or an I-saw-Elvis-ordering-flapjacks at-a-greasy-spoon-diner story. Still, as the day would wear on, inevitably, the veracity of the recounting generally would win over even the most dubious.

Productivity would come to a standstill as word spread of the "Ellie sighting." Group emails would be exchanged, inter-office mail would be self-delivered, so co-workers might take the opportunity to talk to, or about, the new celebrity. Happy hours were scheduled for that evening when a more elaborate and demonstrative description could be told by the hero about how he bravely stared into Ellie's face and was not turned to stone.

On one occasion at an after-hours retelling, perhaps due to the combination of too much alcohol and not enough story, a previously obscure co-worker named Doug Donovan was relishing his newfound fame and trying to raise his image to legend status by adding some embellishment to the recounting of his Ellie encounter from earlier that day.

Holding his vodka and tonic precariously in one hand while engaging his arms in an erratic display of wavings and gestures employed in commanding the attention of his crowd of co-workers, he looked like an air balloon dancer manically flailing and fluttering outside a discount appliance store's grand opening.

Doug told of how he walked right up to "that freakish, high-falootin' miser" and gave her a piece of his mind! He spoke of how he shook his finger in her "pale, stupid face" (for this part, he briefly set down what was left of his vodka and tonic, most of which had sloshed out onto the floor, to demonstrate his finger-shaking technique) and demanded that she acknowledge "her hard-working, talented workers, off whose backs she had gotten stinkin' rich!"

Then, amongst some gasps and some incredulous laughter, he told his new fan base he asked her if "it would kill her to offer a word of praise or thanks!" Sensing co-workers were underwhelmed by that last statement, he adjusted the story on the fly. "And then I really got in her grill and said that everyone deserves a raise or least a Christmas bonus!" At that, his co-workers raised a cheer. He had won them back.

He claimed the only hint of a reaction came at the mention of a

Christmas bonus, but after he had spoken his mind, her acknowledgment was a thoughtful nod and a slight smile as she backed into her elevator. He added that once the elevator doors closed, he could swear that he heard shrieks of laughter emanating from within that seemed to continue all the way up.

Whether Doug's story was true or enhanced or wholly fabricated, no one knew or will ever know, for by the time workers arrived at The Printh Company that next morning, Doug's cubicle had not only been cleared out, but there was a new hire, also named Doug, already in place and clacking away at the computer keyboard. Co-workers who tried to call Doug Donovan got no answer, and those who stopped by his house were met only with a "For Sale" sign and a lockbox on the front door.

The official word from Human Resources was that Doug had quietly resigned and given his notice two weeks earlier, and his departure was planned. Nonetheless, the incident caused all future "Ellie sighting" retellings to stick reasonably close to the factual accounts.

At The Printh Company, there were no holiday parties, no birthday parties, no company picnics, no bring-your-child-to-work days, and certainly no bring-your-dog-to-work days. Unthinkable. Though Ellie might tolerate a child or two as long as they were well-mannered, she had a strong aversion to man's best friend, and they were none too fond of her.

During a visit to an animal shelter several years previous, Ellie had entered the building to the sound of more than two dozen dogs in the back room howling and yapping. While striding through the facility, which her company was considering purchasing and razing, she made her way to the room where the dogs were trying to out-decibelize each other. The suddenly subdued dogs stopped barking. A few squeezed out a weak whimper or two and then... silence. They retreated to the far corners of their cages and warily watched her make her way down the corridor. Not one tail wagged.

Whereas most dogs in shelters greet a visit from a human by barking out, "Pick me! Pick me!" these dogs quietly avoided eye contact with Ellie, but made subtle head gestures toward an obnoxious Doberman named Chief who was in a cage near the far end of a row, as if trying to communicate to Ellie, "Pick him. Pick him." When she had finally made her way out the door, and it closed behind her, the dogs resumed their cacophony, except for Chief, whose feelings were bruised. You see, he had had no idea the other dogs felt that way about him.

Ellie had no delusions about how others of her species felt about her. She knew because those sentiments were of her making. Much like an artist who painstakingly creates an image hoping to elicit a particular emotional response from those who view their work, Ellie had created a masterpiece of a facade she had labored on day by day that prompted a universal reaction of distance and deference.

Moreover, she knew what people thought of her because she employed individuals and devices to monitor conversations and relay all her employees' true attitudes back to her. She would not tolerate a duplicitous person. She had come to learn that in her role and with her temperament, even her more senior colleagues were less than forthcoming, afraid to disagree with her or share an idea because, it seemed, no one honed her tongue to a sharper edge than Ellie Printh. And once provoked and the blade unsheathed, she could verbally slice her victim effortlessly, like an infomercial knife through a plump tomato. Ellie did not suffer fools.

She trusted no one, with the possible exception of Mary Lou, her executive assistant, but that was because Ellie had never caught her in a lie, yet. That made Mary Lou either extraordinarily bright and ambitious, a combination Ellie rarely found in anyone other than herself, or completely honest and loyal, a pairing Ellie had never discovered in anyone, including herself.

Though there is a popular admonishment about judging a book by its cover, in Ellie's case, she was a novel whose ending was pretty much foretold by a dust jacket of her own design. It revealed everything she wanted potential readers to know. Ellie had fashioned for herself a kind of style and appearance that very effectively served as a warning to all human sympathy to keep its distance.

Ellie was the very antithesis of a page-turner from her head to the bottom edges of her feet. Her hair was short and severely straight, with ends uneven and so pointed and sharp it looked as if a toss of her head could lacerate anyone in close proximity (not that there was any chance of anyone getting that close). From the jagged and random lengths of it, one might even assume she cut her own hair with a freshly filed machete.

She dyed her hair blonde, almost white because her natural brown, she felt, was too warm, and it softened her features, which she feared might have the undesirable outcome of making her seem approachable. Her eyes were grayish-blue, the color of thin ice, and they appropriately warned anyone who got too close to "stay off."

Ellie's posture was rigid and straight to portend her inflexibility. She dressed smartly, stylishly, professionally, always in blacks and grays, never revealing, but hugging a-not-unshapely form. Shoes — practical flats, always flats.

The only makeup she wore was to disguise the rosy cheeks that came as a byproduct of the healthier heart. At a check-up a few months after the surgery, her cardiologist asked if she was experiencing any adverse side effects from the transplant. Ellie replied, "only this color on my face," pointing to her cheeks. Then she asked the doctor if there was anything she could take to get rid of it.

If Ellie were a book, she was hardbound and determined that anyone who stumbled across her and wanting a closer look would only find, upon inspection, blank page after blank page. Hers was a life written in invisible ink. She had left no mark, and that was fine with her. She had no desire to ever look back and read what she had written or to reveal it to another human being. And she had no interest in skipping ahead because she knew how the story would end. Alone on a shelf. With an undesirable cover that apprised people to put her down and never pick her up again.

Once upon a time, of all the good days of the year, on Christmas Eve, Ellie sat alone in her office reviewing a stack of eviction notices set to go out in the mail the next week. There were more this month than typical. It had been an unusually frigid November and December in Philadelphia, and that period had been preceded by an historically balmy autumn that had followed an apocalyptically stifling summer. As a result, over a prolonged period, energy bills had been much higher than people were able to pay. More tenants than Ellie could ever remember were months behind on their rent. And that did not sit well with her.

"These people!" fumed Ellie as she looked over and signed each eviction warning, "heating their homes beyond their means and now probably spending their rent money on presents they clearly can't afford. Well, maybe a sleeping bag under the tree would be a good idea for little Johnny. It will fit nicely in the tent these people will be living out of soon enough!"

Ellie's tenants ran the gamut from well-to-do to ne'er-do-well. From the over-employed to the under-employed to the nefariously employed. There were well-heeled country club types who were secretly in debt up to their surgically modified noses, and there were shabby-clothed, weather-worn folks who were unassumingly sitting on their fat assets.

To Ellie, the world was a ship of fools that sailed too often on a sea of red ink. And her tenants were no different, from captains of commerce to passengers in steerage. People were all the same to her. Not that she wasn't a bigot. She discriminated all right, but not by race or creed or color or sexual preference or religion. Her only bias was against people who didn't pay her on time. She despised "those people."

As Ellie was ravenously approving the last eviction notice in the pile, there was a quick rap on her office door before it opened and her assistant, Mary Lou, slid her head in. Without looking up, Ellie impatiently asked, "What is it?"

"Your 3:30 appointment is here."

Ellie reached into the middle of the stack of evictions and blindly pulled out the one she needed, like a magician performing a card trick. She took a look, though, just be sure.

"Ah, yes. Mrs. Fielder. This is going to be good." Then to Mary Lou, "Would you like to stay and watch?"

"No, thank you," said Mary Lou as if Ellie were asking if she would like to drink pickle juice. Additionally, as she was replying, her face contorted in the manner of someone who had, in fact, just taken a swig of pickle juice.

"Well, let's not keep Mrs. Fielder waiting." Ellie was practically singing, and more loud and animated than Mary Lou had ever seen her boss. "Show her in. Show her in!

"Are your heels suitably cooled, Mrs. Fielder?" Ellie yelled to the woman she saw pressing against Mary Lou, peeking over her shoulder.

"Show her in! I'm sure Mrs. Fielder is a very busy woman with much on her plate."

"No. No. I've got no place to be, but I wouldn't mind a little more on my plate… if you know what I mean! Ha! Ha! Ha! Ho! Ho! Whoo! I'm out of breath. Can I sit?"

Those words were spoken by Martha Fielder. She had pushed her way past Mary Lou, who was only too happy to retreat and close the door behind her. Martha Fielder was a woman of forty-two years, of which it appeared the last forty-two had been particularly hard. Her mouse-brown hair was flat and listless, giving the appearance of not having been washed yet this month. Her eyes looked tired and weak, blinking listlessly like two unfit bar buddies who had drunk all night and then tried to run a half marathon on a dare, and were now looking out of their hospital room windows, chins on their forearms, weakly pulling the blinds up and down.

Her blouse was too small for every part of her: arms, torso, midriff. Some random bulges writhed and morphed as she moved as if an eel were slithering around her body under the surface of the shirt. The blouse stretched around the middle, pulling at each button like a kid in a store dragging his mother to the toy department.

Her pants were at least two sizes too small, but the wear suggested that perhaps Mrs. Fielder had purchased them at a time when they were not. Clearly, these pants were a tribute to human ingenuity and invention in that they tested the bounds of man-made fibers well beyond their intended limits.

Ellie looked her up and down with undisguised disdain and finally replied, "If you CAN sit, you MAY sit there," directing her to an armchair on the other side of her desk while also correcting her grammar.

"Merry Christmas!" chirped Mrs. Fielder.

In response, Ellie inhaled through her nose, held the breath in her mouth, letting it fill out her cheeks until it escaped all at once through her lips, forcing a "puh" sound.

Perhaps it was the pronounced expulsion of hot air or the fact that there was no return of her greetings of the season, but Mrs. Fielder's cheerful countenance began to show signs of stress. Her forehead began to buckle into furrowed rows.

Ellie continued… "There is the matter of your back rent, Mrs. Fielder."

"Of course. Of course," said the woman. The pores along her hairline opened in unison like little mouths whose jaws dropped in surprise or fear while beads of retained moisture raced toward the openings to make their escape. "It ain't like we been social, so I was kinda thinkin' you needed to talk to me about something like that," she continued, now twisting her gloves in her hands.

"Two months behind, Mrs. Fielder. It will be three months in just over a week from today. And since I have sent you two separate notices warning of eviction, without any response   you would not make a very good pen pal, Mrs. Fielder — I don't doubt you had at least a hint as to the nature of this conversation."

Trickles of concern were now dribbling down her forehead in the form of drops of perspiration, which were pooling on her brow and glistening there.

An audible gulp reached Ellie's ears.

"Please, call me Martha."

"I have no intention of calling you by your given name, Mrs. Fielder. That would imply familiarity. And though contempt for the

likes of you has been bred in me, it is not the result of any familiarity with you in particular, but with the lot of you. It is the
outcome of your not paying your rent!"

"It's quite warm in here," rasped Mrs. Fielder, now with more
fissures evident on her exterior, as signs of cold dampness could be
seen emerging from under her arms and around her collar. Even the
eel appeared to be breaking out into a sweat as it traversed her
midsection every time she shifted in her seat. "Could you crack
open a window?" she croaked.

"No." A pause, and then Ellie continued.

"I don't want to evict you, Mrs. Fielder. Do you know why?"

"You like me?" offered Mrs. Fielder sheepishly, knowing she
likely did not answer correctly but nonetheless was hopeful.

Another long inhale through the nose, puffed cheeks, and then
"puh!"

"I don't want to evict you because that costs me money. I have to
have the place cleaned and maybe painted. I have to place adver-
tising to find a new tenant. Credit checks need to be run, interviews
conducted. The house may sit empty for months, which means no
income from it for me. So, if we can get this turned around, that is
what is best for me and, though it does not factor into any of my
ruminations, for you as well, I would think."

Now Mrs. Fielder was leaking from every crevice and hole.

"You have children, Mrs. Fielder. Correct?"

"Four. Three are mine and Mr. Fielder's. And one foster child."

Ellie looked through the file.

"Foster child? I was unaware of that. Hmm. Well."

"Is that a problem? I can get rid of her," Mrs. Fielder jumped in,
wondering now if she had ever informed anyone at The Printh
Company of the additional person living in the house.

"I'll need to have your file updated, that's all."

Ellie scribbled a few notes and looked back at Mrs. Fielder. "Do
you have a Christmas tree?"

"Yes, of course."

"Are your presents all wrapped and tied with pretty bows?"

"Not yet. It will get done later tonight. It had better, anyway."

"Where are you having Christmas dinner tomorrow?" continued Ellie.

"My place. Mom and Dad are both gone on accounta the COVID. My brother and his wife and kids will come over. It's cramped, but we'll make do," responded Mrs. Fielder, starting to relax a little. "I bought a turkey and got a pumpkin pie at Bredenbeck's. Do you like pumpkin pie, Ms. Printh?"

"My place? If you're not paying your rent, can you really refer to the house as 'my place?' What money did you use for the presents and the wrapping paper for that matter? How did you pay for the turkey? And the tree? Was it, oh I don't know… your rent money?"

At the end of this line of questioning, Mrs. Fielder's dam burst! Every clear, salty fluid produced by the human body was released. Sweat and tears flowed without restraint.

As she tried to speak, it looked as if she was trying to chew her words and swallow them before they could escape out into the air. Still, up they came forcing their way past the larynx, the pharynx, the undermanned uvula, the tongue, and the teeth, which had instinctively clenched, and finally bursting through her lips and spilling out, at first in no recognizable order. "I, I, I… only… trying… was… you understand… to… surely… you get it… to… to give the kids a good Christmas!" Sniff! Sniff. She paused to order her words to fall in line and to wipe her eyes and nose with her gloves. "Doesn't every kid deserve good Christmas mem'ries? Don't throw us out!" Sniff! Sniff! "Please! I begga ya!"

"Mrs. Fielder, you will not be thrown out today."

"Huh? Wha? Oh, thank you! Thank you! God bless ya!" Mrs. Fielder chirped, rushing the desk and reaching for Ellie's hand, which Ellie quickly withdrew before Mrs. Fielder's sweaty, snotty, slobbery fingers could take hold.

"It's your congressperson that you may ask God to bless. The Commonwealth of Pennsylvania forbids me from tossing you and your family out in the street today. You have fifteen days… or pay your back rent. Now if there is nothing else…"

"Do you have a tissue?"

"I do not. I have no use for tissues. Use your gloves and wring them out once you get outside."

"Outside? So, we're done?"

"Oh, yes. Quite. Go on," said Ellie, making a shooing motion with both hands.

The sodden, soggy, and shaken lady quickly rose and left the office as fast as her thick thighs and bulging calves would permit.

Mrs. Fielder dispensed with, Ellie had not been back into her work two minutes when there was another quick knock on the door. Mary Lou poked her head in.

"What now?" asked Ellie without lifting her eyes.

Immune to Ellie's abruptness from constant exposure, Mary Lou, unphased, replied, "I have been getting questions from some of the employees about whether you are going to be letting them go home early today?"

"Why?" snapped Ellie, looking up at the clock. 3:47 p.m.

"Christmas Eve," replied Mary Lou flatly.

"I know it's Christmas Eve. I've just signed seventeen eviction notices and dated them all December 24th. So, I've got a pretty solid command of the calendar. I meant, why are they asking to be dismissed early? Are they newer employees who are asking?"

"Clearly," said Mary Lou but only with a look.

"I provide them all with an annual allotment of paid time off, which, if they chose to exhaust it for other pursuits, cannot become my concern. They cannot look to me to resolve their reckless planning."

Mary Lou, with her neck stretched and just her face protruding into the office, looking like a turtle, started to retract her head from between the door and its frame when Ellie continued.

"I mean seriously! Did these people not know that Christmas Eve was coming this year? Did they think something would happen that would alter the calendar from its natural course? My strong suspicion is the answer to both questions is "no." And now they are looking to me to erase their dishevelment and release them all, on my dime no less, to their hearths and homes. They left their Christmas Eves to chance and were betting on my benevolence. Well, they lost." Ellie took a deep breath in through her nose, paused, and then exhaled, "puh!"

Mary Lou, believing she had the full answer, again began withdrawing to her protective shell, that is, the space just outside Ellie's office where she had her own desk and corkboard and filing cabinets, and where she was safe from the world on the other side of that door.

As often as possible, she used that door between her and Ellie as a kind of shield. Her boss had a habit of launching items from her desk when frustrated or provoked: a cup full of paper clips, a stapler, a letter opener (that one actually stuck in the door), her cell phone (twice), and a crystal paperweight were among the casualties for which Mary Lou at one time or another had to order replacements.

Throwing things was an involuntary reflex for Ellie. And it would happen so fast Mary Lou had no time to duck or dodge. She was an alert cricket who had to nimbly evade the whip-like tongue of a hungry frog. So far, she had not been zapped with any of the projectiles. Indeed, some had been close enough she could feel the breeze created by the object disturbing the air around her. Some she could even hear whiz past her ear just milliseconds before the ensuing crash or thud or, in the case of the letter opener, thoingggg. To be fair, Ellie was never aiming for Mary Lou, but on the other hand, neither did there appear to be any perceivable intention to spare her.

"They have the whole day off tomorrow... paid," Ellie continued. "And they still want more. Well, I'll tell you what," now adopting a sarcastically sweet tone, "anyone who wants to leave can do so whenever they like... but without pay. And, I'll tell you another thing... I bet no one goes. Oh, they say they want to get home early on Christmas Eve to spend time with their families. But what's it worth to them? Not an hour's wages, I tell you. It's not <u>their</u> time they want to spend with their..." rolling her eyes, "priceless loved ones. It's <u>my</u> time. And since it is my time, I say no. They've already got the paid holiday from me, they'll not get another hour, not another minute at my expense. You can tell them that!"

"Maybe I won't use exactly those words, but I will let them know," mumbled Mary Lou, retreating and closing the door between them.

Though Mary Lou did not, by any stretch of the imagination, slam the door — in fact, she pulled it shut so carefully one could distinctly hear the latch slowly slip inside the strike plate — with its closing came a sudden and furious gust of frigid air. Ellie, who had been standing behind her desk, was blown into her chair.

She could not tell where the wind was coming from. She spun around to see if, impossible as it was, Mrs. Fielder had somehow thrown open the windows during her visit, despite Ellie's refusal to do so.

But both windows in the office were shut tight. Visible through one of them was an overgrown tree branch that pressed against the glass pane. The limb was framed in a dense fog that gave the appearance that the window was frosted, but the scene was as still as if it were a picture.

Inside her office, the wind howled like a wounded coyote and whipped around the room like an arctic hurricane.

It did not feel to Ellie like the cold blast was blowing on her; she felt no force of the gale other than the initial burst. In fact, it was not even rustling her blouse or tussling her hair. No, it did not feel as if it was blowing at her or on her, but rather through her. It was as if the powerful winds slipped through the fabric of her tailored slacks and blouse and entered every pore of her pale skin, icing her bones, organs, joints, and blood to such a degree that Bernice's heart, by comparison, and by far, seemed the only warm part of her innards.

She had never experienced anything like the chill that literally moved up and down her spine and took occupancy in every cell of her being. She wondered briefly if she was the source of the bitter whirlwind ravaging the environs around her, but she was not.

The frozen tempest roared around the office, snatching the eviction notices and scattering them through the air, violently grasping framed black and white M.C. Escher prints off the walls and hurling them across the room, knocking over a floor lamp in the corner of the office and upturning couch cushions, ransacking the place as if it were an intruder looking for wall safes or a treasure map or loose change.

Finally, the blustery tentacles, which were flailing all over the room, spied their collective target and coalesced their efforts into one last outburst of super-chilled air that grabbed hold of Ellie's desk chair, propelling it and its occupant with the force of a bullet discharged from its chamber.

Ellie's head was pressed against the back of the leather chair, and the skin on her face was momentarily pulled back. She looked like an "after" photo in an expose of plastic surgery gone wrong. Ellie was shot across the room, crashing into the bookshelf and coming to a stop at its base. With that, the wind stopped as quickly as it had started.

The impact of the chair against the bookshelf produced two effects. The small, dusty, framed photo of Bernice, long forgotten, teetered and then fell, first hitting Ellie on the head and then falling into her lap. Ellie picked it up and gave it a quick look. Bernice, still struggling to smile, appeared to wink at Ellie.

Ellie closed her eyes and re-opened them. Again, Bernice appeared to give Ellie a cheeky wink. Ellie closed her eyes again, and this time rubbed them, hoping the knuckles of her pointer fingers would act like erasers on a chalkboard and wipe away the preposterous. She then refocused her eyes on the photo with some trepidation—first, a quick glimpse. Bernice was static. Now a more extended look. Bernice's eyelids remained in their upright positions. The eye rubbing had worked.

Ellie felt around the back of her head where the frame had first alighted to check for blood or a bump. Neither. She had already dismissed the winks as a product of her own blurred vision from whipping across the room, the impact with the bookshelf, and the hit on the head by Bernice.

The second effect of the crash was that the ruckus prompted Mary Lou to again poke her head in and check on her boss.

"Everything okay... in... here?" asked Mary Lou, eyeing the devastation. "O... M... G." As previously described, Mary Lou was aware of Ellie's instinct to throw any object within reach when she was no longer able to contain her anger, but she had never experienced her boss throwing every object.

"Yes. Of course! Everything is quite all right," Ellie snapped, also surveying the room.

Mary Lou took one step in, "Listen. Um. For what it's worth, you were right. No one is going to take you up on the offer to leave early without pay." Then a little more cautiously and softly, "Honestly, if I had had even a clue the Christmas Eve question would have been a... trigger... I would have avoided the subject."

Ellie, straightening her blouse and pushing the chair back behind her desk, leered at Mary Lou. "I'm going to need you to stay late and clean this room after I leave," Ellie commanded.

"Yes, ma'am," Mary Lou replied obediently, and again began to retreat.

"Oh, and Ms. Haggarty..."

"Yes, ma'am?"

Ellie had learned not to waste time asking questions to which she already knew the answer, but she felt compelled to persist anyway.

"Did you feel a cold draft or anything of the sort, just recently?" she inquired matter-of-factly while straightening items on her desk. "Any reports of any issues with our ventilation system?"

"No. Is there a problem?"

"No, no."

"I can check with building services if you like."

"No. I would not like," replied Ellie. She had already wasted enough time on this. And she dismissed her assistant with a wave of her hand.

When Mary Lou had pulled back completely into her area, Ellie was alone again. She set about developing a logical, or at least reasonable, explanation for what had just happened. Not that she even knew who Sir Arthur Conan Doyle was. Still, at some point in her life, she had arrived at the same conclusion as Sherlock Holmes: *Once you eliminate the impossible, whatever remains, no matter how improbable, must be the truth.*

The only problem was, the whole thing was impossible. Ellie could not eliminate that fact. She stood and walked over to the air vent and put her hand against it. There was a weak, steady stream of warm air, barely perceptible against her fingers and palm.

She sat back down. Then she stood again, walked to the windows, and felt around them for a cold draft. Despite the low, frigid temperatures outside, there wasn't a hint of cold air around the window's well-insulated frame.

She sat back down. Could it have been a dream or delusion? Yes. But why were pictures off the wall and papers all over the floor, and couch cushions disturbed? And why had some books fallen off the bookshelf from her collision? So, no. There was physical evidence that something had taken place.

Could she have lost consciousness while ransackers invaded her office? No. They could not have gotten past Mary Lou without her noticing something. "Ah! Was Mary Lou involved in the conspiracy?" she questioned. Highly improbable but not impossible. She would need to keep a closer eye on that one.

"Is Mrs. Fielder a sorceress?" Ellie led herself down that path. "If she were a sorceress, she would just conjure up the money to pay her rent. And, maybe, a blouse that flattered her.

"Just stop!" Ellie interrupted herself. And she redirected her thoughts to more practical possibilities.

Ellie lost herself in thought, considering all manner of scenarios. No matter which explanation she tried to press herself to accept, there was not one that she, as a logical human being, could endorse.

Ding dong, ding dong. Ding dong, dong ding.

Ellie became conscious of the peals partway through their

ringing out the hour. In the depths of her contemplation, her recognition of the tones came in waves. First, as some soft church bells far off in the hills of her subconscious...

Ding dong, ding dong. Ding dong, dong dong.

... then came her sensibility of the chimes as emanating from her own mantle clock on her bookshelf, cajoling her out of her rumination.

Dong.

DONG.

That realization turned into full-on horror and astonishment as she became wholly aware and recalled that she had removed those infernal chimes from the clock more than a decade ago!

DONG!

And yet there it was...

Ellie had to cover her ears as each strike of the hour was so much louder than its predecessor.

DONG!

... chiming out in full vigor.

"How can this be," Ellie thought, "I castrated that thing!"

And then, as if in angry reply to that thought, came one final emphatic

DONGGG!

Five o'clock.

"Five o'clock!" said Mary Lou poking her head in, this time without the virtue of a knock first. Ellie shot out of her chair with almost as much thrust as her ride to the bookshelf an hour earlier.

"Oh my gosh — so sorry," said Mary Lou. "I didn't mean to startle you. It's just that it is Christm—, er, December 24th, and I need to clean up in here before I go, so... I'm sorry, I shoulda knocked."

"You didn't startle me!" recoiled Ellie. "I don't startle. For God's sake! You must think very highly of yourself, Ms. Haggarty, to think that you could muster what it would take... because we don't know yet what it would take... to startle me! Really! Really?"

Though Ellie had composed herself outwardly, her thoughts

were flying without any navigation. Her mind was like a middle-schooler rushing to class when cruelly tripped from behind by a bully. Now it was frantically clutching at the wall and doorknobs and anything else it could use to remain upright and avoid the embarrassment of tossing its books and planting itself, face first, on the linoleum.

Ellie recognized herself in the sharpness of her response to Mary Lou, and that had served to bring her back into balance. She took in a deep breath through her nose. Held it. "Puh!"

"I'm just going to pack up. You can come in and straighten everything up — quietly — while I'm doing that."

"Yes, ma'am."

Mary Lou ventured all the way in. She rarely spent time in Ellie's office when Ellie was there. She compared it to being a circus hand who had the good sense to move the lion out of its cage before mucking it out. But, there she was, alone with the lioness without a whip or a chair at her disposal.

As Mary Lou made quick work of collecting and stacking the eviction papers, replacing the cushions, and rehanging the pictures, Ellie started gathering some files and articles to review at home. She reached down under the desk and pulled out her briefcase, unclasped the latches, and lifted the smooth brown leather top with the embossed initials, *E.P.*

Out of the corner of her eye, she saw it. There in her briefcase. Impossibly. But there it was! Bernice's picture!

"I returned that to the bookshelf!" thought Ellie. "Or did I? I can't remember. I don't know what I did with it, but I didn't put it in my briefcase. What the...?"

"Oh, are you reading this?" asked Mary Lou, cutting through Ellie's bewilderment.

"What? Oh. What?! Reading what, for heaven's sake?"

Mary Lou, who had been replacing the dislodged books to their slots on the shelves, was leafing through the book in question.

"*A Christmas Carol*. You know... Dickens?"

"No! Why would I read that? Gawd!"

"You've never read *A Christmas Carol*?"

"Ms. Haggarty, you are on very thin ice."

"May I borrow it? I'd like to read it to my nephew tonight."

"Ms. Haggarty, I do not waste my time reading publications or periodicals that have no benefit to me or my business. I suggest if you want to get further in life, that you adopt a similar attitude and instill the same in your nephew. I'm not sure about you, but there may still be time to spare him."

Having stymied Mary Lou, Ellie looked back down at her briefcase and at Bernice's pained eyes and forced smile. "How?" she thought.

Meanwhile, while struggling to get the book back on its shelf, Mary Lou dropped it, once again [nearly] startling Ellie.

"Oh, for the love of… Just take the book! If it gets you out of my office any sooner, take the book! I'll want it back, of course, because it is my property. But right now, take it and go. Leave me at once."

"Yes, Ms. Printh." Mary Lou blew some dust off the top of the gilded pages and placed the book under her arm. She carried it with her out the door and away from the space where it had sat untouched since the day Ellie moved into her office, seventeen years earlier.

Ellie did not hear Mary Lou leave or even pay any notice to her re-entry (head only) to wish her boss the "blessings of the day, tomorrow." Ellie was singularly obsessed with the object she now held in her right hand, turning it over and over as if it were a Rubik's Cube, and she was trying to figure out where to start solving it.

There was nothing unusual about the cheap metal frame with gold paint fading to dull gray in random raised spots on its surface. On the back was the thick, black cardboard that fit snugly into the groove of the frame. There were little hinges screwed into the backing, securing the flap that extended, allowing the photo to stand for display. And nothing else. No strings or wires. There was nothing the least bit suspicious about the frame that would explain any trickery involved in depositing itself in Ellie's briefcase.

"How?" questioned Ellie again, her eyes fixed on the photo's previously permanent place on the bookshelf. She then tried to imagine some sequence of falls and bounces and ricochets that could have convolutedly transported the frame from where Ellie had placed it after the collision (though Ellie was now applying not a small amount of pressure on her memory to recant that one bit of testimony to aid in the postulation of a host of other reasonable theories) to the bottom left corner of a latched briefcase which had been sitting under her desk and literally inches from her legs. Even then, it would have had to have passed through the leaves of a ficus tree and a solid cherry wood desk and into the clasped leather brief-case. The Warren Commission could not have devised a plausible explanation.

Once you remove the impossible... At first, it seemed improbable that Ellie's own recollection had betrayed her. But faced with other unsettling answers, she was quickly warming to that explanation.

"I must have been mindlessly carrying this thing about," reasoned Ellie, referring to the picture, "and at some point, I must have stuck it in the briefcase. I don't remember doing that. I don't know why I would have done that. But it's what must have happened. The events of this last hour must have played a part in my distraction. Of course, they did."

Further satisfying Ellie with this conclusion was her rational-izing that on those occasions when she drove to work (though often, since the transplant, she would walk the previously unman-ageable distance), she would frequently arrive with no memory of stopping at red lights or proceeding through green lights or yielding to a pedestrian on the crosswalk (only because it was the law) or slowing her car as it crossed over the Belgium block stones of Germantown Avenue. She was certain those things happened; she just had no recollection of them.

She reckoned that there were many activities and actions her conscious mind delegated to the back of her brain during the course of the day, so she was freed up to engage in more critical, higher-level strategic endeavors. The photo's placement in the briefcase must have occurred during one of those times her frontal lobe was otherwise occupied — while pondering the maelstrom, most likely.

Ellie decided to resolve that matter thusly and put it behind her. She had mindlessly placed the photo in the briefcase. There was no other logical explanation, and although improbable, it was not at all impossible.

Ellie, somewhat out of sorts for her, but nonetheless still high-functioning in relation to most people, took one more quick look at the picture of Bernice and placed it in her top desk drawer, and locked it in. And then, for good measure, she pushed in her chair as far as it would go against the desk as if to provide some additional resistance should Bernice manage to undo the lock from the inside and try to force open the drawer to slip out.

A rare fantasy crossed Ellie's mind. She imagined herself placing the frame in a tiny straightjacket, wrapping it in little iron chains (she envisioned paper clips), and slipping a heavy lock through the links. Then she pictured herself making a show of throwing away the key and placing that whole package in the desk drawer, locking it, and shoving the bookshelf across the room and up against it, for good measure.

"Ha!" She saw herself saying in her reverie, "Let's see you get out of that, Bernice!"

Ellie's mind had done a little more delegating while she had been lost in this fancy. For, as she reclaimed her awareness, her laptop was shut down and in her briefcase, and she was slipping her folders into the sleeve of her attaché. "See," she thought, further reassuring herself she had accurately solved the Curious Case of the Bernice in the Briefcase.

She latched the briefcase, grabbed her coat and scarf, left her office, and locked the door behind her. Locking her office was not a common practice for her. Though she would not have admitted it, the safeguard posed an extra challenge for Bernice should she pull a Houdini act and get past the desk chair. Ellie had already convinced herself she had only taken the extra precaution because of the sensitive nature of the eviction notices sitting in the open on a corner of her desk.

Christmas Eve morning had been as bright as an inquisitive child and as cold as a stuck-up debutante, with a sky as blue as the mood of a jilted groom on his wedding day. Therefore, Ellie had walked — more accurately, marched — to The Printh Company that morning, past coffee drinkers braving the chill and sitting at tables outside the Chestnut Hill Coffee Company, by commuters running for the local train that would take them to 30th Street Station and then on perhaps to New York, Harrisburg or Washington, DC.

She passed shopkeepers readying their quaint stores for what they were sure would be a busy day. She saw police officers, one on each side of the street, walking in opposite directions, but the peace was keeping itself this hour of the morning. And she breezed by shoppers arriving early on the Avenue hoping against hope some shops would open up before their advertised hours so they could start crossing off items on their long to-do lists.

Though Ellie noticed little, she observed much. That may seem like a contradiction, but one may be observant without placing any thought or motive behind what they see. So it was with Ellie. She was attentive to the fact that everyone within her view that morning seemed weary and joyless and just going through motions as if programmed to do so. But she gave no thought to it. She was like a video surveillance camera, recording everything but applying no judgment to anything.

She spoke to not one of the scores of people she encountered. She made eye contact with no one. And likewise, no one wished her good morning or even glanced her way, despite exchanging holiday greetings with other apparent strangers in their paths.

Despite the spectacle of a long, lean woman in a knee-length black overcoat with the tail of gray scarf trailing behind her, walking at a pace at which she seemed to be overtaking a sidewalk slab with each step, she made her morning trek as if invisible.

That was the morning. A lot of drama occurs in the average person's life between getting up and going down. Ellie was not the average person, so looking down from on high upon her inferiors, she was often amused at the way they seemed to invite trouble. Take Mrs. Fielder, for example. Spending her rent money on Christmas presents and a turkey would soon land her and her family in a homeless shelter.

This day was different in that the trouble and chaos Ellie believed her fellow humans invited to their own doorsteps, through a host of poor judgments and emotion-charged decisions, must have gotten the wrong address. Not only had they knocked on her door in error, but they walked in and made themselves right at home in her office. Their welcome was overstayed the moment they arrived.

The world to which Ellie was walking into at the end of the day was far different from the one she experienced on her morning hike into work. Sometime around two in the afternoon, clouds had arrived to snuff out the child's natural curiosity, encourage the debutante in her haughtiness, and worsen the groom's disposition to battleship gray.

Once the clouds had paved the way in the mid-afternoon hours, the fog came rolling in like tanks. It was a heavy fog. Odd for such a cold day, but it lay on Philadelphia thick and sinewy like pillow stuffing.

Seemingly suspended throughout the haze were minuscule shards of ice whose frosty talons latched onto the faces and hands of the hustlers and bustlers and then dissipated almost instantly upon contact with exposed skin, still stinging nonetheless.

The little icy fragments clung to the lampposts and made them glassy. They settled on the stone blocks in the streets and made them as slick as personal injury attorneys. Not a few procrastinating gift wranglers, going in or coming out of the trendy shops, had the fog to thank for obscuring from others' view, and potential amusement, their ridiculous contortions as they attempted to keep themselves upright when their unsuspecting feet hit the glazed Belgian block.

Adding to their degree of difficulty was the concurrent juggling of boxed cakes or wrapped presents, or crates of clanking wine bottles.

In contrast to everyone else's struggling through the elements, Ellie was at ease in the foggy, frigid, frosted evening. She glided so effortlessly and confidently, it was as if she floated above the sidewalk and through the lumbering legions of last-minute shoppers. It could easily have appeared that she was suspended under each arm by two invisible bodyguards, one on each side, lifting her up and ferrying her down the avenue. She was most definitely in her milieu.

Ellie found sublime comfort in the darkness of winter's late afternoons. She put on the dark and cold like she was slipping into an old cozy sweater and well-worn slippers. Whereas most people started grumbling about how short the days were getting by late September, Ellie would be satisfied with December's pre-five p.m. sunsets all year round.

Though she had long ago shredded and incinerated and thereby disintegrated any happy thoughts of her early life, some impression had been made on her soul from a time when this hour of the day in this season of the year was spent waiting at the front window of her childhood home for her father to return from work while not-so-secretly worrying about his traversing the snow-covered roads.

The windows would fog up from the warmth created by her mother making dinner on the stove in the kitchen. From her little chair set in its position to keep watch for her dad, Ellie would draw mostly zoo animals on the steamed windows with her frail finger. When her dad's Pontiac made the turn into the driveway, its headlights shone through her elephants and giraffes and lions, bringing them, and Ellie, to life.

From a very early age, Ellie had a dark premonition that her daddy would be taken from her too soon. On those winter evenings, the lights of his car provided immediate relief from that doleful despair in her heart.

She had no conscious awareness that this nightly relief in her long-vanquished childhood was the reason she drew comfort from the early dusks of cold winter; she had given it no consideration. She just preferred it.

There was still the same mix of shoppers and storekeepers and commuters, but by this hour, it was a different shift. But all were still frazzled and scurrying about. There was an even drearier gloominess pervading their countenances, which drew a sharp contrast to the backdrop of the festive lights and fresh greens in the shop windows and over doors than Ellie had observed in the morning.

Everyone looked wearier. Some looked hopeless, running out of time to procure that perfect gift or find fresh cranberry sauce before every place closed up for the night. But they all trudged along, marching to the front in the procrastinators' band, all horns and percussion, drowning out the peals from the large bells from the church tower high above the crowd and the clangs from the little handbell of the Salvation Army Santa in the thick of the throng at his post on the corner.

November's bright brigade of revelers had devolved into this now haggard, agitated, warring, and battered battalion as they had advanced throughout the exhaustive modern two-month holiday shopping campaign. This initially peaceful troupe had long ago taken up their credit cards and waged battle on the home front at their computers and smartphones, or on the foreign soil of malls, discount stores, gift shops, and specialty boutiques, then ultimately settled on the most personal of presents… the gift card.

And now, at long last, they were limping into the campaign's final fight where their fate would be decided. That judgment would take place, as it did every year, at the front known to all as Christmas morning.

Ellie didn't care about any of that. Christmas was a day to get caught up on work and to be left alone. So, as she passed the arctic sea of humanity on her way home, and as the cold air cleared away that "nonsense" from the office, she decided she would take her usual dinner at her usual table at her usual tavern, McNally's.

The restaurant was more crowded and festive than on a typical evening. Ellie made her way, squeezing past the barflies who were downing one last dose of liquid encouragement before heading home for what could be twenty-four consecutive hours of family time. "On second thoughts, I'll have one more," Ellie heard one loving husband and father say.

Ellie noticed there was a new presence behind the bar this particular evening. She recognized him as a former business rival that she had not only bested but clearly, based on his current occupation, completely annihilated. She avoided eye contact, turning her head away and partially concealing her face with her hand.

If it had been a normal day, she would have enjoyed gloating over her conquest by sidling up to the bar and ordering an obscure cocktail like a Basil Fawlty or Pimm's Cup in an effort to befuddle and frustrate this new bartender. But this had not been a normal day, and as much pleasure as she might have derived from a victory lap, Ellie felt it would be much more enjoyable if she waited until a day when she was feeling more herself.

She made her way past the crowded tables on her right, usually set snugly for a maximum of four diners, but tonight some were supporting five or six. No one seemed to mind the lack of any personal space. The days of social distancing were behind them.

"Merry Christmas, Ms. Printh," said Anne McNally, the tavern proprietor, greeting Ellie. Anne knew everyone on a first name basis and greeted everyone that way. But Ellie had established a boundary years earlier, and Anne abided by it. Ellie was a Mr. Peterson in a bar full of Norms.

"I assume, despite your volumes this evening, my table in the back is available," replied Ellie.

"It sure is," replied Anne.

"Fine," said Ellie, "I will have the salmon, well done, with the béarnaise sauce on the side. And do you have asparagus?"

"Of course," said Anne.

"Fine. I'll have that too. And I'll seat myself while you get me my S. Pelligrino."

"It's already waiting for you at the table, with your glass, filled three-quarters of the way with ice. And your order has already been placed."

"Presumptuous! But, since you were correct, my disdain for your brazenness will not be reflected in your server's tip."

"Thank you," replied Anne, turning her head away from Ellie for the sole purpose of rolling her eyes. "But you know, if it's Wednesday, it must be salmon and béarnaise sauce. Just trying to be efficient."

Anne began to walk away, but Ellie stopped her. "Ms. McNally. A moment?" she said, bidding Anne come her way.

"Yes?" asked Anne.

"You have a new man behind the bar?"

"Yes," answered Anne, knowing where Ellie was going with this line of questioning.

"That is David Burke? Yes?"

"It is. Is that a problem?"

"Well, it's just… why is he working here? I mean, he used to be my biggest competitor. Now he's tending bar at a tavern? Oh wait, is this one of those charity evenings?"

Anne hesitated, not knowing exactly how she wanted to respond. Then, resolved, she said, "From what I heard, you stole his company out from under him and left him with nothing."

"Is that what you heard? Well, let me set this story straight. I didn't steal his company. I outmaneuvered David Burke, fairly and squarely. He trusted people he shouldn't have trusted, which is none of my affair, but it did create an opportunity that I took full advantage of."

Ellie continued: "And if he were a good man of business, he would have seen it coming. Being trusting is quaint, but it is not conducive to success in the business world."

"I can't say as I agree with any of that. I've known David for a long time. Things haven't been going well for him. Whatever happened supposedly made him damaged goods, and he hasn't been able to find work."

"I thought his wife had a good job. Surely she can support him?"

"She is in the process of divorcing him. They have two young kids. I don't really need another bartender, you know, but I'm just trying to help."

Ellie looked at Anne square in the eyes and said earnestly, "Let me give you a little piece of advice, Ms. McNally. Restaurants, even one as apparently popular as yours, have very thin margins. Though it may seem a nice thing to do for someone, you know, down on his luck, you must also think of yourself and your patrons. If you hire every person with a sad story who walks in the door, you will need to raise prices or lower your standards to make ends meet, and either way, you will lose even your most loyal customers. Restaurants are houses of cards, Ms. McNally. Houses of cards. And if you staff yours with jokers like David Burke, it will all come crashing down on your head."

"David is a good man," replied Anne with conviction. "Good people make any business better. I'm happy to have him here."

"I'm just saying… Do what you will with your business, but I would hate to have to find a new regular spot."

"No worries," said Anne as she smiled and walked away.

Ellie slid into the back booth, obscured from the rest of the diners, but if Ellie chose to, she could crane her neck to look around the corner at the rest of the tavern's clientele. Of course, she never did. Why would she want to do that? She found that most people had no table manners at all.

One evening, while bending over to pick up her napkin, which had fallen off the side of her lap, she accidentally caught sight of a woman licking mayonnaise off her fingers as if they were sugar-coated lollipops. It so turned her stomach and dispatched her appetite that Ellie rose, walked over to the finger-licking woman, handed her the napkin she had retrieved from the floor, and said, "I no longer have a need for this," and walked out.

Since that episode, Ellie took every precaution against even accidentally glimpsing another diner. But this particular evening, as Ellie sat reading emails on her phone and waiting for her meal, her concentration was repeatedly interrupted by the most heinous wailing she had ever heard. It sounded to Ellie that the sobbing was emanating from a woman, but it could also have been a wounded animal, or perhaps a World War II-era air raid siren.

Ellie tried to ignore it. She expected that some busybody in the restaurant would seek to comfort the distraught woman. Only the bawling continued. Louder and shriller. Ellie took a deep breath and held it. "Puh."

Whereas most people would want to sneak a peek if only out of curiosity, Ellie decided it was time to shoot this caterwauler a stern glare that would effectively further dampen her low spirits and hopefully the volume of her despair.

She took down one of the menus she was using to shield herself from the mass of humanity and peeked around the corner. At the table closest to her was an old couple with an even older couple. Parents with their adult son and his wife, she concluded. The matching buck teeth and enormous ears of the old man and the older man had confirmed the conjecture.

Oblivious to Ellie was a sadness that weighed heavily on the older couple, which the husband and wife were making an effort, if not a wholly successful one, to obscure from their son and daughter-in-law. The son, whom Ellie, within three-tenths of a second of laying eyes upon him had assigned the name Bucky, Jr., and his wife, Ugly Hat, were not unmindful of the parents' feeble attempt to soldier on. That scant effort to conceal their feelings gave the younger couple license and cover to ignore whatever issue was pervading their evening.

Bucky, Jr. and Ugly Hat knew the reason for the anguish that hung over the parents like clouds besieging mountaintops — relegation. The old couple had been bumped to Christmas Eve. They had never missed a Christmas morning with Bucky, Jr. ever since they brought him home from the hospital more than six decades ago. But Bucky, Jr. and Ugly Hat had downsized earlier this year, and now the new, smaller house would be cramped with just their children and young grandchildren. So the conversation had taken place a couple of weeks earlier.

"How about we celebrate Christmas with dinner at your favorite place on Christmas Eve instead of your coming over on Christmas Day?" Bucky had told his mom over the phone from the green of the seventh hole at Whitemarsh. "It's getting too much for you. And with all the kids running around... It'll just be better all the way around."

Despite his mother's initial protests, it was decided. And although Bucky, Jr. felt a little tug at his heart when he thought of his mom and dad alone all day at Christmas, exchanging no gifts, for those days had long since passed, and eating dinner in front of the TV as if it was just any other day, here they were at McNally's on Christmas Eve, waiting for the check in silence. They looked like a bank of security cameras, each surveying a different quadrant of the restaurant, but never pointed at each other.

Ellie, eyeing that foursome, wondered why they didn't all have their focuses trained on the woman doing the obnoxious blubbering. "Perhaps they are too polite?" thought Ellie.

Ellie slid a little further out of the booth to spy another table. Here was a young couple. It looked as if they were grabbing a bite to eat before going to a party, obviously at the home of a hostess who is a notoriously bad cook. This was confirmed when another couple, just leaving, paused at their table. The man said to the seated couple, "Going to Becky's party?" They nodded affirmatively. "Us too. Hey, could you not tell Becky you saw us here having dinner?" They all laughed. The seated woman replied, "We won't if you won't!"

These couples were also paying no heed to the loud lamentations.

"I'll have to take care of this myself, I guess," Ellie said out loud to herself in a determined manner. She slid all the way out of the booth, this time intent on locking eyes with the source of the sobbing. Whereas Ellie was prepared for just about anything, she was not prepared for nothing. Though the wailing continued, there was no source of it to be seen.

Bearing in mind the unusual occurrences of the afternoon and observing the disinterest from the first two tables she had surveyed, a suppressed fear surfaced that she was the only one for whose benefit the yowling was intended.

At that moment, Meg McNally, Anne's sister and co-proprietor, arrived with Ellie's salmon and asparagus.

"Are you all right, Ms. Printh?" asked Meg, finding Ellie out of the booth and frozen in mid-step. The question had the effect of silencing the offending boo-hooer.

Ellie quickly collected herself and shifted her eyes to meet Meg's.

"Of course I'm all right. My napkin blew off my lap. This establishment is terribly drafty, Ms. McNally. Why, if I don't weigh down my napkin, I could probably work off all the calories from my meal from the constant retrieval of it. If I wanted to get up and back down with this frequency, I would attend a midnight mass."

Though it was not intended as a joke, Meg laughed.

Ellie slid back into the booth, and Meg set Ellie's meal down in front of her.

"Can I get you anything else?" asked Meg.

Ellie did a quick inventory of the table. Salmon, béarnaise sauce, asparagus. "No. No. That will be all."

Meg turned to leave.

"Oh, Ms. McNally. Let me ask you…" began Ellie in a slightly hushed voice.

"Yes?" replied Meg, intrigued. It was highly unlike Ellie to speak in a confidential tone.

Ellie, seeing the extent of Meg's interest, decided against continuing. She was only going to ask if she had heard what sounded like a cat being tortured.

"Nothing. Never mind." Then, referring to her dinner in front of her, "You can put this on my tab. And, I think service tonight warrants the full 15% gratuity. No demerits."

"Thanks," said Meg as cheerfully as possible, then continued under her breath, "Now, let me get out of here before I say or do anything that might cause you to change your mind."

Ellie ate her dinner quickly, anxious to get home and be home.

By the time Ellie exited McNally's, most of the stores on Germantown Avenue had closed, and there were only a few stragglers out and about. The Salvation Army Santa was still clanging the handbell and trying to encourage some last-minute donations into his big red kettle.

Ellie buttoned up her coat, wrapped her scarf around her neck, and headed in the direction of home. As she reached the corner where the Salvation Army Santa was stationed, Ellie stopped to look both ways even though the streets were empty. She always looked both ways since she was a little girl.

She looked to the left, nothing. She looked to the right, nothing. She looked back to the left. And there, standing right next to her, was the Santa. She did not permit it to show, but she had been shaken to her core. She looked back to the right at the location he was standing a split second earlier. The kettle was unmanned. She looked back at the Santa, standing next to her, head down and face turned away. As Ellie began to cross the street, the Santa grabbed her arm.

Ellie froze momentarily, not from fright or impudence, but from the unfamiliar sensation of being touched, if that is what you could call it through his gloves and her multiple layers of clothing. Still, when was the last time anyone had squeezed her arm or even tapped her on the shoulder? She had no idea.

As she turned toward him, the Santa lifted its face toward her.

She recognized the eyes at first, but then when Santa pulled down the beard…

Ellie let out a quiet expression of surprise, but inside she screamed, "Bernice's face!

Bernice's face!"

Ellie again turned to cross the street. This time, the Santa spoke to her.

"Sorry, ma'am. I didn't mean to scare you."

Though she had never heard Bernice speak, she knew that could not have been Bernice's voice. So she stopped and turned to look again at the Santa. This time, she was looking at a middle-aged

African-American gentleman who had now removed his cap and the entire beard, as if trying to reassure Ellie that he was not going to kill her, or mug her, or put her on the naughty list. (He would have been too late for that anyway.)

"My phone died. And I need to text my wife to pick me up," explained Santa with a broad and warm smile. "It's probably not safe for me to be out here too much longer; there's a lot of cash in that kettle. Could I trouble you to, you know, help me out? Can I use your phone?"

Ellie looked him in the eyes. He had very kind eyes like any Santa should. They twinkled in the glow of the street light. She could not mask the relief that washed over her. She looked down at her feet and took a careful step in the direction of the fake Santa, reached into her coat pocket, looked up again into the sweet face of the Salvation Army volunteer, re-establishing eye contact, and said, "No," in a flat and emphatic tone.

Then she pulled out a small air horn from her pocket and gave it one short, loud blast that would have knocked the three wise men off their camels. She turned, looked both ways perfunctorily, and walked toward home at the briskest pace she could sustain.

She could not say this had been the worst day of her life. No, she knew that date all too well. But it had been the most uncomfortable and uncontrollable day in all her adult life.

She felt like she was unraveling. She knew that what she had experienced in the past few hours could not have really happened.

"Things like that just don't happen," she told herself. "It is impossible. But everything seemed real. "Are people conspiring against me? Could it be Mary Lou? Mary Lou is hardly a mastermind, but there is no shortage of ex-employees who might want to take me down. I had to be hallucinating or losing my mind. Impossible! Have I snapped?" These were the brand-new thoughts occupying her mind as she paced purposefully and hastily to the sanctuary and, she hoped, sanity, of her own home.

She paused only once in her rush to get to her house. And that was when she came to a stately million-dollar home with what appeared to be another million dollars' worth of tacky Christmas lights and animatronic reindeer. Plus, there was any number of inflatable Santas, including a giant Mickey Mouse in a Santa suit going down a chimney while Minnie Mouse stood by adoringly. There was a large toy soldier, Rudolph the Red-Nosed Reindeer, Frosty the Snowman, and Elf. It was a veritable Who's Who of the secular Christmas illuminati.

As Ellie beheld the spectacle in disbelief and disgust, a little girl stepped out from behind a bush.

"Hey, lady! My dad did all this. Ain't it the most greatest thing you ever saw?" asked the beaming child.

"It's atrocious!" responded Ellie.

"Thank you!" said the girl, who obviously did not know the meaning of the word.

Ellie's house was a large stone estate built with the area's indigenous Wissahickon schist. It sat in a neighborhood of similarly constructed homes, all set back from the street a good distance, and each of them fenced in, some with white picket, some with wrought iron, some with thick hedges. A visitor to the tree-lined neighborhood, recalling the old adage about fences, would assume that these separators made all of the residents the best of neighbors.

Ellie's property was a fortress. Hers was the only home with a stone fence, about five feet high and extending all the way around the property, except for an opening for the driveway and an old carriage house-style door, originally placed there as a more attractive entrance for visitors who were entering from the street. That door was now ornamental only; Ellie had had it bolted to the stone walls on both sides of it.

Spanning the driveway entrance was a large iron gate with a substantial gold lion's head set right in the middle. The gate latched and locked on the right-hand side and swung in toward the house when opening. When Ellie drove, she could use the programmed button on the car's overhead console to open the barrier from the comfort of her heated seat. On the days she walked, she needed to use the key and manually release the latch to gain entry.

And so it was on this Christmas Eve evening that Ellie's steps finally turned into her usually sleepy neighborhood, now wide awake with music and lights and laughter emanating from almost every house. Ellie, striding at a speed skater's pace, was fast approaching that gate with the gold lion's head guarding her darkened house.

Still a few yards from her driveway, Ellie began reaching for her keys. She had had enough of the outside world by this hour every day, but that feeling was especially keen this day. She just wanted to get on the other side of the fence and shut everything and everyone out.

In her haste to pull the gate key from her pocket, the same pocket that contained the air horn and a can of mace, she snagged the key chain on the inside lining. She tugged at it with such force she not only freed it from the threads it had caught on but also from her own grasp. The keys flung out of her hand and flew into the darkness.

First, she heard metal against metal. That would be the keys hitting the wrought iron. Then, as she expected would follow, she heard metal hitting pavement. That would be her keys landing on the driveway.

Ellie could only hope the keys had alit on her side of the gate. This was unfamiliar territory for her. These kinds of things just did not happen to Ellie Printh. She had always made quite certain of that. Yet, here she was, at the mercy of a carom, perhaps about to crawl around on her hands and knees on the wet, cold macadam or maybe scale a wrought iron gate.

"Puh," she expelled.

Pulling out her phone, she turned on the flashlight app and looked around. She spotted the keys right away and quickly assessed there was a downside and upside to her situation. Downside: the keys were on the ground on the other side of the locked gate. Upside: they looked to be within her reach.

Ellie squatted and reached her arm between the bars. Her fingers were a good three inches from the keys. From this position, she could not retrieve them. Her knees were in the way. Not to be denied, Ellie lay prostrate on her stomach with her left arm gripping a wrought iron bar, the side of her head pressed up against it as well. Her right arm and most of her shoulder were through the gap to utilize her full extension, which to her relief was more than enough to retrieve the keys.

She got to her knees and whisked off her coat, then got to her feet and brushed off her knees and slacks. When she rose and straightened her back, she found herself eye to eye with the lion's head.

As she paused there for a moment, fixated on the gold lion's face, nothing happened. "Yeah," whispered Ellie to the lion and perhaps to Bernice, "don't even think about it."

She quickly unlocked the gate and slipped inside just as soon as it had opened wide enough for her slim frame to do so. Once through, she stopped the gate's momentum and pushed it back into the latched position, and locked herself in behind the safety of the bars and under the protection of her new and only friend, the lion.

Ellie walked swiftly to the front door, lifted the cover of the alarm keypad, and punched in the code, 2-7-1-8-1-2, which sounded like "boop, booop, beep, boooop, beep, boop." At the end of the last "boop," the front door sprung open, and lights came on inside the house.

Ellie entered, closing the door immediately behind her. She reached for the keypad on the wall, quickly pushing numbered keys in the right succession: boop, booop, beep, boooop, beep, boop. Ellie could hear the door latch and the lock engage. The digital readout on the keypad read "SECURE." She was home.

Ellie caught a quick glimpse of herself in the hallway mirror. She had never seen herself disheveled before and almost mistook her own image as an intruder. She would deal with her appearance later, she thought.

The house was quiet, and that was how Ellie liked it. Usually. This night, not so much. She owned a television, but it was rarely used. Some mornings she would watch CNBC while she ate her Special K, sipped her black coffee, and read her Wall Street Journal.

Never had she turned on the television in the evening, until this evening. Before she even took off her coat and scarf, she went to the coffee table, took up the remote, and turned on the set.

Shark Tank was on, but she didn't care what it was; she wasn't looking for anything in particular. She wasn't going to watch it. She was going to use television in the way most Americans used it, as a substitute for thinking. She turned up the volume and set down the remote. Kevin O'Leary's acerbic put-downs, which were never a source of consolation to hopeful entrepreneurs, were sweet comfort to Ellie this night.

She picked up a different remote control and depressed two buttons simultaneously. Instantly, blinds which were built into every window in her house began to descend, creating a whirring sound throughout the home, drowning out Barbara Corcoran's offer to the inventor of something or other. All the blinds reached the bottom pane at the same time, creating a loud "thwup" that sounded as if Ellie had just sealed herself in a giant Tupperware bowl.

Ellie unbuttoned her overcoat, slid her shoulders out, and just let the coat fall off her to the ground. She unwrapped the scarf and dropped it on the coat, took off her gloves, and mindlessly flung them on the pile as well. If she didn't get to it, the housekeeper would pick them up the day after next.

Ellie went to her room and quickly changed into pajamas and a robe, and slippers. Most nights, Ellie stayed in her work clothes until it was time for bed. Most nights, she sat at her desk in her study upstairs and read business publications and did paperwork. She sent emails to employees just to see who responded after hours, and she would take note of who waited until the next morning to reply.

But after what she was calling her "hallucinations" from earlier in the day, she thought she might take a night off from work and just rest her mind.

Her plan for this night was to light the fire in the fireplace, fix herself a pot of herbal tea, sit on the couch and engage in some mind-numbing activity — and she considered television viewing to be novocaine for the brain — until she was tired enough to go to bed, fall asleep, and have this day behind her.

With each extraordinary happening that had occurred in her day, from the windstorm in her office to Bernice's photo ending up in her briefcase, to the woman crying at McNally's, to the image of Bernice's face on the Salvation Army Santa, Ellie had been able to convince herself, with increasing certainty, that there was a logical explanation for each incident. And, with each passing minute from the latest bizarre encounter, she had actually begun wondering if the whole afternoon might have just been an elaborate daydream.

Still, not one for undisciplined thought, she knew that if she had indeed been letting her mind wander, it was likely due to fatigue. She was also convinced that a night of uninterrupted sleep would be conducive to her welfare and the reclamation of control over her mind.

Ellie never liked tea. And with her first sip, she was instantly reminded of that fact. She seldom drank it, couldn't remember the last time she had made it. Further, she had no idea how long this herbal tea had been in her cupboard. But she needed something to warm her bones and soothe her spirit, and she knew she did not want coffee if she were to make an early night of it.

She set the tea down and picked up the remote control. She flipped the channel. "It's a Wonderful Life" was on. The actor was Jimmy Stewart, and his voice was recognizable enough, thought Ellie, but that did not look like Jimmy Stewart. She leaned in a little closer to the screen. It was Jimmy Stewart's body, but, "Ack!!" she shrieked. It was Bernice's face, and those were her lips saying hello to the old building and loan!

Ellie quickly turned the channel. Here was Rudolph the Red-Nosed Reindeer. "Only," she thought, "that snowman's face... my God! It's Bernice singing about silver and gold!"

She turned the station again, now frantic. Again, Ellie could not believe her eyes. Bernice was telling some round-faced boy in horn-rimmed glasses that he'll put his eye out! "What?!?!?!"

Click. Now there was an old man in a nightgown and nightcap sitting alone by a fire, eating soup. Ellie was sure she had seen this movie before as a kid. "That's Scrooge," she recalled.

Her heart was racing at this point, and she was inclined to turn off the TV, but instead, she threw down the remote and started pacing back and forth behind the couch. She thought about calling her doctor, but she was not ready for anyone to know she had gone mad.

On television, every bell in Scrooge's house started peeling, and he was covering his ears. The noise distracted Ellie's train-wreck of thought briefly. Then she began pacing again and wringing her hands.

"There is a reasonable explanation," she was telling herself, "and I will figure it out." She had begun once again the process of convincing herself that nothing had happened, that probably she had just started nodding off and dreamed the whole sequence. She had just made the decision, and mustered the courage, to take back up the remote and turn the station to the other programs to prove that to herself, when she heard a loud,

BOOP.

"What the hell was that?" Ellie said out loud to no one or maybe to Scrooge, who appeared to have an expression of a blend of quizzicality and horrification on his face as she imagined she must have on her usually stoic face as well.

BOOOP!

"Where is that coming from?" thought Ellie. "It's not a car horn. Yet I know that sound."

BEEP!

"Oh my God!" said Ellie in her head. "It's the security keypad."

BOOOOP!

Ellie's back straightened and stiffened. She was not one to shy away from confrontation. She was more than ready to take on whoever or whatever was responsible for throwing off her day. She welcomed a showdown. It is more difficult to wage battle within yourself than to fight an enemy outside. Finally, she would face her abuser.

BEEP!

"Bring it on!" she said.

Ellie walked toward the door and took up her position.

BOOP!

Ellie's front door unlocked and swung open, and at that instant, a gust of bitterly cold air blew, in carrying leaves and other debris. Ellie stood still and resolute in the midst of it. After a few seconds, the wind subsided, and the door closed and locked. There was nothing else.

Ellie stood there quietly for a moment, still looking at the door curiously when a quick, thunderous "BOO!" exploded against her left ear like the sonorous blast of a tugboat horn. She felt hot, stale breath on her skin and was nearly felled by a foul stench that, if she had not been so preoccupied with fear, would have made her wretch.

Ellie jumped and turned abruptly, coming face-to-face and nose to nose with Bernice. Bernice had clearly derived great pleasure from giving Ellie such a fright, for now she was having no trouble lifting both sides of her mouth in a ghastly grin. In fact, she tried to laugh, but it seemed she did not know how and ended up doubled over, dry heaving.

"It's a good thing you have my heart instead of your old pump, or you would have been joining me on this side tonight," said Bernice, pulling herself together. Her voice was gruff. It sounded like her words had to ride out of her mouth in the back of a pickup truck traversing a gravel road. She doubled over again, trying to laugh, but nothing was coming out. It was a gruesome sight, and Ellie looked on in horror.

"This really is Bernice," Ellie had to admit to herself. But not Bernice, really. More like a hologram of Bernice. Her ghost, Ellie conceded.

Ellie could see the television through Bernice's capacious torso.

She could see that Scrooge was confronting a ghost of his own, right at that very moment. His visiting specter was fettered with chains and cash boxes. Bernice was not likewise encumbered.

Ellie dispensed with the initial shock and filled its void with anger.

"What is this?!" asked Ellie harshly. "What are you? What do you want?!"

"Shut up!" commanded Bernice. She said it with such force that Ellie's fire was immediately doused. She cowered a bit, like a disobedient dog familiar with the back of its master's hand, raised and ready to swing. Ellie took a step back, partly in fright and partly due to the odor that came out of Bernice's mouth along with her remonstration.

"If you think ghosts are timid little floaty things, you're sorely mistaken, Ms. Printh," continued Bernice. "I've had my way with you all afternoon."

"So, you are Bernice?" Ellie asked, looking for some verification since the two had never been properly introduced.

"I would say 'in the flesh,' but that would not be quite accurate, now would it?" growled Bernice. "Now, I could turn myself to flesh and bones if you'd like, but I've been gone seven years, and that would not be a pretty sight, and if you think my breath is foul, well…"

"I can't believe this! This cannot be happening!" Ellie told herself out loud. She moved to the couch and sat with her back to the apparition. It was a weak attempt to ignore it out of existence.

"You don't believe it, huh?" Bernice asked. She floated through the couch and stood in front of Ellie again. She positioned herself in front of the television. Ellie could see and hear Scrooge asking his ghost why spirits walked the Earth.

Ellie looked up at the apparition and confronted her. "It's my mind playing tricks on me. Everything I know tells me that you are not real and that there is a psychological or physiological cause for all of this. I could be dreaming, or I could be hallucinating. I could be crazy. You could be the result of something I had for dinner that sickened me. The salmon, or maybe the sauce. There could be more béarnaise than Bernice about you."

At this, Bernice raised her arms and shook her fists. Her face contorted and distorted, and she let out a loud wail that sounded like the crying Ellie had heard at McNally's earlier in the evening.

"Stop! Stop it!" demanded Ellie, covering her ears.

"You know in my heart," said Bernice, reverting to her previous form and adopting a more measured tone, "who I am and what I am. It was not easy for me to get here. I had to make a case for this, and I don't have much time. So stop fighting. Trust your eyes and, I suspect by now, your instincts.

"Why are you here? What do you want with me?" asked Ellie, regaining her composure and rigid posture.

On TV, Jacob Marley was leading Scrooge over to a window.

"I am here to help."

"I don't need any help. I do quite well on my own," argued Ellie. "From your wailing in the restaurant, it sounds like maybe you are the one that needs help."

"You idiot! That was your pain I was channeling," countered Bernice.

Ellie reacted as if she had just been slapped across the face, but she said nothing in reply.

Bernice continued. "Once I crossed to the other side of the veil — that's what it is like, a thin curtain between these two worlds — I could see everything clearly. I realized I had it all wrong my whole time on this side. It was devastating, really. It's such a short time and to get it all completely wrong... well..."

Bernice's voice trailed off, and she looked as wistful as she was wispy. She exhaled a loud, plaintive sigh that woke her from her own reverie as, in life, a prodigious snore might have woken her from a deep sleep.

"You see that ridiculous looking ghost on your television right now, with the chains and the shackles?" Bernice, now revived, asked, pointing to the television.

Ellie looked over at the apparition with Scrooge then back at Bernice.

"I don't appear to have those constraints, but I am weighed down by something much heavier and far more inescapable. Regret. It was there to meet me on the other side. It attached itself to me from the start of my new life, and I fear I will carry it forever. Though I'm not sure. I can't say I know how things work on my side. The communication is awful." She said this last part as an aside to Ellie and with a pronounced eye roll.

"I have no regrets!" Ellie insisted. "I do what I want when I want. There's just me. I'm all I need to worry about and take care of. And I do that with full vigor!

"I would say I am quite content," Ellie concluded.

"Then you don't know the meaning of the word," charged Bernice. "How can you be content when so many around you are hurting and in need? What you are is self-satisfied. You think of yourself as a shark swimming through life, daily surveying the riches of your ocean fiefdom, but through the filter of the veil, you are more like an oyster, alone, holed up in your work, inhaling regret like sand."

"That is absurd!" retorted Ellie. "Who is in need around me? I maintain a workforce of over a hundred people! I pay them. That allows them to put food on the table and buy Christmas presents. I own scores of properties which are roofs over family's heads and warmth in the winter."

"That's business. All business!" Bernice rejoined. "I was all business. I was a fool. Like you."

"I hardly think…"

Bernice ignored Ellie's protest.

"If you can help just one person in this world, what a difference it can make!" Bernice now appeared anguished as she thought on these words. "I helped no one in my life. Not one soul.

"Oh, the weight of regret is torturous!" she lamented.

"You donated your organs, for Christ's sake!"

Bernice looked sheepishly at Ellie and blinked and nodded,

conveying that there was more to that portmanteau than she cared to unpack at the moment.

"And your children told me you left them millions of dollars! Surely, that was a help to them."

"Heh! They went through all of that in no time!" Bernice explained. "Money is the least of the treasures of this world. Kindness, compassion, charity, forgiveness, love — those are the forms of wealth you can take with you, and there is none of that in your portfolio, I'm afraid. And when you arrive at your ultimate destination, those are the only currency with a favorable exchange rate. My blind pursuit of money left me empty-handed."

"Yes, I left my children a lot of money, but in life, I never knew them well enough to anticipate they would squander it. I thought I was an example of fiscal responsibility for them. I didn't teach them. I didn't take care of them, nurture them, love them. Not my children. Not my granddaughter. Not my husb... Well, my husband, that's another story.

"The point I am trying to make is, this world is about loving each other. It's about helping one another. It's about spreading joy and giving hope. It is so clear now. It's so simple. It's the whole message of Christmas. I didn't see it. You don't see it.

"It is so painful and frustrating not to be able to go back and fix things. You are being given a chance to make things right — a chance and hope of my procuring. You're welcome!

"And I tell you, though my burden on the other side is great, the cargo of regret waiting for you is already so much more abundant. I've seen it. I don't know your story, but whew!"

The wind outside had picked up noticeably. Ellie could hear it blowing hard against the house and causing tree branches to scrape against the windows.

Bernice heard it too and began to talk with more urgency and with observable melancholy. "Oh, the pain of being back here, even for just a few minutes, despite being with someone as unpleasant as you! I wish I could just come back and start over with what I now know!"

The gale outside roared. "My time with you is nearly done," said Bernice, "and I have not yet conveyed what I need to tell you."

Ellie rose and took a carefree stroll over to the fireplace. She now sensed desperation in her visitor. And even though her intuition told her Bernice's intentions were pure, Ellie could not help but exploit her vulnerability.

"I am still not sure whether this is really happening," Ellie lied nonchalantly to the vision while poking at the logs. "I may be dreaming or having some sort of psychotic break.

"But it would be a shame, in any event, if I did not hear what you came all this way to say before you leave, or I wake up, or I run screaming into the night. So, proceed."

Bernice spewed back at Ellie, "You're telling me to proceed? Why, you…" She caught herself, knowing she did not have time for a cat fight. Bernice continued, trying to emulate Ellie's casual air but failing.

"You will be visited by three spirits…"

"Wait, wait!" cried Ellie. "I think I know this story."

Bernice interjected with more imperativeness as she began drifting toward the door. "It wasn't just a story! It really happened, and now it's happening to you. You will see soon enough. I don't have time to explain."

BOOP

"You will be visited by three spirits. The first will come at one a.m." Bernice was still floating toward the door, clearly against her will.

BOOOP

"Another one an hour later and the last one an hour after that, at least I think they are hours. I'm not certain. Time is not really a factor on the other side," said Bernice, frantically looking for something, anything to grab onto to slow her impending exit.

BEEP

Bernice was now speaking with a panicked tone, her eyes darting toward the door and back to Ellie. "Ellie, listen closely," she said more familiarly, for effect. "I have secured this chance for you. But it is only a chance."

BOOOOP

"If you have a change of heart, you can alter the course." Bernice was now next to the door and sounding more distressed, wanting to tell so much more but having only seconds.

BEEP

"Why are you doing this for me?" asked Ellie, hoping she could at least get that answer before Bernice was gone.

"I'm not permitted. . . " shouted Bernice with vehemence. "I mean, I'm out of time!" she said exasperated, glaring at Ellie. "Hopefully, you will figure it out."

BOOP!

The front door flung open. Bernice was being pulled from the house by a boisterous blast of cold air that roared like a thousand airplane engines. She grabbed the door frame and held on for dear afterlife, but the suction was too great. At the last second, Bernice turned her head toward Ellie and shouted over the tumult. Ellie could barely make it out.

"The reason will be clear!"

Then her fingers released, and Bernice was gone.

The wind immediately ceased, and the door swung closed and latched. And just like that, aside from the voices on the TV, the house was again quiet and still.

"Puh!" said Ellie. "Nice to meet you, too."

STAVE 2: THE FIRST OF THE THREE SPIRITS

Ellie Printh was not one to be easily shaken or stirred. As she lay in her bed, sipping a martini — she had moved on from tea — waiting for sleep to come on, she was not overly anxious despite Bernice's foretelling of impending visits from other spirits.

"After all," she thought, "this is what I do — take difficult meetings with difficult people under difficult circumstances — and I always come out on top." She was good at it. She could be whoever she needed to be to get what she wanted. She could feign being polite and patient and even naïve, even if, all the while, the performance was nauseating to her. Or she could stare down a so-called titan of industry or pillar of the community, showing her more natural inclinations of aggression and deviousness. Either way, the outcome was always favorable to Ellie Printh.

The only variable was the condition in which her adversary left the meeting. She had no problem letting someone depart thinking they had gotten the better of her or leave feeling quite ruined and undone, just so long as she got what she wanted out of the exchange. She was fine with losing battles in order to win the war.

So, as she lay in bed awaiting separate visits from three different spirits, she thought of each one like a meeting. She would dispense with these three ghosts one at a time in whatever manner necessary, and when it was over, she would have what she wanted: to go back to her normal life where she was in complete control.

Because of this reasoning, she was relatively calm while waiting for her "one o'clock" to arrive. There was actually some excitement growing within her. She easily dispensed with other mortals she went toe-to-toe with. She was anxious for some stronger competition, and after a deity well, wasn't a spirit the next best thing?

The day had provided her with plenty of frights. Oh yes, she would admit to that and give Bernice her due. When she thought back on her reactions to Bernice's antics, particularly the Santa Claus, she laughed out loud. Now, with the knowledge of what was behind all of these happenings, she could find some humor in it.

"Well done, Bernice," said Ellie out loud while raising her glass and then downing the last vestiges of her martini.

There was some amount of relief in that toast because it confirmed the conclusion at which Ellie's analytical mind had arrived regarding all the weird happenings of the day. She had not been hallucinating, nor had she gone mad. No, she had been haunted this day by a frumpy, ill-tempered ghost with a severe case of halitosis.

That she had been tormented by Bernice's spirit was a tidy explanation for everything. Even earlier that evening, on her list of theories for the day's unexplained occurrences, she would have categorized "haunted by a ghost" under the "impossible" heading. But over the span of a few hours, she had inched that conjecture over to the improbable column. But "improbable" was not "impossible," and she had come up with nothing "possible" or "probable." She had run through plenty of other story lines as she lay there sipping her drink, and more and more, she had become satisfied with this "haunting" conclusion.

The worst-case scenario, Ellie had decided, would have been if she had been imagining and hallucinating every occurrence of... what?... paranormal activity? She could handle taking meetings with ghosts. She could apply skills she had honed over the years to deal with that. She was on solid footing there. She had no frame of reference to deal with being crazy.

She would have needed to learn how to hide her madness from business rivals, associates, and employees. It would have meant doctor visits and treatments, maybe long needles, daily medications, brain scans, and perhaps, worst of all, counseling. In any event, it would have been a lengthy process, and she did not have the time nor inclination for any of that.

But now, because Bernice's ghost and its shenanigans were real, she only had to suffer visits from three more otherworldlies, and this would all be over. And nobody would ever know because she certainly was never going to speak of it to any living soul.

Ellie would only put up with the visits because it seemed she had no choice. She would go through the motions, feign interest, shake hands, "thanks, but no thanks," say goodbye, and get back to work. This would be like going to a timeshare presentation. She would buy nothing, take her enticement and go.

Though, if she was honest with herself, she would have had to admit that there was a small voice inside her, a little girl's voice, coming up as from deep in a well, that was desperately yelling for change. Ellie was honest with herself, and so she shouted back down into the pit, "not going to happen," which echoed back in agreement, "not, not, going, not, going, to, going, to, happen, to, happen, happen."

Ellie's thoughts turned to Scrooge. She was reasonably certain that was the book she let Mary Lou borrow — A Christmas Carol. She decided to run through everything she knew about the story before she drifted off to sleep. Not because she was worried or afraid, but out of habit. Familiarizing herself with details was how she prepared for every adversary. She wasn't even concerned enough with her situation to watch the rest of the Scrooge movie. She had turned it off as soon as her front door closed on Bernice.

So, what did she know? She reckoned if there was some parallel with her and A Christmas Carol, it seemed a foregone conclusion that she was the Scrooge role. (Any of Ellie's employees familiar with *A Christmas Carol* could have told Ellie she certainly was not up for the part of Old Fezziwig.)

About *A Christmas Carol*, Ellie knew there was a clerk, and he had a sick boy, Tiny Tim, and that Tiny Tim says, "God bless us, everyone." And did he also sing "Tiptoe through the Tulips"? She looked over at her martini glass on the side table.

She knew there were three ghosts — Christmas Past, Christmas Present, and Christmas Future, or something like that. Lastly, she knew that Scrooge underwent a transformation at the end and became a kind old man who loved Christmas, and probably butterflies and unicorns and poor people.

She would not be sorry to disappoint theatre-goers everywhere, but this would not be the feel-good movie Bernice and the other ghosts, and whoever or whatever was behind them were hoping for.

Ellie wanted to be awake when the first spirit who was foretold arrived. She had set the alarm on her phone for 12:45, and the alarm on her watch for one a.m., in case and in hope the martini would have the intended outcome of dulling her senses enough to cool her mind enough to relax her body enough to become heavy enough to sink deep enough and then deeper enough into the soft, luxurious marshmallow of a mattress and... off... to... sleeeee.

When the chimes on Ellie's iPhone started going off at a quarter to one precisely, she sprung right up and hit the stop button. She raced into the bathroom and brushed her teeth, then headed to the kitchen to make some coffee. She would wait for her first guest in the living room.

Had she fallen back to sleep, the additional backup of the watch alarm would have been unnecessary. The light display that poured into Ellie's living room precisely at the stroke of one, filling it with a blinding, dazzling, white brilliance, would have been visible from the International Space Station. It was pure, unfiltered, unearthly, full-spectrum illumination. From where Ellie sat, the brightness seemed like a hundred police helicopters shining spotlights through her windows, despite the room-darkening blinds being drawn!

Ellie shielded her eyes and squinted, trying to see what was happening, but to no avail. It was as if the sun had decided to pay a visit and parked itself right outside her living room window. She ran into her bedroom, leaped onto her bed, and pulled the covers up over her head.

The bedding provided little protection from light that seemed to find its way through the high thread-count sheets Ellie insisted on. She had sensed at first that the light was outside and was circling her home, but now it seemed it had come through solid walls and windows and was in her bedroom and still rotating violently, yet producing no wind or noise. Ellie's room was the center of a vortex of light that was gradually getting narrower and narrower at its base.

The light began to diminish slightly, and Ellie, extricating herself from the covers, could see the outline of a whirling funnel, wispy at the bottom but robust and violent at the top.

It was now just beyond the footboard of her bed. She could see it touch down, bounce up, and crash to the floor, bursting into a million stars that flooded Ellie's bedroom with sparkles that exploded around her, blinding her momentarily, and then floating around the room like dust particles in a sunbeam, before fading away.

When Ellie regained her vision, she saw, standing in the same spot where the tornado of light had just disintegrated, a diminutive and benevolent-looking being. By all measures, it had alighted from that very funnel which had apparently served as its transport. Ellie regarded the being through bleary eyes as they readjusted to the lighting in the room.

The creature stood shy of five feet tall and wore a white turtle-neck, long in the sleeves and waist, with gray slacks that gathered at the ankles and partially covered black athletic-style shoes with black rubber soles. It looked like someone who was up and dressed for an early trip to the market.

"Hello!" said the visitor. Its voice was as bright as its entrance.

"I presume you are the first of the three spirits who will be darkening my door."

"My dear," it replied, "I would hardly consider my entrance a 'darkening' of anything.

Ellie thought. "I suppose not," she allowed.

The spirit acknowledged Ellie's concession with a wry smile. Then it pronounced, somewhat grandly, "I am the Ghost of Christmas Past."

"Uh-huh," uttered Ellie nonchalantly, trying to gain the early upper hand by appearing unimpressed. That was a little difficult for her to pull off, though; she had just watched the form ride in on a dazzling whirlwind of illumination. However, Ellie did a commendable job of seeming blasé. She continued, "So when you say, 'Christmas Past,' do you mean the history of Christmas? Are we talking about the manger here and working our way up to the present day?"

"Your past," said the ghost a little less cheerily.

"Shall we get started then?" asked Ellie. "Shall we sit in the kitchen? I have the coffee on. Can you drink coffee?"

"I can," said the spirit. "I am corporeal."

"You have ranks in your ghost world?" This was Ellie's attempt at humor. Wit was another device she would employ to disarm a foe, though very rarely, and then not very effectively. Humor from Ellie was unexpected and uncomfortable for everyone.

"No. Corporeal, not corporal. It means I am flesh and bones, er, at least for this. But, I don't wish any coffee, thank you, dear."

"I know what corporeal means. I was just... never mind."

Ellie's eyes had fully recovered, and she was getting a clearer look at the apparition. It had short-cropped hair, its face was youthful but with just enough wrinkles to give it character. Ellie could not guess its age or gender. The fact that she could not discern basic information that should easily be obtained through observation was a great source of frustration to someone who prided herself in the ability to instantly size up her rivals. And for Ellie, that meant everyone.

But its characteristic that was by far the most prominent and mesmerizing was the spirit's eyes. They were radiant and lively and something like blue. They were not exactly blue or any other color found on Earth. Ellie found herself drawn to them and safe in them and warmed by them. She looked away.

The ghost's eyes seemed to contain and emanate wisdom, empathy, kindness, knowledge, and peace as if every good thought from every good life was stored up there.

"Child," said the Ghost of Christmas Past, "let's take a walk."

"Outside? Now? I'm not dressed for it!" protested Ellie.

The ghost waved its arm and instantly, an opening, like a well-lit hallway, appeared in the middle of the outer wall of Ellie's room.

"Walk with me," said the spirit.

"I'm not going in there," insisted Ellie. But then she locked eyes with the ghost and felt something she had not felt since she was a little girl: trust. She relented. After all, she reminded herself, she just wanted to get this over with, and any protest would only serve to prolong the affair.

She walked over to the Ghost of Christmas Past, who was standing next to the portal. "Is it safe for me to go in there?" asked Ellie nodding toward the opening. "I am not like you, you know."

Bear but a touch of my hand," said the spirit, "and you shall be upheld in more than this!"

Ellie recoiled at the suggestion of touching its hand, but the sincerity and empathy in its eyes again weakened her objections. She placed her hand on the spirit's hand, and together they walked into the light.

At first, she was blinded by the brightness, but as she and her guide came through something like a short tunnel, she found herself on a street in a neighborhood of small ranch-style houses. All of the homes were decorated with multi-colored Christmas lights hanging from gutters, candles in windows, green garland strung around lampposts and over doorways, and many with plastic, lighted Santas with sleighs and reindeer, or snowmen or nativity scenes in yards.

There was a fresh, frosty, alabaster blanket covering the ground that, although it was evening, looked almost as white and pure as the light that led them there, except under the eaves where the tinted illumination created the illusion of watercolor snow.

On this particular block where the traffic only ran in one direction, there were half a dozen houses on one side of the street. The ghost and Ellie had entered on the other side of the road, where there was a small park with some benches and a playground.

When Ellie beheld the setting, she knew immediately where they had arrived. Her mouth dropped open, and she covered it with both hands while her eyes blinked away warm, salty moisture that, if allowed to develop, would become small droplets, known to everyone but Ellie Printh as tears.

"Do you know this place?" asked the ghost.

"It's, um,... of course," said Ellie softly and then clearing her throat. "It's my old neighborhood. It's where I lived when I was a child.

"This is well done. I certainly didn't expect anything like this."

The spirit led Ellie across the street and into the yard of one of the houses. It was the least attended to of the homes that lined the block.

This house was the awkward, old bachelor uncle of the street, who shows up at the wedding in the same wrinkled, ill-fitting suit that he's worn to every family event in the past two decades. He spends no thought, or energy, or care on his fashion. He puts on the coat and tie, not to look nice, but only to meet the expectations of him for the occasion.

So it was with this house. The same strings of lights, with the same burnt-out bulbs as the previous year, plus a few more, were clipped to the gutters haphazardly so that they sagged in some spots and clung tight to the roof, as for dear life, in others, looking more like war-torn bunting than festive holiday illumination. For the bulbs that did remain lit, they appeared to do so without any enthusiasm, their darkened brethren serving as a constant reminder of their imminent fates.

On the ground, one of the two reindeer pulling Santa's sleigh was also missing a light, making it much duller than its counterpart.

That is not a commentary on which one would be more engaging at a dinner party, but rather another observation of the careless manner in which the holiday display was set up.

"This is the house you grew up in?" confirmed the spirit. It had asked the question because Ellie had been warily eyeing the street and the front lawn of the house just next door. The ghost's inquiry brought her attention back to it and her immediate surroundings.

Ellie looked at the spirit but only nodded. She reached out to examine one of the reindeer, the brighter one. She had expected her hand to pass through it, but instead, it came to rest on the reindeer's snout. She withdrew it quickly as if she had touched a hot stove. Ellie had imagined that she was inside some elaborate hologram, but everything, including her, was really there.

"This is real?" She asked the ghost with increasing incomprehension. "How can this be real? How are you doing this?!"

She looked down at herself as if expecting to see a little girl's body, but she was still herself and still in the robe and slippers she had changed into earlier in the evening when she was hoping for a quiet and restful night at home. It was now becoming apparent that she was in for anything but that.

"You are here in the actual time and place," said the ghost, placing its hand on her shoulder in an effort to calm her. "No one can see or hear you. We are here as this is happening, but sort of on a different frequency."

"I... I... I..." Ellie could only stammer.

The spirit, assuming Ellie's stupefaction was the result of not comprehending his explanation, continued, "In your realm, you only know time as linear, but in actuality,…"

Ellie waved the ghost off. "Well, I can't go in there!" she declared, referring to the house, as if, surely, that could not even be what the spirit was intending. "I can't! Don't make me. I'll do anything. We don't need to go any further." Ellie could not believe these words were coming out of her mouth. It went against every natural instinct to give over control of a situation to an adversary.

"We must," replied the spirit taking Ellie gently at the elbow. And just like that, they glided through the wall and into the home.

Ellie immediately saw her former self. She was setting the table in the kitchen. Her mother was at the stove stirring pasta in a large pot. Ellie could smell the tomato sauce cooking. She could hear the television in the living room. It was Walter Cronkite's voice.

"Ellie," said her mother, glancing at the table, "If you're not going to do the job right, just don't do it at all. This is a mess. I'm going to have to redo the whole thing.

"You know what I would like for Christmas? A daughter who could be a help around the house. Do you think I'll get that in my stocking?"

"No, ma'am," replied Ellie honestly.

"I don't either."

While she was berating her daughter, Ellie's mom moved some forks and knives around and replaced a spotty glass.

"There! See! It doesn't take any more time to do the job right," she said, softening her tone and her look.

"Your dad should be home soon. Why don't you sit in your chair and wait for him."

"Yes, momma," said little Ellie in a weak voice. Despite her frail appearance, she skipped over to a little chair by the front window. The glass was steamed up, so Ellie made two small circles side by side, like binoculars, with her little hand so she could peer out and see the street and the driveway.

She took a quick look and saw no sign of her dad's car yet. So she began to draw with her finger in the beaded condensation. Around the eye holes, she drew the head of a giraffe and then the long neck. The neck was so long she had to make the body and legs disproportionately shorter as if it were being viewed from the perspective of the highest branch of an acacia tree. Little Ellie admired giraffes because she saw them as majestic and beautiful and strong, all things she someday hoped to be.

She took another look outside, this time through the giraffe's eyes. Still no sign. She began wringing her hands and fidgeting.

"Mom?"

No response.

"Mom?!" she cried again in a raised voice.

"What is it?" her mom yelled back. She was now sitting at the kitchen table, leafing through a magazine and clearly aggravated at the interruption. "I'm busy making dinner! What could you possibly need now?"

"Never mind," said little Ellie.

"Oh, let's not play this game, Eleanora! Tell me what you want!" shouted her mom. Then to herself, she sighed, "As if I don't already know — 'when will Daddy be home?'" Then to Ellie again, she warned, "You know it's Christmas Eve. You need to be extra good, or Santa won't come tonight."

Ellie began, "But…"

At the same moment Ellie started to reply, the phone rang. Ellie's mom got up from the table, now even more annoyed to be separated from her *People* magazine, and picked up the receiver of the moss green Trimline phone hanging on the kitchen wall.

"Hello, this is Claudine!" she answered in a tone that immediately signaled to the person on the other end that "this had better be good."

At her first recognition of the caller's voice, Claudine's entire countenance unstiffened. She began to fuss with her hair and straighten her top as if the person on the other end of the phone line was able to see, as well as hear her, and she was determined to make a good impression.

A casual observer might have had to wonder if she had lost control of her pelvis. The raising of one hip in conjunction with the lowering of the other made it look as if her haunches were playing aggressively at seesaw.

A cautious observer might have to worry that the constant and rapid rubbing together of her thighs in that manner might, like two dry sticks employed in that same fashion, start a fire.

"Well, this is a nice surprise!" Claudine sang in what could easily be mistaken for a lilting southern accent, even though she had never in her life stepped foot anywhere south of Cape May, New Jersey.

…

"Merry Christmas to you, too!" she said in more of a hushed and careful voice. "But why are you calling me at home at this hour? What if Henry had been here?"

…

"Ohhh. I didn't know he was stopping there. Did you speak to him?"

…

"You said what to him?!" asked Claudine, alarmed.

…

Now relieved, "Don't kid like that! Oh my gosh! I believed you!"

…

"No. I'm not mad at you." Claudine had now returned to her softer voice and, covering the space between her mouth and phone with a cupped hand, she continued. "How could I ever be mad at you?"

…

"I'm so glad you called!"

…

"I'll miss you tomorrow too, so much!"

…

"I wish that, too! By next Christmas, for sure!"

…

"Okay. That's a promise I'm going to hold you to!"

…

Now even quieter, "I love you, too."

Ellie's mom held the receiver next to her heart for a few seconds, smiling.

She was brought out of her reverie by a little girl's voice:

"Mommmma!"

"OH, WHAT IS IT?!" Claudine snapped, like an alligator coming out of the water after an oblivious duck.

"Where's dad?" asked the oblivious duck. "He should be home by now!" pouted Ellie, impatiently.

"Listen," said her mom, now standing inside the living room with her hands on her hips, now at rest above her cooling thighs. "There's only one kind of wine I want tonight, and I don't mean the kind that is coming out of your mouth right now."

"But, I'm soooo nervous," whimpered little Ellie, stomping her feet and twisting her shirt.

"You're going to stretch that out, and I'm not going to buy you another one!" screamed Ellie's mom as if the little girl had taken a ball-peen hammer to a priceless family heirloom.

"I'm sorry, Momma! But where is daddy? Something's wrong. I just know it."

"Nothing's wrong," said her mom, exasperated, "He made a stop on his way home. That was one of mommy's friends on the phone just now, and he said he saw your dad at the store. He should be home any minute now. Okay?! Can you stop worrying now? Maybe if you weren't such a little worrywart about your dad, your heart wouldn't be so sick, and we wouldn't have to spend half your dad's paycheck on..." Mercifully, Claudine did not finish the sentence, and now looking at her helpless daughter, felt a deep and hopeless sting of remorse.

It was not Ellie's fault she had been born with a heart abnormality, so why did she blame her daughter for ruining all the expectations and promise of pregnancy? Claudine wanted a baby. But not a baby with issues. When she decided to go forward with the pregnancy, she had never even considered anything but a perfect outcome. If she had, maybe she would have given up the cigarettes and wine coolers while the child was developing in her womb.

From the moment her brand new "doll" had come out of the box damaged, and she couldn't return her to the store, Claudine could not hide her disappointment, not from herself, not from her husband, and not from her daughter. And she knew it would probably just be better for everyone if she were to pack up and leave town.

The little girl shrank but stared sorrowfully up at her mom and then hung her head. "I'm sorry my heart doesn't work like it's s'posed to, Momma."

Claudine walked over to the child and gave her a quick squeeze. "Me too," she said and meant it more than anything she had ever said in her life.

Then she turned Ellie around in the direction of the window, patted her bottom, and said, "Go watch for your dad. He'll just keep circling the block unless he sees you at the window."

The spirit looked over at Ellie, who had been standing quietly, stoically watching this scene unfold. Still, the Ghost of Christmas Past saw in Ellie's eyes a crest rising quickly behind the trough. As it glided toward her to provide comfort, their attention was diverted by the loud screech of a wooden chair against a wooden floor.

The little girl was up and scurrying toward the front door, the same front door Ellie had been keeping her own nervous watch on. This had been a scene that played out night after night in her youth, so Ellie knew what was coming next. She had sensed the girl's relief when the car lights appeared. She allowed herself to feel her height of euphoric expectation — one more time — just before the door opened, aware that this was an altitude to which she was unaccustomed, and the ensuing fall would be devastating.

As the door creaked open, the little girl started running toward it. At first sight of her father, both girls, Ellie and her former self, cried, "Daddy!"

The little girl ran into her adoring father's open arms, while Ellie stood frozen and shaking. Seeing her father and seeing the pure joy in the little girl's face, her own face of youth, Ellie was overtaken. She tried to speak but could not. She tried to motion to the ghost for assistance but could not lift her arms. The world around her started wobbling and quivering as if the walls and the floor were made of Jell-O.

Suddenly, her face felt as hot as it did that summer day her mom had left her sleeping on the beach. When she had woken up alone, crying in fear and anguish, the salty tears had made a stinging trail down her cheeks. She felt those tears again, retracing the path like scalding streams.

She squeezed her eyes shut, pressed her lips together tight, and folded her arms taut around her torso in a useless attempt to contain the flood of emotion erupting within.

Long-suppressed torrents stored for a lifetime in saturated clouds of grief, loss, and disappointment rolled through her. Every levee and wall she had painstakingly built and put in place over the years to protect herself from any surge like this were, in this one moment, leveled.

Ellie dropped to her knees and sobbed, appealing to the spirit, "Please, please, no more."

The Ghost of Christmas Past, who had not foreseen the ferocity of her reaction, took Ellie by the waist and bore her out of the house. They floated back over the yard and crossed the street into the park. There, the spirit led her to a bench and sat her down. The ghost seated itself with her and patted her back, and offered some soft words of comfort.

Ellie raised her head but did not look at the ghost.

"All better now?" asked the spirit.

"All better?" replied Ellie angrily and turning toward the ghost while avoiding its eyes. "I'm pissed off!!"

The spirit recoiled.

"I told you not to make me go in there. I begged it of you!" cried Ellie, who was now up and stomping back and forth before the spirit. "Now look at me! Is this what you wanted? Why did you do that to me?

"Why is any of this happening to me?! Are you trying to shock me into conforming? You are wasting your time! I will tell you that right now! I am perfectly happy the way I am."

"My dear, first of all, I have no way of knowing how you will react to what I show you. I can only see the past. I would have stood nearer by if I had had any inclination that your feelings about this time and place were so raw. I could have been more of a help to you."

The ghost continued, "It is painful enough for any person to return to a place that holds fond memories of a time in their youth. How much more painful to go back to that place at that time and relive it? I can only imagine.

"Each time I take someone back, and they see themselves in their lives as they used to be, they experience an almost unbearable wistfulness that can be useful to my purposes. Though I will admit, there is something much more acute in your sorrow than I have seen in any of a long line of others."

"Wait. There have been others?"

"Every Christmas Eve, there is another."

Ellie shook her head. "What am I caught up in?"

Ellie had been pacing back and forth in front of the ghost, who was still reclining casually on the bench.

"Sit with me," it said, patting the area next to it as a pet owner might entreat his dog to join him on the couch.

Ellie did not want to comply, but she was exhausted from trying to fight the tsunami of intense sentiment that had swept her away, so she took a reluctant seat on the bench. All at once it occurred to her that she was sitting down on the very spot she often occupied as a child, sitting next to her dad on summer evenings, watching other kids play on the swings and the jungle gym.

To her now, that bench was just a lonely pew, left behind when its fellow pews, the congregation, and the entire church, upped and moved to a happier place. "Did they even know it was missing?" she wondered.

"There are... unpleasantries... that happen in people's lives that, if not dealt with, resolved and accepted, are like brier hedges," the ghost said with compassion. "They make your way difficult and prickly, and as they grow, untended, their branches, with their thorns and thistles, become like barbed prison bars that keep you locked within."

"Doesn't matter!" returned Ellie. "There's nowhere I need to go. Nowhere I want to go. There's nothing for me on the outside. There's no... deeper fulfillment... or whatever you want to call it, that I need to achieve. I have me. That's all I've ever had. That's all I will ever have. It's all I will ever need."

"Look at me," said the spirit calmly.

Ellie, wanting to prove to the ghost and herself that she had freed herself from whatever hypnotic power its eyes had possessed over her earlier, looked the spirit right in its baby blues.

"You and I both know that none of that is true," said the spirit emphatically.

No one ever challenged Ellie, and the ghost's protestation spoken with the full vigor of truth in its eyes left her uncharacteristically speechless. Having no rebuttal, she simply looked away.

The Ghost of Christmas Past, satisfied that it had gotten its message through, decided it was time to move on.

"That was your mother's last Christmas with you, wasn't it?" it inquired of Ellie, though already aware of the fact.

"Yes," replied Ellie softly and with a pronounced melancholy. "She left us for the man, I guess who was on the telephone just then. He was our insurance agent, I was told. They ran away together a couple of weeks after Christmas. I never saw or heard from her again.

"I think I was just too much of a burden for her. She was only a child herself when I was born. She and my dad were high school sweethearts. My mom said they got carried away one night after a dance. Neither of them finished high school. Her parents disowned her and even moved away. My dad was raised by his grandparents who were too old to be of any help.

"My dad worked two jobs, so she had to do everything for me. My mother couldn't stand that I was often sick or too tired or weak and that I wouldn't go out and play like other kids. She called me boring and lazy."

Ellie then added in her own defense, "But I heard the doctors tell them that I shouldn't get over-exerted. So I was cautious. They said I could die."

The spirit looked on empathetically and touched Ellie's arm, encouraging her to go on. Ellie detested the show of sympathy but continued, nonetheless.

"She just never took to me. She just couldn't love me. I think she tried, but she couldn't love someone as weak as me. Maybe I was more feeble than I needed to be. Maybe if I had been more like other kids… I just don't know."

They remained in silence for several seconds until the spirit broke the quietude.

"It's time to go," whispered the spirit to Ellie. "I have more to show you. The next scene will be distressing. You know what I am referring to, don't you?"

Ellie, who had been sitting on the bench with her head bowed, nodded yes as tears began to fall onto her robe, the belt of which she was unwittingly wringing in her hands.

"We will go back inside. It is Christmas morning, two years later," informed the ghost.

"I know," said Ellie, and she stood. She bent over and placed her hand on the cold bench next to where she had been sitting. It was the same spot her dad had occupied on those warm evenings.

She stood and slowly raised her eyes, communicating to the spirit, "Okay. Lead on."

She followed the ghost like a condemned prisoner might follow a priest to the gallows. She shuffled as if she was shackled at the ankles and wrists, her head slightly bowed. Her hands were clasped in front of her waist, and she took slow, steady steps as she and the ghost retraced their earlier path.

As they moved back across the street, the night turned to dawn. The Santa and reindeer that had been on the lawn had been re-lit and moved to the roof, which made room for a new, jollier, more vibrant Santa with a raised, welcoming black-mittened hand. He was situated as if to give the impression that he was signaling hello to two hard-plastic families who had recently moved into Henry Printh's holiday front yard display.

One family consisted of a carpenter and his wife and their infant son, and the other was a trio of snow people, also parents and a child, occupations unspecified. However, the father's top hat and cravat gave a distinct appearance of his being quite gentrified. The apron around the good snow-gentleman's wife suggested she was a homemaker. The snow-child had a mischievous grin of painted-on pieces of coal.

They were all caged in by tall candy canes, staked into the ground, and spaced about three feet apart around the front of the house and up the driveway to the brick walkway leading to the front stoop. It was a lot for the eyes to take in, especially crammed into such a small yard.

The lights on the house were now hung straight and taut. The bulbs must have been replaced recently as all of them were alive and vibrant. Easily the brightest on the block. Leafless trees stood as sentries over this holiday mélange. And the whole scene was glazed in a thin layer of icy glass from freezing rain that had fallen earlier that morning.

A dazzling Christmas tree with what looked to be a thousand colored lights was featured in the same front window where little Ellie would sit at evenings and watch for her dad. It did not appear possible that there was room for one more bulb or that there was any color of the spectrum not represented.

All of the lights seemed to be twinkling with glee at their participation in this holiday production. The tree itself seemed to bristle with pride in its adornment. Instead of allowing its limbs to sag under the weight of copious bulbs and wires, it had the bearing of a weightlifter flexing his biceps, as if asking its admirers if they had their tickets to the "gun show."

The tree was framed in the cozy, gilded glow produced by the living room lamps that were already on at this early hour, proudly brightening the room and coloring it with soft gold hues. Everything had a role in the play, and they were performing their parts with aplomb for the audience of one.

A cynical passerby might only take note of the otherwise unexceptional house for its singular tackiness and might even describe it, like Ellie had deemed the overly bedecked mansion she encountered on her way home earlier that evening, as atrocious. But Ellie, observing her childhood home now, knew it was a house decorated by a man who loved his little girl and created the scene to please no one but her.

She felt a twinge of regret that showed on her face. The observant spirit asked, "What is the matter?"

"Nothing," Ellie replied mindlessly. Then she offered, "There was a young girl earlier this evening who asked me how I liked her decorated house. I... I just wish I had walked home a different way."

"Not where I thought you were going with that, but all right," said the ghost.

Ellie observed that, despite the frosty, cold, frigid exterior of her girlhood home on this chilly morning, there was no doubt of the warmth which existed inside.

By all estimations — his parents', his teachers', his bosses', his wife's — Henry Printh was a person who was, and had always been, unremarkable in almost every way. He was a man of average height, average weight, average looks, average intelligence, average ambition, average prospects, and average means. Those assessments, underwhelming to begin with, were significantly lowered when he became a husband and father at the age of nineteen.

By the estimation of his daughter, Henry Printh was extraordinary. He knew that he was the tallest, strongest, handsomest, smartest, bravest, richest, and most ingenious person on the planet to his daughter. And she almost made him believe it as well. To her, he was Walt Disney, Superman, and Mr. Rogers all rolled into one.

Perhaps, with the love and faith of a good woman, he may have achieved something beyond the commonplace. But Claudine could not muster much enthusiasm for a fumbling and bumbling husband whom she married more out of defiance of her parents than for any feelings she had for the boy with whom she had been going steady, for the most part, since eighth grade.

As Ellie and the spirit reentered the home, Henry Printh was busy putting the finishing touches on the Christmas tree. He was dressed in sweat pants and a tee-shirt, and he was wearing a Santa hat. He looked like he had been up all night... because he had, but that had not dampened his spirits. The radio was on, and Bing Crosby was singing "It's Beginning to Look a Lot Like Christmas." To which Henry Printh, admiring his tree, replied, "It sure is, Bing. It sure is."

Henry looked at his watch and said out loud to himself with genuine excitement, "It's time! It's time!"

He arranged the three gifts that were under the tree as if trying to make it appear that there were more. He tried unstacking them and spacing them out. Then, stepping back and looking at them, he decided to create a "pile" with two and place the third a little to the right. "Perfect," he thought.

Then, up the stairs he bounded, taking them two at a time!

Ellie and the spirit remained downstairs but could hear Henry opening the creaky door to little Ellie's bedroom and saying enthusiastically, "Princess! Princess!"

Ellie turned to the ghost and said, "I had forgotten he called me Princess."

Henry continued, "Princess? Guess who came last night?"

With a lot of sleep still in her voice, little Ellie matched her dad's exhilaration and provided the answer he was looking for. "Santa!" she said as loud as she could.

"Let's go downstairs and see what he brought you," said Henry. "Here, I'll carry you down."

Ellie turned to the ghost with tears in her eyes, "He loved to carry me. I was such a frail little, little thing."

"Cover your eyes," said Henry to little Ellie, as they reappeared on the stairs to their onlookers.

They reached the bottom of the steps, and Henry set Ellie down and guided her to the front of the Christmas Tree.

"Okay! You can look!" he said.

Ellie removed her hands from her eyes and opened them. When she beheld the tree, she could not contain herself.

"A Christmas tree! A Christmas tree!! I thought you said we couldn't have one!"

"Well," replied Henry, "your mom couldn't stand the smell of pine, as you well know. And last year, I forgot to ask Santa to bring one for you, and I felt real bad about that. This year, I remembered to tell him. I said to him, 'If ever there was a little girl who deserved her very own Christmas tree, it's my little princess!' And, he must have agreed because here it is."

"I love it! I love it! Thank you, Daddy!" The delicate little girl leaped toward her dad, who had been kneeling down next to her admiring the tree. She wrapped her thin arms around his neck and planted kisses on his cheeks that he could feel all the way down in his heart.

"All right then," said Henry. "We're not done yet. Santa left some presents for you there, and I have a surprise for you that should be showing up in..." he stopped and looked at his watch, "oh, boy, about five minutes. It's not a houseful of brothers and sisters like you've been asking for. But it will have to do for now."

Ellie opened her first present. "Lite Brite!" she cried.

"I think Santa wanted to get you something we could do together. How about we play with that after breakfast? Though," intimated Henry, "you may not want to after you get your surprise."

"I can't wait!" said Ellie.

At that moment, as if that line were a stage cue, the doorbell rang. Little Ellie won the race to the door but hesitated there. She looked at her dad, who nodded.

"Go ahead. Open it. I have a feeling it's for you," he said.

Ellie turned the knob and flung the door wide open and found herself looking up at an older woman she recognized as the next-door neighbor, "Mrs. H." And standing next to her, obscured from the waist up by a large red box with a big white bow, was, presumably, her husband, known to Ellie as "Mr. H." The galoshes were a dead giveaway.

The box in Mr. H's arms was apparently unwieldy and unsteady, and the old man was struggling to maintain control of it. Clearly, something was moving or rolling back and forth inside.

"They lived next door," Ellie informed the spirit. "The Harrisons, Don and Irene."

"Merry Christmas!" sang Mrs. Harrison cheerily.

"Can we come in?" asked Mr. Harrison. "I think Santa accidentally left something at our house for you," he told Ellie.

"She knows it's from me," said Henry.

"I told you that!" Mrs. Harrison scolded Mr. Harrison. "Why do I even bother talking to you if you're not going to listen to a word I say?"

"That's one of the great mysteries of my life," snarled Mr. Harrison. "Why don't we set this down somewhere?"

The box was obviously becoming so unstable in Mr. Harrison's arms that the concern had grown high among all of them, including Mr. Harrison, that he might just drop the present, revealing its contents before the little girl had a chance to open it. So everyone rushed to take a corner of the box and guide it to safety in front of the tree.

Ellie looked at her dad and then to Mr. Harrison and Mrs. Harrison. They were all standing around her with the joy of expectation all over their faces.

"Go ahead, Princess," encouraged her dad. "Open it."

Ellie didn't hesitate. She untied the bow and removed the top from the box, and up jumped a rambunctious and wiry springer spaniel puppy who immediately licked little Ellie all over her face while wagging its tail vigorously and thumping it against the inside of the box.

Ellie screamed with excitement! "A puppy!! A puppy!! I can't believe it! I love him already!! Can I hold him?"

"Of course," replied her dad. "he's all yours."

"Be careful, my dear," said Mrs. Harrison. "That one's a handful."

Ellie reached in the box and grabbed the dog under its front legs. As she starting pulling him out, the dog leapt, knocking Ellie onto her back. The puppy slipped through her hands and darted around the room, jumping up on the couch and then back down on the floor, running between the legs of the side table, then under the tree knocking off some low-hanging ornaments.

Henry and Mr. Harrison tried to corner the spry puppy, but he squirted between them. Henry dove at the dog as it passed, trying, but failing, to snag him.

"Close the front door!" yelled Mr. Harrison to Mrs. Harrison.

In the eagerness and joint effort to get the box inside and the anticipation of watching Ellie open it, no one had even noticed the door was still open.

It was now a race between a seventy-five-year old woman, who in the privacy of her own home, used a walker to get around, but whose vanity would not permit her the same assistance in public, and a six-month old puppy who had been cooped up in a box for almost half an hour while Mr. Harrison tried one more time to pee before heading to the Printh's.

The dog won. The puppy was out the door before Mrs. Harrison had made two steps in that direction. Henry, who had gotten to his knees after diving for the dog, was now up on his feet and giving chase. He was followed by Mr. Harrison, who was surprisingly fast for his age. Mrs. Harrison was a distant third. She was followed by little Ellie.

"Stay in the house!" the little girl could hear her dad shout from outside.

That admonishment was unnecessary. When little Ellie got to the front door, she stopped. The scene that was playing out in front of her — her daddy running into the road, her neighbors in pursuit, and, out of the corner of her eye, a car speeding down the one-way street in the wrong direction, going too fast for the icy conditions — was a gauzy vision she had known subconsciously all her young and fragile life. And now here it was coming together in pellucid, vivid reality and taking place right before her eyes.

Ellie, in the doorway, still in her pajamas, knew instantly that this would be the moment she had feared her whole short life.

She could not move. She could only stand there and watch.

It may be cliché to say that the entire incident took place in slow motion because of course, it didn't. But adrenaline coursing dangerously through Ellie's weak heart and her veins and arteries caused her brain to process all that her eyes were sending its way so rapidly that it was as if she was witnessing this tragedy frame by frame.

She saw the dog sprint down the icy walkway toward the street with her daddy running after a few yards behind.

She saw a red sports car coming the wrong way down their one-way street.

She saw the driver, a man wearing a red velvet coat with white fur around the collar and a matching hat with a white tassel on the tip. He had a fake beard hanging around his neck, and he had thick, black stubble on his face. She could even see that the coat was open, revealing a dingy white tee-shirt underneath. He looked like an off-duty Santa Claus.

She saw the Harrisons halt in their tracks and heard Mr. Harrison yell, "C-a-a-a-a-r-r-r-r!"

She saw the alarm in the driver's face as he saw the dog in the street.

She saw the driver's fists tighten on the steering wheel, saw his knuckles turn white, and saw his body stiffen against the back of his seat.

She saw the automobile's wheels lock in place though the car was continuing on its same course.

She saw the little dog leap to safety onto the curb on the other side of the road.

She saw the brief flash of relief on the driver's face as he realized he had averted killing a puppy on Christmas morning.

She saw her daddy slipping on the ice while trying to stop himself from going into the street after the dog.

She saw the driver mouth a profanity as his attention turned to his right, spotting the man skidding on the sidewalk and heading into his car's path.

She saw her daddy falling to the ground and sliding uncontrollably, and coming to a stop in the street, trying to right himself to get back to the curb.

She saw the driver turning the steering wheel desperately to the left.

She saw her daddy frantically lunging for the curb and trying to stand, only to have his legs slip out from under him again.

She saw the back end of the vehicle swinging out from behind the front, and the car, now out of control, spinning down the street.

She saw her daddy's eyes open wide as he saw the back bumper of the car careening toward him.

Then, she saw a look pass over his face of what she could only interpret as resignation of the outcome and... peace?

She saw the Harrisons frozen in horror like statues in a haunted wax museum.

She saw her daddy give one last glance over his shoulder toward the front door, toward his little princess.

She saw a message in his eyes: "I love you! I'll miss you! I'm sorry."

She saw the impact.

She saw her daddy thrown backwards into the neighbor's yard... and beyond the veil.

As the Harrisons, now released from Medusa's spell, ran toward Henry Printh's vacant body and the car came to a stop and then sped off, little Ellie took three deliberate steps backward inside the house. She calmly and slowly closed the door between her and the awful scene, between her and the world, and between her and unconditional love.

And then she locked it.

Ellie and the spirit had stayed this whole time in their same positions against the wall. The ghost watched what had transpired through the window, obscured somewhat by Christmas tree branches. Ellie only relived the accident with her eyes on the little girl's face, which betrayed very little, but more than enough to take Ellie back to that moment and see it all again.

Little Ellie walked over to her favorite chair, from where she had kept a nightly watch for her dad. She turned its back to the window and now sat facing the Christmas tree under which lay an empty box that only minutes before concealed a happy, exuberant puppy and the joy that comes with it. Next to the box was a Lite Brite set that would not be played with after breakfast, or ever, and two other lovingly-but-shoddily-wrapped presents that would forever remain unopened.

The Ghost of Christmas Past looked at Ellie. Her eyes were wet, and her face was wearing unmistakable grief. But she was holding up.

"The police had to break the door down," Ellie said. "I spent the rest of that day with the Harrisons and then for a couple of weeks after that. They kept the dog. I didn't want him…" Ellie explained to the ghost as she walked over to her former self, circling her curiously and then kneeling in front of her and putting her face inches from the little girl's face, which was colored by the lights of the tree. She stayed that way for a short while, studying her former self, and then placed her hand where the child's cheek was. The little girl reached up and scratched her face where Ellie's hand was caressing it.

"They tried to find my mother, but she never turned up. I was an orphan. I guess I still am."

As sirens could be heard mixing with the church bells of a Christmas morning that, until then, had been oblivious to the tragedy, Ellie rose and spoke to the spirit.

"I can't believe I'm saying this, but on some level, spirit, I appreciate what you are trying to do here. I had forgotten how I was. And seeing this," she said, looking back at little Ellie in her chair, "I'll confess, I would very much like to be as I used to be — happy, hopeful, loving,… loved." Her voice strained on the last word as she confronted the reality that she was unloved. "But too much has happened. I became an adult on this day. This little girl has been locked way down deep inside of me ever since. I locked her up good and tight. She is not retrievable."

The spirit shook its head, "Huh! Adult? Well, this is exciting for me. I've never met an adult from your world!

"No, my dear. You are all really just children acting out your parts — relishing your roles and losing yourselves in the characters you've written for yourselves. It's not so much 'retrieving' the child, but rather giving her some lines, a voice, and placing the rest in proper perspective."

Ellie did not regard the ghost's commentary but continued on as if it had not spoken at all. "This child was jailed in me a long time ago, and the person I became stood guard to make sure she could not escape. Both are me, I know.

"I don't doubt that as a child, I placed myself in the cell — went in more than willingly, but I also don't deny that over the years, I have heard the cries of this little girl, pleading to be let out, and have ignored them until they stopped altogether. I imagine this poor child," Ellie again turned and looked at her former self, "retreating to a lonely corner of her cage where she, helpless and hopeless, could only watch as the life she would have liked to live slipped by.

"I have to think it is not very much a child's nature to give up, but at some point, she did. So she must have been very tired, or I must have been very stern with her — as I know I can be."

"If it is a prison, as you describe it, then it is of your own making," said the spirit to the little girl, not the one in the chair by the Christmas tree, but the one who had just been speaking. "You are free and have always been so. You only need to be the person you want to be. Who's to stop you? You have the key."

Ellie returned, "That's very naïve on your part."

The ghost laughed.

"The world now has the key. There are... expectations. People know me as I am. My nature has been set, and that's that."

"Nonsense!" said the spirit.

"Even if I could change, and I really don't believe I can. Nor do I want to. But even if I did, if I would be suddenly different, people will only think I have gone off the deep end!" argued Ellie. "Don't you think if I start crying at coffee commercials and going ga-ga in the street over babies in strollers, given my current disposition, people will think I've lost my mind?"

"Who cares! It is your life!"

"I'm not a child. This is who I am," she said, gesturing toward herself like a magician demonstrating she had no tricks up her sleeves. "And I've gone too far down this road to turn around. I'm comfortable with who I am. Even though people don't like me, they are familiar with who I am. Give me a compelling reason to upset my whole world. You can't. There's too much to lose and nothing to gain."

"But how can you..." the ghost started its rebuttal, but Ellie interrupted definitively.

"No. No," she continued, waving her arms, "Just no!"

Then, stiffening her spine, wiping away the remaining moisture from under her eyes, and taking a last, hardened glance at the little girl, she looked the spirit in its eyes and challenged, "What else have you got for me?"

The ghost and Ellie held their gaze for a short amount of time. Ellie was determined not to be the first one to blink. Her bearing and defiance had been an effort to convince the spirit, and herself, that these memories had had no effect on her. But now, she was forced to turn her eyes away from the ghost before it saw the truth in them.

"Puh! This is not my day!" said Ellie, throwing up her arms. She was genuinely disappointed with herself. "I was looking forward to going head to head with you and your kind. And I expected I would put up a better fight than I have thus far. I pled with you not to make me come in here. I never plead with anyone. Ever. I mean, ever.

"Then I break down and cry uncontrollably at the first sight of my da... my father. I don't remember the last time I cried." Ellie paused. "That's not quite true. I do. I do remember. But that was a long time ago, and it has not happened since.

"And then just now, my heart aches for this little girl for the endless trials ahead and for the woman she will become, compared to the woman she thought she'd be.

"But I grow stronger and more resolved against any transformation as we go along, spirit. Yes, I do. I am proud of what I have accomplished. I am comfortable with who I am. I am. So, I say, let's move on."

"You may believe that, dear," replied the ghost, "but I have been doing this a long time, and I observe that there is something at work in you whether you want to acknowledge it or not. But we shall see."

And so said, it lifted its arm and opened another illuminated portal, and as the spirit reached to take Ellie's hand, she withdrew it. She stepped into the bright arch ahead of the specter, who, amused by Ellie's bravado, followed her in.

Although Ellie had entered the passage first, the Ghost of Christmas Past was already there waiting for her when she emerged.

"Finally!" the spirit said with feigned agitation. "I thought you got lost. No matter. You know this place?"

Ellie needed a moment to comprehend what had happened. She had only been in the "hallway" for half a second and had entered well ahead of the ghost, yet here it was leaning against a wall, looking annoyed as if it had been made to wait for hours. Or perhaps eons?

It took a moment for Ellie's eyes to adjust to the low lighting in this new scene. She and the ghost were standing in a quiet living room. One whole wall was filled with Christmas cards that had been taped up for display. There was a fake Christmas tree in front of a large sliding glass door at one end of the room.

Despite, understandably, having no fondness for December 25th, Ellie did have a fascination and affection for Christmas trees. Even while eschewing any celebration and decoration for the holiday, it cannot be said that Ellie did not intentionally linger in areas where a real, live Christmas tree was displayed. She could spot a fake tree just as quickly as she could smoke out a dishonest man.

It did not require any keen insight to spot this particular tree as a fraud. It was white and luminous, and alternately yellow, then green, then red, then blue, back to white, and so on. Trees like that don't grow in the wild. Show me the forest where such a tree grows!

A spotlight trained on the tree, and shining through a rotating wheel of colored glass, created the various hues. It also provided all the illumination Ellie needed to identify her surroundings. She and the spirit were in the Poole family's living room.

"Ahhh!" said Ellie, "The tree is a dead giveaway. I had never seen anything like it before, or, gratefully, since. And the Christmas card wall. Tacky.

"But I know this place, this was the home of my first foster family, and though I have not thought on it in many a year, I'll admit, spirit, that it now brings back a fond recollection of what, as a little girl, I always dreamed Christmas would be."

"Okay, oldest to youngest," said Mr. Poole to his children, who were milling about in the hallway, squinting from the bright light of the video camera he would use to capture this Christmas morning's proceedings on 8mm film.

Ellie and the ghost turned their attention away from the tree to the parade of Pooles exiting the hallway in single file.

Into the living room came Paula Poole, the first of the five Poole children. She was twelve and the only one of the kids of an age at which it was unfashionable to believe in Saint Nick. So for her, the onus of the gift selections was squarely on her parents. And later that morning, as Ellie was now remembering, Paula's mother would take the brunt for two or three articles of clothing that were not the right size or not on her color palette.

Next in was Patty Poole, almost nine, who was the same age as Ellie was that year and who had become the closest thing to a sister Ellie would ever have in the short time they had known each other. Patty smiled for the video camera and went and sat in front of her pile of presents, as she had been around the block enough times to know the Christmas choreography.

Patty was followed by Peter Poole, the first boy, tall for seven years old and all arms and legs, lean and gangly, almost to the point of emaciation. Wiping sleep from his eyes, he wandered aimlessly looking for his tower of presents; he looked like a shell-shocked war orphan who had just emerged from a bombed out building.

Mr. Poole motioned for the next child to enter. That was Penny, Peter's twin sister, though they bore no resemblance. It was hard for friends and acquaintances to believe that Peter, blond and fair, had been wombmates with the black-haired and dark-eyed Penny who favored the complexion of the rest of her family. Because of the aberration, it had been joked more than a few times to Mr. and Mrs. Poole that there must have been a mix-up at the hospital, and they were raising someone else's child while someone nearby was raising theirs.

Though it was always spoken in jest, it did prompt Mr. and Mrs. Poole to inquire at St. Dunstan's Hospital whether or not something like that was a possibility (they were assured it was not). Nor did it stop them from scanning other similar aged children at malls and schools and fairs, over the years, for a young man who more closely resembled their daughter Penny.

Finally came Mrs. Poole, who had gone back down the hallway and emerged with three-year old Preston Poole. He was still half asleep and hiding his face in the nape of his mother's neck, looking up and around only long enough to wave off the home movie camera capturing his Christmas crankiness for posterity and for the showing off to at least two future girlfriends, neither of whom would ever become Mrs. Preston Poole.

Here was the Poole family: Paula, Patty, Peter, Penny, and Preston, with dad, Philip, and mom, "Pea."

"Okay!" announced Mr. Poole, "Go ahead and open!"

"Wait!" cried Patty. "What about Ellie?"

"Your father and I discussed whether to wake her to open presents," explained Mrs. Poole, a bit annoyed at having been challenged on this point, "but there are only two presents for her, and we didn't think it would be appropriate to make her sit and watch all of you open all of yours."

"But Mom," pleaded Patty, "She won't care. She's never opened presents with a family before. She will feel left out. It will be worse if she comes out and we did all this without her, and then we watch her open her presents. Why did Santa only bring her two?"

"Well," replied her mom, "We figured Santa wouldn't know she was here, so we bought her presents. We only got her a few things because, well, we are only allotted so much money, and she's only been with us a few months..."

There are times in life when you don't realize you are on the wrong side of an issue until you are faced with having to defend your position, and then, realizing you have the weaker argument or no argument at all for your stance, you have no choice but to change sides. This was now the case for Mrs. Poole, who looking at Mr. Poole, found no rebuttal in his eyes or on his lips, and so she had no option but to relent, and thus she continued, "and you're absolutely right. My God, I feel terrible."

Patty scanned her gifts and picked out a couple. "Can I give her these?"

"Yes! Oh, Patty, thank you! I'm sure Santa will replace whatever you give her!"

"I'll give her one of my presents," said Peter, then adding, "if they are clothes."

In turn, each of the Poole children removed a present or two from their piles and placed it on little Ellie's.

Ellie turned to the Ghost of Christmas Past and whispered (unnecessarily), "This explains the See 'n' Say and the wood burning set. I didn't know any of this. I just thought they were terrible gifters."

"Patty," said Mrs. Poole, "Go wake Ellie and tell her it's Christmas morning, and Santa came, and there are presents here for her to open."

Patty jumped up and darted toward Ellie's room.

"Tell her not to worry; there are no puppies in any of the boxes!" yelled Paula sarcastically. Patty turned around and shot Paula such a look of disapproval that Paula, first searching her parents' eyes for any hint of refuge, and finding none, had to put her head down and stare at her lap rather than make eye contact with anyone the whole time little Ellie was being roused.

"Puh! Rude!" said Ellie and then informed the spirit, "she never liked me."

Paula was also the only Poole not to part with any of her presents. Even Preston, only three, took a box from his mound of gifts and set it with Ellie's. When his mom and dad and siblings clapped at the gesture, he went back to his stack for another gift and then another. If it were not for Mr. Poole surreptitiously returning that same gift to Preston's pile and thus replenishing it as fast as the toddler could deplete it, out of generosity or adulation, his entire inventory would have been gone before a single present was opened.

In a few moments, Patty returned hand in hand with little Ellie, who, though appearing reluctant to participate in the Christmas morning festivities, also seemed determined to make a brave show of it.

"Merry Christmas, Ellie!" said Mrs. Poole. That was followed by the rest of the Poole family chiming in with their merry Christmases too.

"Oh, um, thanks," said Ellie shyly.

"You're s'pposta to say 'Merry Christmas' back," instructed Penny.

Little Ellie said nothing.

"It's fine," interjected Mrs. Poole. "Any response is fine."

"Well, what are we waiting for?" cried Mr. Poole, clapping his hands excitedly. "Let's see what Santa brought you all!"

The Poole children went about ripping the paper off the presents revealing the gifts underneath, and then sharing that intelligence with their mom or dad. Excited cries of "Mom, look! A chemistry set!" and "Dad, look, a baseball mitt," and the like filled the room as the kids tore into their wrapped presents efficiently and methodically. Despite a large number of gifts to be opened, the entire process took only a few minutes.

Except for Ellie. She was cautiously opening each present as if the contents of any one of them might spring out unexpectedly and turn her world upside down again.

The See 'n' Say, she gave to Preston. The wood burning set, she re-gifted to Peter. She kept the curling iron, the Etch-a-Sketch, and the walkie-talkies that were intended as a gift for her and Patty so they could communicate from their respective rooms. There was "Operation," which she and the Poole kids would play with later in the day. And there were clothes, most of which "Santa" had intended for Patty.

Little Ellie unwrapped these presents and first viewed them through watery eyes. It had only been a year earlier when her Christmas morning was anything but the happy, normal, family Christmas the Pooles were trying to make her a part of.

"She is so brave," said Ellie to the Ghost of Christmas Past. "Look how she is holding it together. Even at this early age, she is able to hide her emotions."

"Oh, is that a good thing?" asked the spirit, looking sympathetically at its companion.

The children were all busy playing with toys or taking stock of their Christmas haul when Mr. Poole announced, "Okay, time to get ready for church."

"Do we have to?" whined Peter.

"Yes!" said Mrs. Poole. "It's Christmas Day!"

"Jenny's family doesn't go to church on Christmas!" argued Patty.

"Jenny's family is Presbyterian. Protestants don't go to church on Christmas," explained Mrs. Poole.

"Why can't we be Protestants?" protested Peter.

"Let's go," said Mr. Poole. "It's just an hour."

"Not if we have Monsignor Latimer," sighed Paula as she and the children abandoned their gifts and headed to their rooms to get ready for church.

The spirit and Ellie watched the rest of this Christmas Day unfold side by side with very few words passing between them while the scenes seemed to move by at the speed of life.

The ghost had decided they would stay in this time until Ellie could see no more and asked to leave. That request never came. Even though Paula's worst fear that old Monsignor Latimer would be delivering the homily had come true, the request never came.

They were with little Ellie and the Pooles at the church for mass. They were with them in the station wagon on the way home with the whole family singing Christmas carols along with the radio: *Angels We Have Heard on High, O, Come All Ye Faithful, Joy to the World...* Ellie was surprised to see her former self singing right along with them. "How does she even know the words?" she thought to herself.

The sight of the child singing along to carols with words long forgotten to her, laughing and smiling, stirred a medley of emotions in Ellie, not the least of which was betrayal. How could her former self have forgotten what had transpired only a year earlier? There was another feeling that Ellie had not yet identified as regret. Regret for having given up on childhood and on her dreams too soon.

They were back at the Poole house to watch the kids revisit their gifts, play with their toys, and participate in a couple of rousing games of Operation while waiting for dinner. Thanksgiving and Christmas were the only two days of the year when the Pooles had their big meal in the middle of the afternoon. A long dining room table was moved into the living room, and a card table was also set up and placed at the end of it to form one long table. Several extra places were set.

Mrs. Poole had prepared an Italian feast of rigatoni and meatballs, stuffed shells, beef braciola, and fresh-baked bread. Mr. Poole was in charge of the salad. His heavy hand with the vinegar and the salt was enough to elicit scalp sweat on all takers.

There was so much food! Were they expecting the Italian army? When the doorbell rang promptly at three p.m., it was not exactly an infantry from Rome that had arrived, although one could stretch to call it that. Rather, it was a waddle of nuns from Saint Dunstan's Convent who were invading the Poole household.

In marched Sister Mary Margaret, Sister Mary Josephine, Sister

Mary Louise, Sister Mary Patricia, and Sister Mary Carol, all in their long black robes with rosaries dangling from the waists with their habits and wimples covering every part of their heads except their cherubic faces.

They entered in high spirits, chattering and jabbering and obviously happy to have somewhere to go for dinner and be with a family on Christmas Day. They looked as if they could be from the chorus of a community theater production of *The Sound of Music*. One might expect them, at any minute, to put their hands together as if in prayer and break out into a rousing version of "How Do You Solve a Problem Like Maria?"

"Oh, yeah, the nuns," said Ellie to the spirit. "Funny, I had completely forgotten, but looking at them again, I don't know how that is even possible." A small but genuine smile broke out across her face.

The smile turned into a full-on laugh a short while later when Peter, accidentally walking in on Sister Mary Carol in the process of relieving her bladder in the bathroom, came running out into the living announcing his new discovery that "Nuns have legs!"

The whole dinner party erupted in laughter and then again even more uproariously when the four remaining nuns at the table, in unison, reached down and pulled up their robes, revealing calves and a generous portion of thighs. (Enough to make an uncomfortable Mr. Poole avert his eyes.)

Sister Mary Patricia then announced to Peter, "We nuns do show our legs from time to time, but we try not to make a 'habit' of it!"

There was some polite laughter. Sister Mary Patricia was crestfallen, thinking she would score a much bigger response, but her reach for the pun had only served to cool off the room.

"Saw that one coming from a mile away," Ellie said to the spirit.

"It is quite unfortunate," the ghost replied.

The afternoon passed by. The nuns had coffee and dessert, sat patiently while each child showed them the presents Santa had brought him or her, took turns making a fuss over Preston and bouncing him on their respective knees, which Peter earlier in the day had established were, indeed, part of a nun's anatomical makeup, picked at cookies that were set out for their ongoing enjoyment, and in every way possible, blessed the house and family that had blessed them with a welcome spirit of Christmas.

Throughout the afternoon, the nuns had made a point of taking private moments with little Ellie to express their joy at seeing her with such a loving family as the Pooles. Each of them ended their conversations by placing a hand on Ellie's head and asking the Lord to grant her a life full of love, laughter, and family.

"Obviously, the blessing did not take," Ellie said to the spirit.

"Not yet, anyway," replied the ghost.

Ellie rolled her eyes.

After having finished up in the kitchen, Mrs. Poole entered the living room and turned on the lights.

"You don't have to sit in here in the dark," she said, loud enough to wake the nuns, all of whom were dozing in a variety of positions on couches, in armchairs, or on the floor.

Sister Mary Carol, who seemed to be the leader of this "away team," quickly noticed it was now after 5:30 and announced they needed to get back to the convent for their own Christmas celebration.

"Let's walk them out," said the Ghost of Christmas Past. When they exited the Poole's, Ellie found herself all at once in front of another house. It was an old, quaint, dark brick structure with a large and welcoming gray porch that looked like it would, on hot summer days, beckon passersby to sit a spell with a tall, cool glass of lemonade.

The neighborhood was comprised of similarly styled houses situated close enough together that borrowing a cup of sugar from one's next-door neighbor may not have required either party to leave their home.

This particular house on this particular street was filled with particularly festive revelers. And among the celebrants was the Poole family. And among the Poole family was little Ellie. Therefore, the Ghost of Christmas Past led his charge through the brick wall and into the living room of the DeCiminero family.

Mrs. Poole had been born Liliana Paulina DeCiminero, the youngest of six children. Her birth order and birth weight earned her the nickname "Peanut," which, before the age of two, had been shortened to just "Pea." And though teachers throughout her early school years tried to impose her given name Liliana on her, by high school, even the most fastidious and peculiar of teachers scratched out "Liliana DeCiminero" on their class lists and penciled in just "Pea."

Pea's large family begat six large families. Her brother and her four sisters all married, and no pair produced fewer than four children. All of the families lived within a fifteen-minute drive from each other. There were twenty-seven cousins in all, ranging in age from twenty-two years old to three years old, all of whom appeared to be as close as if they were siblings.

And so it was this Christmas night, as it had been every Christmas night for as long as anyone could remember, that all roads led right here to the original family home still occupied by the patriarch and matriarch, John and Mayme DeCiminero.

The house was considerably too small to hold this family of forty-one plus little Ellie. Despite the windows being cracked open a little to allow in some cool air, the room was stifling and close. Sweaty kids, their hair matted to their scalps, chased each other on a circuit from living room to TV room to kitchen to hallway, back through the living room again and around and around — contributing screams of delight to the polyphonic symphony of disparate conversations, sporadic laughter, and the raised voices of two or three loud talkers, that all contributed to a baroque composition that filled the house with an unwavering din.

The slightly older kids played school on the steps that led to the second floor. Patty played the teacher and placed a wadded-up piece of paper in one of her hands behind her back and then offered both fists to the students on the stairs. If the pupil guessed the fist with the paper correctly, he got to move to the next step. If not, he had to stay put. The first one to get to the top of the stairs was the winner. And the graduation prize was taking over as the teacher for the next round.

Little Ellie was the winner of the first game, amid protests from the cousins that Patty helped her win. Certainly, little nods, eye movements, and the further extension of the fist holding the wad of paper than the fist that was not likewise inhabited were observed by Ellie and the spirit.

Little Ellie, however, in her turn as the teacher, did not return the favor to Patty. In fact, she "flunked" Patty by seemingly goading her into choosing the fist with no paper in it. And Patty wasn't the only one. Little Ellie had served to introduce guile into this family's innocent little game of school, and it would never be played the same way again. Her future self looked on approvingly.

"I am sad to see your heart so closed off at such an early age. Patty was the first friend you had ever known, and yet you deceived her."

"I remember now that I was only going to fool her the first time, as a joke. She trusted me completely. You saw the look on her face when the paper was not in the hand I had extended the furthest and bent my head toward. She couldn't believe I had done that to her. Do you know what I felt? Power. For the first time in my life, I was controlling an outcome! Not just sitting on the sidelines, forced to accept events outside of my control. And it felt good. I couldn't stop."

"Yes, but you also had the power to let her win, just like she let you win. That would have been the same kind of control."

"No. We don't see it that way," replied Ellie, gesturing to little Ellie and back to herself. "If you return every favor, you end up with nothing."

The older kids of high school and college age were in the kitchen, standing around sipping from bottles of Nehi sodas or RC Cola and chatting about school and crushes and cars and clothes.

Amid the teenagers was Uncle Leo — the self-proclaimed "fun uncle" — always ready with loud and sarcastic interjections into conversations not intended for him. And he punctuated each of his comments with his own laughter, which he aimed at the sky by throwing back his head. His guffaws rose like auditory flares through a thick cacophonous fog to find clear, unoccupied atmosphere where their explosions could be heard by everyone in the house and all the ships at sea.

Most of the grown-ups were seated around the large kitchen table where at one end, a generous charcuterie was set out along with other cold cuts and rolls. At the other end was what looked to be a million cookies comprised of a thousand varieties — pizzelles, snowball cookies, biscotti, glazed lemon knots, chocolate crinkles, chocolate chips — too many to itemize. But were there enough to feed this brood? At the rate hands reached in and over and up to take cookies, and at the still early hour of the evening, that question could not yet be answered.

The men mostly sipped some Old Granddad bourbon. Red wine was generously poured from large ceramic jugs set out on the kitchen counter next to a coffee percolator plugged in next to the stove. On that stove sat a large vat of homemade sauce and meatballs.

These two disparate scents — percolated coffee and tomato sauce — intermingled to create a unique aroma that endured through time, not in the air, but in the hippocampus in each family member's brain, so that whenever it was even closely duplicated in some other setting, no matter where they were or at what stage in life they were, just a brief whiff would bring every one of them right back to that kitchen on a Christmas evening at Grandma's and Grandpa's. And it would produce in them the warmest feelings of family and belonging and simplicity, weighted only slightly with that yoke of melancholy that human beings must bear with any thoughts of the irretrievable.

And it was now with Ellie as that essence was now completely enveloping every room in the house and triggering her own olfactory neurons that she was consciously sensing, remembering, and living that Christmas with the Pooles more comprehensively than ever before.

"This was what I always thought Christmas would be," Ellie said to the spirit, "even before I ever had a Christmas. I think it's what my dad was trying to give me before... you know...

"I can remember those days after this Christmas, the Pooles had visitors every evening — family, friends. Mrs. Poole put out pepperoni and cheese and crackers every evening. And the kids would show all of the company — that's what it was called back then — company. 'We're having company,' she would say. Anyway, the Poole kids would show everyone what Santa Claus brought them. And the Pooles would go visiting, and I would go with them, and it was just something everyone did. It was nice. And Christmas went on like that for a week. And right here and in this moment, I remember it all; when, if anyone had asked me about this last week, I would not have recalled any of it."

Ellie sensed it was about time to leave, so she took another look around the room and her eyes came to rest on her former self, who was clearly having a great deal of fun tricking younger children into selecting the fist without the paper in it.

"It's very nice for them. And it's very nice for people with large families. Good for them. But that's not me, spirit. I'll never have this now. Though this was a nice memory to revisit, I'll give you that. That's not how things worked out for me. But I am completely fine with how my life turned out and where I am. I am quite... comfortable."

There was more resignation than conviction in Ellie's voice, and though her words were spoken to the ghost, her eyes remained fixed on little Ellie with a longing in them as if she would have liked to have been able to go to her and get a message through to her.

"If that were true, we wouldn't be here," replied the spirit. "You'd be home snug and warm under your blankets, and I would be visiting someone else's past with someone probably less obstinate than you."

The ghost looked into her soul through her eyes. "I think it is best at this time to make one more stop. I was hoping to end my time with you here, but I think if we are to have any chance of being successful tonight, there is another Christmas to visit."

"How much more time do we have?" asked Ellie. "I'm expecting other spirits tonight! And we've been here a whole day."

"There's no such thing as time," replied the Ghost of Christmas Past flatly, "Not where we are. Nowhere really except in your world, and I can manipulate that however I want.

"So, don't concern yourself with getting home in time for your, as Mrs. Poole might say, 'company.'"

"Let's get it over with then," demanded Ellie with some of her characteristic impatience and agitation making itself known in her tone and cadence. "I know where we are going. There is only one other Christmas of any note in my life, and I'm not pleased, by any stretch of your spiritual imagination, that you would choose to take me there. I'm surprised though, because if this were a trial, I would be using the Christmas I presume you are taking me to in defense of my disposition. But since I know any objections on my part would be overruled by you, carry on."

Most of this conversation took place in the bright, tubular hallway the spirit had been using to move from one time to another. Ellie had become so familiar with it that when the portal appeared at the DeCiminero's, she stepped in as casually as if she were stepping into her private elevator at her office.

When the gateway closed behind them, they were exactly where Ellie had thought they were going.

"I'm one step ahead of you, spirit!" Ellie gloated. "I knew this is where you were taking me."

"You got me!" replied the ghost with a sly smile and a spread of its arms in acquiescence. "I wanted it to be a surprise, but you're just too clever," it continued wryly.

Ellie returned the spirit's gaze curiously.

They were in a large, lavishly appointed bedroom with a canopied bed serving as its centerpiece. Against the far wall from where Ellie and the ghost had entered was positioned an ornate dressing table and mirror. It sat between a large bank of windows, curtains drawn, obscuring the late evening Philadelphia skyline, and a set of double doors which opened to a walk-in closet the size of which, in square footage, fell somewhere between Delaware and Connecticut. Of course, if it were a state, its name would be Hyperbole.

There was a plush lounging sofa at the foot of the bed. A grandiose dresser, an imposing wardrobe, a petite writing desk, a lampstand table for each side of the bed, an accent chair, and a floor lamp rounded out the rest of the contents in the spacious room. And yet, even with all of those furnishings, there would still be enough floor space for a boxing ring.

A light spilling out onto the floor from the lavatory to the right of the bed suddenly went out and from out of that darkness emerged a young woman. She appeared to be in her mid twenties. Her hair was long and curly and pulled back tightly and held in place by a gold headband. She did not seem to be a woman who fussed with her hair.

She made a frail appearance despite there being life in her blue eyes and purpose in her step. Her black dress was likely a size zero, and it probably hung more loosely on her than it had on the hanger. She moved to the dressing table and sat down to apply makeup to give her hollow cheeks some show of ruddiness.

She was tired but obviously had some miles of an obligation to go before she could sleep.

"Going out?" asked the ghost to Ellie.

"I was getting ready to go to my fiancé's parents' house for Christmas Eve dinner," a clearly irritated Ellie replied. "If I'm not mistaken, Nate will be entering shortly."

At the speaking of these words, a man's voice could be heard in the outer room. "Ellie!… Ellie!" He yelled with anger and urgency.

The younger Ellie stopped applying lipstick mid lip, but only briefly. She looked at herself in the mirror. In the young woman's reflection, the spirit and Ellie saw a brief look of disappointment and hurt pass quickly over her face. She then continued with the lipstick, placed the cap on, and pressed her lips together, making a "mwah" sound.

The bedroom door flew open, and in walked Nate with a thick, bound document in his left hand, which he held up and pointed to with his right.

"What the hell is this?" he ranted as he moved to what would have been center ring.

"Don't you mean, 'good evening, darling?'" Ellie replied, giving herself one last "mwah" into the mirror and then turning in her chair to look at her betrothed.

Nate glared at her. "I was with your lawyer today to go over the prenup agreement you had her draw up. I thought you said it would be typical… cookie cutter. It's not. My lawyer says it's punitive, ingenious, and ironclad."

"You've been a busy boy, Nate. I only mentioned to you this morning that it was ready and asked you to make an appointment with Sarah and your lawyer next week to review it. Anxious much? If only your job search was carried out with such voracity."

Nate took a couple of aggressive steps toward Ellie's corner, but she did not move nor change her expression.

Desperate, Nate went down to one knee. "Listen, uh, sweetheart… I'm sorry. I know I'm worked up, but this agreement is insulting. I mean, you intend for me to get nothing if we don't stay married. Understood, I guess. But even if you die! That's unheard of. I'm not even sure that's legal."

"It is," replied Ellie emphatically. "Did your lawyer not tell you that? What difference does it make? You are marrying me for love, not for my money. I built my fortune without you."

"You mean you stole your fortune without me!" Nate seethed.

"No," responded Ellie calmly, "I told you what happened. There was an opportunity, and I took charge. I was shrewd and deliberate, and I controlled the outcome to my advantage, legitimately and legally.

"And here I am," boasted Ellie, surveying her surroundings. "And the others are not."

"Well, I heard…"

"I don't care what you heard! If I were a man, I'd have been slapped on my back, not talked of behind it, for my cunning maneuvering. But when you are a twenty-three-year old woman…"

"Regardless, why should you feel entitled to anything I've acquired to date? You will live well while we are together. You plan to work, right? Well, you can save all your money. You won't need to spend a dime of it while we are together. I'll take care of everything. And if I die first, which as I know you are well aware, is quite likely given my bad ticker, all the wealth I created will find its way back to my business through corporations, trusts, and other machinations Sarah has devised. I'll be running The Printh Company from my grave. You'll take your savings and have plenty of money to live out the rest of your days pining away for me. I believe this is quite fair. I mean, I could make you pay for half of everything while we are together."

Nate stood up and flung the prenup on the bed. He paced around the room like a boxer waiting for his opponent to come out of the corner and engage him.

The younger Ellie now rose and continued a little more softly, "Honestly, Nate, I'm surprised at this reaction. After all of your declarations of love and devotion, I am rather upset to see your attitude toward this… agreement. What difference does it make?" Here young Ellie took a deep breath in, held it, and let it out. "Puh! You told me you would love me even if I was poor and had nothing."

Nate turned and seized Ellie by her frail arms. His face was red, and his eyes were wild in contrast to her pallid skin and controlled demeanor. He looked like a man who had sacrificed a couple of years of his life scheming for one big payoff only to see the plan fall apart just as he was about to cash out. And that is precisely what he was.

Ellie was caught off guard by the abrupt attack. Nate was in her face, and her frame went limp.

"I told you that…" Nate needed a moment to relax his jaw enough to respond but could not hold back long enough to unclench his teeth before continuing, "I told you that because that's what people say. No one would say, 'Gee, Ellie, good thing you have money, or I wouldn't even give you the time of day!' Would they?"

"Is that really the way you feel?" asked Ellie, trying to free herself from his grasp but generating no resistance.

"You have nothing I am interested in other than your money. I loathe you! My God! The only thing I liked about you was that you worked so much all the time that you didn't have time for me. That was a perk!"

Nate released Ellie, who spun dizzily but righted herself with both hands against the dressing table. She was able to maneuver, somewhat gracefully under the circumstances, into the chair, or she might have otherwise fallen to the floor.

This match had turned suddenly, and it was Nate who was getting in the verbal body blows and Ellie hadn't the strength to raise even a frail defense.

Now, Nate's gloves were off as he continued pummeling her. "You have no friends of your own. My friends can't stand you! You have no family. My mother detests you!"

"What about your father?" young Ellie tried feebly to parry, "I can't have mistaken his kindness toward me."

"You're the means to a new fishing boat. That's all. After he met you the first time, he told me I'd need to have a girlfriend on the side because you were colder than anything he had ever brought up ice fishing in Maine."

The punches were landing, and young Ellie was against the ropes when Nate went for the knockout.

"He even said to let him know who the girlfriend is, and he'd name the fishing boat after her as our little joke. I told him he could plan to name it 'Marlena.'"

"After your cousin?" asked young Ellie, but she wished immediately she had not said that out loud, showing such gullibility.

Nate spread his arms and gave her a triumphant look. "Didn't you ever wonder why someone like me — I mean, look at me — why someone like me would even take an interest in someone like you if it weren't for the money? Who are we kidding here? And then you pull this?" Nate had again picked up the bound prenup that he had tossed on the bed earlier and threw it maliciously at Ellie, barely missing her but striking the mirror and cracking it diagonally from top to bottom.

Nate walked to the door and grabbed the knob but stopped and turned to look back at young Ellie, who had not only regained her composure but who had already adopted an air, a stiffness, a resolve that was visible on her face. Nate was momentarily startled by her hardened features but quickly recovered.

"Even if there was no prenup and even if I had access to your vast wealth and even if you drew up a will that left me all of your money and your company and whatever else, I think it might still have been too steep a price for me to pay to have to live out however many years with you!"

With that, Nate walked out and slammed the bedroom door behind him. Ellie waited until she heard the outer door close with a similar but muffled bang.

Ellie picked up the phone on the dressing table and punched in four numbers. "Yes, it's Ellie Printh. I will need my locks changed this evening."

"Yes, I'm aware of what time it is and what day it is. Just make it happen!"

Ellie hung up the phone. She looked at herself in the broken mirror. The angle of the crack split her face in two between her eyes and to the left of her nose. She inhaled deeply. She held it for as long as she could, trying to decide if it might be best if she just never exhaled and if she should just make that the last breath she would ever draw. Deciding against it, she released the hot air with an extended, "puhhh, huh huh."

Young Ellie was unable to suppress another "Puh." Another followed and another and another until they had turned into sobs.

To her own surprise, she was crying despite her fiercest effort to hold it in. Tears flowed, and she made audible wails of despair. She was unable or unwilling to take her eyes away from her image in the mirror. She was mesmerized by her own anguish.

Within seconds, it was over. Young Ellie dried her eyes, removed her headband, and shook out her hair. She spoke to herself in the mirror, wagging her finger, like a mother admonishing her daughter: "I don't want to see this ever again. Never, ever again."

Ellie and the Ghost of Christmas Past had watched the proceedings in silence. Ellie had her arms folded the entire time and looked like an obdurate child who was dragged to church against her will.

When the young woman had composed herself, Ellie turned to the spirit.

"Are you satisfied? Did you get what you wanted?"

The spirit started to speak, but Ellie interrupted. "Take me home. I want to go home... NOW!"

This time there was no portal, no bright light, no delay. They were instantly back in Ellie's own living room. It happened so quickly, Ellie had to wonder if she had ever left her house. It was still enough for Ellie to formulate a plan and a proposal for the Ghost of Christmas Past.

Though she had full recollection of the time she had just spent with the spirit, which included a whole day with the Pooles, it did not seem as if she had been away from this room for more than a few minutes. She looked at the clock. 1:42 a.m. They had been gone for less than an hour! Ellie could not wrap her brain around it, but that was the least of the perplexities on her growing list of inscrutabilities.

At first, Ellie feared the spirit had sent her back alone. Then she saw the Ghost of Christmas Past standing near the couch and motioning her to come nearer.

"I'll stand over here by the fire," she said in response to its gesture.

"That was not how I wanted us to part. I built in some time," said the spirit. "I cannot be here when the next ghost comes, so we don't have very long. If you have questions... "

"Questions! Okay," said Ellie heatedly, "here's one for you. If you are trying to get me to change, why did you show me that last memory? Everywhere you took me were reminders that I have been abandoned every time I have allowed someone in. First my dad, then the Pooles. What you didn't show was that February after Christmas, when I was told that Mrs. Poole was pregnant with their sixth child and they, unfortunately, needed my room. I would need to go to a new foster family.

"I mean, my God, she already had five kids! I couldn't have been their sixth? Why not me? I wasn't good enough? They preferred to take their chances with a new kid?

"And after I left them, I was sent to five different foster families in eight years until I just packed up and ran away because my last foster 'dad' was a little too grabby, and my foster 'mom' was far too oblivious.

"You had the opportunity to leave me with a… I'll say it… a fond memory of Christmas, a dear remembrance that maybe, once I was back here and thinking about it, might have started to work on me… maybe. But then you decide to take me to the most humiliating moment in my life, the moment when, now that I think about it, my nature was cemented for good. Seeing it again sets me only harder. You're really not very good at this."

"You had already dismissed any good the Poole memories had stirred in you as pleasant but unattainable," replied the spirit in a compassionate manner, in complete juxtaposition to Ellie's harshness.

Ellie and the Ghost of Christmas Past locked eyes briefly, but that was long enough to loosen Ellie's anger's grip.

"Sit," beckoned the spirit.

Ellie relented.

"How old are you, child?" inquired the ghost.

"Forty-eight," replied Ellie, not opposed to being called 'child.'

"No, you're not," countered the spirit.

"Fifty-three," Ellie confessed.

"You're not that either," answered the ghost.

Before Ellie could protest that she was indeed that age, the spirit continued.

"You are as old as life. Yes, you have been in this world for fifty-three years, but you have always existed, and you always will. Since you'll be spending all of Time with yourself, it's probably a good idea to like yourself. Your short period here is crucial to that. Live the life you want to live; be the person you want to be. Don't waste this time."

"I can't live the life I wanted. That opportunity was taken from me right out of the gate. I was born with a deformed heart that made me watch the world go by through a window. I couldn't play outside, so I had no friends. My mom ran off. I watched my dad die on Christmas morning. Then with the Pooles, just when I was starting to feel like I was part of their family, they replaced me with a new baby and sent me packing.

"The man I thought loved me and who for the first and only time since I was nine, made me think that maybe, just maybe, I was lovable, actually loathed me and only wanted my money.

"And I couldn't help that any of those things happened to me. Which one was my fault? Which one did I have control over? All of it happened to me, not because of me!"

Ellie had been raising her voice but regained her composure and finished, "Okay, am I happy? Is this the life I imagined I would have as a little girl? No. But for all I've been through, I've made the best of it."

"True, your life has been shaped by what has happened to you. Those events have pushed you off the path of your childhood hopes and dreams. You are farther off track than you know, and you will only walk deeper into the woods if your course is unaltered. You will be lost forever."

"I assume you and your fellow spirits do not want that for me, or there would be no point to this evening," Ellie began her negotiation.

"That may or may not be true," replied the ghost. "I've explained my assignment. It involves no rooting interest."

Ellie persisted. "I have a proposal for you. It is a very generous offer, in that I take on all the risk, and you walk out of here with a win, and your two colleagues don't even need to show up."

"I'm intrigued," lied the spirit.

"Yes. I thought you would be. It is simple. You just give me a do-over. Let me go back in time to the minute just before I opened the box with the puppy in it and live my life again from there. I know I will be a better person. I think I have made that argument."

"I cannot do that."

"Of course you can. You said you could. You said you could manipulate time however you like."

"I cannot take you back through time. In your world, time is current that only flows in one direction. You can't go back. Just like sharks can only move forward in the water, people can only move forward in time or drown in a sea of anguish over not being able to either change or replicate what was. You can't go back and change things; you can only change what is in front of you."

Ellie saw her hope of a deal slip away.

"But how? I've been this person for so long?!"

"You can only live a day at a time. And only an hour of a day at a time. And only a minute of that hour at a time. And only a second of that minute at a time. You don't need to change anything for the rest of your life. You just need to change it for that second and then the next and then the next. Be in each moment. Be your best self in each moment. And you will be your best self for the rest of your life."

"I don't think I can change. I really don't want to."

As bright, white light began to swirl around the room, the ghost rose. It turned to Ellie. It, too, was illuminated, and its voice now sounded as if it were from some distance away. "There is no time when adults are nearer to the child they used to be than at Christmas time when they are closer to the pure joy and wonder and hope of childhood. This is your best chance."

"What will happen to me?" asked Ellie of the spirit.

The ghost was now mostly obscured and enveloped by the whirling funnel of gleaming particles. It was leaving the same way it came. Only this time, the light was not blinding Ellie, and the outline of the spirit was still visible to her as it replied.

"I don't know. You have worn a deep rut. One of the most cavernous I have seen."

Ellie looked like a patient who had just bravely received a poor prognosis from her doctor. She stood and took a few fearless steps toward the brilliant cyclone and, looking up into the face of the Ghost of Christmas Past, said, "It's just as well, I don't think I would even know where to go if I did get out of it."

At that moment, the funnel ascended, the light was gone, and, with it, the spirit.

Ellie stared at the void left by the ghost's departure. As she began to turn away, a sudden, brief, spinning, bright vortex dropped from above, its narrow fingers bouncing up and down on the hardwood floor, like a one-handed pianist tickling the ivories, producing a cloud of fluorescent debris. And from out of the light came the ghost's voice saying...

"The child will show you the way."

And then, Ellie was once again alone and in the dark.

STAVE 3: THE SECOND OF THREE SPIRITS

*E*llie looked at the clock. 1:56 a.m. She had four minutes until the next spirit was due to make its appearance.

The tornado in which the Ghost of Christmas Past departed had sucked all the energy and light out of the room, except for what the now-meager fire was producing. In the void created by the spirit's absence was a palpable silence and stillness that made Ellie uncomfortable in a distantly familiar way.

She knew this feeling. It had been a long time since she had experienced it. But the childhood memory came instantly to her... of waking up frantic in the middle of the night with trouble getting her breath and with a cough that made her sound like a barking dog... of her mother's annoyance at having been disturbed from her sleep,... of her dad running hot water in the shower to steam up the bathroom... of his worried look when her struggle to breathe persisted despite the damp air... of his bundling her up and putting her in the car and rolling down all the windows and driving her off into the crisp autumn night... of catching some deep breaths and falling asleep in the car... of waking up in the back seat to a bright sunrise... of her dad stopping the car at a park... of his carrying her, still in her pajamas and slippers and wrapped in a blanket, to a bench overlooking a placid, pristine pond... of her looking out over it amazed at how shiny it was and how the colorful leaves on the trees were mimicked by their watercolor counterparts on the small lake... of how unsure she was whether what she was looking at was really water or a sheet of glass cut to the shape of the pond... of an insatiable need to end her confusion... of picking up a rock and taking a few steps toward the water's edge and hurling it in just to assure herself that what she was looking at was real... of her relief and disappointment when the stone made a loud "splunk" followed immediately by a splash... of her dad being startled from dozing on the bench and asking her why she did that. And of her response, "It was all so peaceful and beautiful, I thought maybe I died, and this was heaven. I just had to make sure this was real, and I was still alive."

"No reason I have to stay in my pajamas for all of this!" Ellie spoke this thought loudly.

It had the same effect as throwing the stone. Her voice shattered the silence, and reality was confirmed.

The statement served a second purpose as well. Now spoken, it confirmed to Ellie that she did not want to sit and wait the eternal four minutes for the next spirit to show up.

She went to her bedroom, pulled out some comfortable slacks and a matching top, and an oversized cardigan. She slipped into a pair of loafers. She called this her Katherine Hepburn look. She ran a straightener through her hair quickly and took a good look in the mirror, sighed, and then applied some wrinkle cream under her eyes. "Just because I'm being haunted, it's no excuse to look like h..."

She was halted in this thought when she was all at once aware of a bright, flickering orange glow in the hallway. Retraining her eyes back to her reflection, she could see a wave of emotion move across her face in the span of a moment.

First, the low trough of confusion furrowed her brow, followed by the rising crest of alarm which raised her eyebrows with it; then finally, the crash of realization that these golden hues foretold the arrival of the second ghost. As quickly as it came, the wave receded, pulling any visible show of feeling with it out to sea with its undertow.

"Showtime," she said to herself in the vanity mirror, and she pushed herself up from her chair with both hands.

"Coming!" she shouted without solicitation.

"Take your time," came a friendly reply from the living room.

Ellie wasn't sure what she was expecting, but she knew this wasn't it. She had some vague memory from the movie she had seen as a little girl that the Ghost of Christmas Present was a large, gregarious man with a booming voice. She hadn't laid eyes on this current iteration, but the tone in the reply that entreated her to take her time was soft, gentle, and cheerful.

Before this evening began Ellie, in one of her rare and brief moments of what she would call weakness (when her thoughts would escape and run on beyond her to the places she had clearly communicated were off-limits, and before she could catch up and drag them, like spirited but disobedient children, back inside) would try without any success to remember the sound of her father's voice. It was always irretrievable.

Earlier in the evening, when the Ghost of Christmas Past had led her to her childhood home, she at once realized that it was the same place to which her truant thoughts were always heading, just to try to hear his voice, if only a fragment, to bring back and have forever.

If nothing else, her journey with the spirit provided her that gift.

This second ghost's voice was not her dad's voice, but it contained the same qualities and characteristics of his manner of speaking, which immediately endeared him to her, sight unseen. Though she instantly resolved that the ghost would see not one sign of that inclination from her.

Ellie made her way down the hallway, slowing as she approached the living room. She stopped short of the doorway and peeked around the corner to try to catch a glimpse of the Ghost of Christmas Present without being detected.

He was standing, warming his hands, by a robust fire that just moments ago was barely embers. She could make out that he was tall and lean, slightly stoop-shouldered; well maybe, after all, he was leaning over the fire. He had thick, wavy black hair. That's all she could tell from her vantage.

His manner of dress was also a surprise to Ellie. No robe with fur around the trim. No robe at all. He was wearing beige slacks (possibly corduroys) and a red and green tartan plaid wool sport coat over, what Ellie could see from the exposed collar, a red and white striped shirt.

"Is this the Ghost of Christmas Present or a sartorially-challenged English professor?" Ellie thought to herself.

"Come on over by the fire and have a warm, Lord bless you!" The spirit spoke these words without turning around. Ellie was startled. She had made no sound, and he had given no indication that he sensed her presence.

Ellie took a couple of falsely confident steps toward the fire, but the ghost crossed the room in three giant strides with his hand outstretched.

"Come in! Come in! And know me better! I am the Ghost of Christmas Present."

He grabbed her hand from her side with both of his and nearly shook her arm out of its socket. It is safe to say that no one had ever greeted Ellie with such enthusiasm and warmth.

"Your hands are cold," remarked the spirit.

"By comparison only," assured Ellie.

The spirit made no reply but only guided her to the fireplace.

"There, that's better, isn't it?

They were now both warming their hands. Ellie was spying the spirit out of the corner of her eye and wondering why she was complying with his insistence.

He had a smile that incorporated his whole face. His lips and teeth and cheeks and eyes all took part enthusiastically. There was something so overwhelmingly kind and paternal in this being that Ellie was in the unaccustomed position of having to fight an instinct to like him.

That poor little instinct didn't have a chance. The naïve impulse was quickly dispatched by Ellie's experienced misanthropic tendencies.

"Listen," said Ellie as she broke out of the brief hold the spirit's charm had had on her. "My hands are just fine at their natural temperature."

She walked away from the fire and toward the middle of the living room.

"You've got quite a handshake there," she said, still thinking about his greeting. "You are flesh and bones?"

"Flesh and bones-ish," he replied. "It would be difficult to explain. So let's leave it at that."

"So, you are the Ghost of Christmas Present? What is that like?" asked Ellie, in a not-so-subtle attempt to learn more about an adversary she was uncharacteristically reluctant to call a foe.

"I am not quite sure," replied the spirit. "It's my first — and only — day in the role."

"What?" Ellie did not hide her surprise but then continued nonchalantly, "Why is that?"

"I'm only here for you, for this. Just like my brothers and sisters before me, it is one Christmas and done. It's a limited engagement."

"I should say. Your siblings have also been Ghosts of Christmas Present? How many in your family?" asked Ellie. Here, finally, was some information she might be able to use.

"Nearly two thousand."

"Impossible!"

"No, no. I assure you. Each member of my family is brought into your world to usher in Christmas, and when it is gone, so too is each of them."

"I do not understand," Ellie said haltingly. Those were not words she often spoke, so they came out of her mouth as dissonantly as a quartet who had never sung together before.

"I thought the Ghost of Christmas Past would have enlightened? Did the procurer of this chance not explain?" asked the spirit, referring, Ellie assumed, to Bernice.

"Yes, to a degree. My interpretation is that I am living the story about Scrooge, and I'm Scrooge. Since that is impossible, I am insane. That is my interpretation of what I have been told.

"Yet, here I am. And there you are," Ellie admitted. "And you are real to me. Perhaps more real to me, at this moment, than I am to myself. The idea that I have been placed into elements that resemble a fictional story has been a point of consternation and disbelief, I must say. And it gives credibility to my theory that I am experiencing a break with reality."

And then, to herself, she asked, "But are people who are having a break with reality this aware they are having a break with reality?"

While Ellie was alone with that thought, the spirit was alone with his own considerations. They both emerged at the same moment.

"Why don't you have a seat, Ellie," he said in a fatherly tone that instinctively compelled her to comply.

"I don't think I would be breaking any trusts if I gave a bit more in the way of explanation," he began. Though spoken to Ellie, he was also declaring his final ruling in the deliberation he had been having in his head a moment earlier.

Ellie was seated on the couch, hands folded on her lap, and eager. Eager to gather more information, and eager to know what this was like. "Is this how it would have been to have a father when I was growing up?" she wondered to herself. There was something in this moment that she was cherishing.

"Go on," she said, trying to take back control.

"*A Christmas Carol*, right? You know the book by Charles Dickens, with Scrooge and Tiny Tim and Bob Cratchit? That's the *fictional* story you think you have been placed in?" The Ghost of Christmas Present just wanted to establish this before proceeding.

Ellie ignored her instinct to reply sarcastically, "No, no. I was referring to 'National Velvet.'"

Instead, she politely answered, "Yes. Ghost of Christmas Past. Ghost of Christmas Present. The other one." Typically, Ellie would have stopped there, not giving her opponent any more information. However, she wanted the spirit to fill in as many blanks as possible, so she continued. "If I'm being honest, I never read the book. I vaguely remember watching the movie a long time ago. I have some familiarity with the character Scrooge from having that epithet directed at me on more than one occasion. Unfairly, I might add."

"Fairly, unfairly," said the spirit, shrugging. "Will any of that matter after tonight? Maybe, maybe not.

"It's important for you to know that what you are living out right now is real. You have not stumbled into a storybook. The missing piece to your thinking that changes everything is, *A Christmas Carol* is based on a *true* story. Scrooge was real. Though, that was not his actual name, of course. As I understand it, someone familiar with the incidents that occurred on that particular Christmas Eve told someone else who told someone else who told Charles Dickens about what had taken place — probably all started with the old miser's nephew. That's my guess. Anyway, that's immaterial at this point. Dickens quickly fashioned the account, adding a few literary embellishments, and turned it into one of the most famous stories in all of literature."

The spirit paused here to try to read Ellie's reaction. There being absolutely none, he continued.

"What Mr. Dickens did not know, how could he, because neither Scrooge nor his nephew knew, how could they, was that Scrooge was not the first miserable wretch…" The spirit looked sympathetically and apologetically at Ellie. "… no offense…"

Exasperated, Ellie threw up her hands and dropped them heavily back on her lap. "Go on."

"Scrooge was not the first… uh… *misguided* human to have such visitations and to be given a chance at reclamation. This had occurred every Christmas Eve for hundreds of years before him and every year since.

"There's an allusion to it in Dickens' story." The ghost reached into his coat pocket and pulled out a book — remarkable in that the tome was much too large to have fit in the pocket! As he opened the book, Ellie could clearly see it was, of course, *A Christmas Carol* by Charles Dickens. The book fell open to the specific page the spirit was looking for. He cleared his throat and placed his finger on the place on the page from which he was about to read.

"Blah, blah, blah,... here it is... *'You have never seen the like of me before, exclaimed the spirit.*

"'Never,' Scrooge made answer to it.

"Have never walked forth with the younger members of my family; meaning (for I am very young) my elder brothers born in these later years?" pursued the phantom.

"I don't think I have," said Scrooge. "I am afraid I have not. Have you had many brothers, spirit?"

"More than eighteen hundred," said the ghost.

The spirit finished his recitation, closed the book with a loud clap, returned it to his coat pocket effortlessly, then looked at Ellie.

Ellie returned the gaze, shaking her head, "I don't get it. So that ghost was one of your brothers? And now the family has grown to nearly two thousand?"

"Yes," replied the ghost, "a different Ghost of Christmas Present for every Christmas since very early on. Scrooge wasn't the first. He wasn't the last. You will not be the last, presumably."

Ellie would need to think about all of this. It was too much to consider given the day she had had and its extension into the wee hours of the next one. Still, she felt some compulsion to collect more information.

"That would explain my experience with the Ghost of Christmas Past. I didn't think it quite knew what it was doing."

"Actually, the Ghost of Christmas Past, as well as the Ghost of Christmas Yet to Come, are permanent. They are the same spirits from time immemorial."

"Well, that hardly seems fair," Ellie tried commiserating.

"Oh? I think it is very profound. Think about it. The present is really just a moment, isn't it? It's fleeting. Once this moment passes..." The spirit held out his hand to highlight his brief pause, then he continued, "... it belongs to the past.

"And the next moment still belongs to the future until you take it. And what you do in each moment is like a chain reaction for every moment after it. Unfortunately, there's nothing you can do in that moment to change the past, but each twinkling of time holds the opportunity to alter what's ahead."

Ellie persisted in order to see if she could find out anything about the next specter she would face. "Because the past is not going to change, the Ghost of Christmas Past is the same being forever. Because the present is brief, the Ghost is Christmas present is short-lived. What about the Ghost of Christmas Yet to Come? Isn't the future always in flux? The future can change by what happens every second. You just said so yourself. How can that phantom even pretend to show me the future when it is impacted by what happens in the here and now?"

"Do you know the best way to predict a person's future behavior?" asked the spirit, not planning on giving Ellie time to answer. "You look at their past behavior. The future is not as fluid as you might think. The Ghost of Christmas Yet to Come is like an actuary on steroids. It will guide you through the most likely scenario based on billions of permutations, not just of your own behavior but of literally countless others who have walked this plane before you. Predicting other people's futures isn't that hard, really. People have the ability to change their projected future, but it is highly unlikely. It's hardly ever done, even when they desperately want to."

"Why are you telling me all of this?"

"I don't know. I thought it would help you to move beyond your insanity theory. You're not hallucinating. You're not experiencing a psychotic episode. You're not in a 'fictional story,' as you called it. You're in this moment. You have been given a rare and remarkable opportunity. I thought that was important for you know."

"What makes you think I won't tell people about this?" asked Ellie, half threatening.

At this, the ghost laughed heartily.

"Well, first of all, who would you tell?" he asked with a nod of his head and shrug of his shoulders. "But also, if there is no alteration in you after tonight and you disclose to anyone what happened, they won't believe you and will think you really have lost your mind, especially when you recount the other parts of your day."

Ellie agreed.

The Ghost of Christmas Present reached out his hand. "Shall we go?"

Ellie stood and looked at the ghost expectantly. She didn't want to have to ask, but despite her hesitation, she inquired of the spirit, "And if the evening has your desired outcome, which I must tell you, and as you have just confirmed, likely will not. But what about if somehow it does?"

"Oh, oh. Well, if we are successful, you will have no need or reason to tell anyone."

"Scrooge told someone." Ellie countered.

"Maybe. Or perhaps it was part of some plan. I really don't know. But it had not happened before, and it has not happened since. The Dickens story actually makes it less likely for someone in your position to be believed if you do relay the account. And you really won't want to. You'll know, and that will be quite enough for you."

Ellie considered the ghost's words, but finding them unrelatable, she discarded them as irrelevant.

"Let's be off!" said the ghost. "Touch my sleeve."

Upon the instant of Ellie's fingers coming into contact with the fabric of the spirit's jacket, her surroundings became a blur. She and the ghost were walking, but in one step, they were out the door. In two steps, they were already at the gate where the lion's head was standing guard.

"Some protector!" Ellie thought.

It was as if while they were strolling in one direction, the world was spinning past them in another. She had the sensation of moving backward against the pages of a flipbook.

She and the spirit were advancing at a casual pace, but the scene was hurtling by. Zip. Zip. Zip. And though it had been the middle of the night when they left Ellie's house, the sun was now making an appearance on the eastern horizon and rising with measured precision like the second hand on an old pocket watch. Tick. Tick. Tick.

Another couple of steps and they were on the same street that a few hours earlier was bustling despite icy and foggy conditions, and where she had abandoned a Salvation Army Santa in his stunned bewilderment of her rudeness.

Another step, and they were passing large homes in tree-lined neighborhoods. Or were the big houses and towering trees gliding by them? Ellie didn't know. Both?

The world began to slow down around them. After another couple of paces, they came to a stop in front of a humble house in a tired and dull part of town.

The whole walk may have taken five seconds judging from the sun's position low in the sky, about two "ticks" above the horizon. It cast a long shadow of her, but only her, up the walkway leading to a front door of a residence she did not know.

"We are here!" announced the Ghost of Christmas Present. "Do you know this place?"

"I do not," replied Ellie. "Are you sure you have the correct address? I'm sure I don't know anyone who lives in this..." Ellie looked around with distaste, "... neighborhood."

"This is the home of your assistant, Mary Lou Haggerty," informed the ghost.

"Oh," replied Ellie, simultaneously performing a quick visual inspection and mental calculation. "Oh... well, this is not bad at all for what I pay her. I'd say she has done quite well. Not good, of course, but quite well for what I know her earnings to be."

They walked to the front door, but before they entered the home, the spirit stopped and reached his hand into his coat pocket, from which he removed a large torch, again much too large to have fit in the coat's pocket. Also, the torch was aflame.

Ellie noticed he looked very grim and severe for the first time since they had been together.

The spirit raised the torch and made a sweeping motion over the archway of the entrance to the home, releasing from its fire what looked like that fine day-after snow that blows off roofs and ignites into sparkles upon catching the sun's rays. The delicate particles hung in the air over the archway like stars hold their position in the firmament, twinkling and shining, until absorbed into the morning sky.

Ellie stood in awe at the sight. "Oh, my! What was that?"

"It is Christmas cheer. And it's the least I can do for the poor soul inside and also the most I can do, unfortunately."

"Mary Lou? A poor soul? Oh pish. I rather doubt it."

The ghost dropped the torch back into the pocket.

"Enter with me." His good nature now restored, the spirit held out his arm. Ellie touched the sleeve of his coat, and the two of them stepped across the threshold into the modest home.

They entered into a cluttered living room. There were blankets and pillows on the couch, suggesting someone had slept there the previous night, and there had been no time or no effort to straighten up.

A small, misshapen, artificial Christmas tree, perhaps four feet high, was adorned with a garland of popcorn and cranberries, homemade ornaments, colored lights, and tinsel. It stood awkwardly in front of a bay window, looking like a child trying to climb on the seat to have a look outside.

Mary Lou was not immediately visible, but from the smell and sound of crackling bacon and the loud rattling of plates, her whereabouts were easily discerned.

In front of the Christmas tree was a young boy, still in his flannel Santa Mickey pajamas, sitting on the floor amidst discarded wrapping paper, games, and toys. He was playing with the newest iteration of Hess truck and an Iron Man action figure.

"Breakfast, Ben!" cried Mary Lou.

"Can we eat in here?" pleaded Ben.

"I guess! But only because it is Christmas!" said Mary Lou cheerfully as she entered the room carrying two plates piled high with scrambled eggs, bacon, fresh fruit, and toast. Then she added, "But it must be our secret. I don't suppose it would go over well at your mom's house."

"Heck no," replied Ben, exiting his imagination and rejoining the real world in time to see his aunt setting a plate down on an end table at one side of the couch and the other plate on the arm of the other side of the sofa.

"You take the table," she said after little consideration. She walked over to Ben, squatted behind him, and from Ellie's viewpoint, appeared to be hugging him until she lifted him with no small effort, and dragged him to the couch and set him on it.

"I'm not going to be able to do that much longer!" rasped Mary Lou, heading back to the kitchen for her coffee as Ben quickly repositioned himself on the couch so he could eat.

Ellie looked at the Ghost of Christmas Present and rolled her eyes. "Really? Seriously? I guess Ben is my Tiny Tim?"

The spirit replied, "There are few parallels to be drawn. Other than the three spirits, everyone's story is different. This woman is not your Bob Cratchitt; this boy is not your Tiny Tim."

Just as the ghost had finished speaking those words, Ben whooped, "God bless us, everyone!"

And both he and Mary Lou said in unison, "Amen!" They both chuckled, and then they started on their breakfast.

"I can't believe my good fortune! I have you for almost the whole day! What do you want to do after breakfast, Benny?"

"I'd like to play with my toys, but maybe you could keep reading to me from that book you started last night. I'd like to know what happens to Scrooge," said Ben.

"Yes. We need to finish that today. I need to return it to my boss tomorrow, or she might have me thrown in jail for stealing," Mary Lou replied with some theatrics.

"Is your boss really mean?" asked Ben. "You don't talk about her very much."

"Is she mean? Hmmm. That's a difficult question," Mary Lou answered. "On the outside, she gives every impression of being mean. And I can't say that she has ever given me or anyone else any reason to think that it doesn't extend to her very core. But I don't know... there's something. No one is either all good or all bad, in my opinion. I'm always suspicious of people who come off as all nice and holy, so why wouldn't I have doubts about someone who appears to be the opposite extreme?"

"Wise woman," the ghost said to Ellie. "I like her."

Ellie briefly glanced downward but made no comment.

Ben seemed to ponder Mary Lou's opinion on the subject for a few moments.

"Aunt Mary Lou?"

"Yessir?"

"I think I may be a totally bad person."

"Oh, no, no, no. You are absolutely not a bad person! You are a very good person and a brave person and such a sweet young man!" she replied emphatically as her eyes swelled with tears, and she slid down the couch to put her arm around her nephew. "It breaks my heart that you would even let a thought like that enter your head! Why on Earth?"

"Well," started Ben, "since the accident, I have only been pretending to not blame my dad. But really, I hate him for doing this to me. I hate him!" Ben's voice raised, and his face colored with crimson.

"He ruined everything! For me, for our family. I've been acting like I am okay, so maybe Mom will give him a break, and they can get back together. And maybe his boss will give him his job back and things can go back to normal.

"But really, I wish he had died in the accident! I wish he was dead and had a big insurance policy, so we had lots of money, and mom didn't have to work on Christmas Eve and Christmas Day."

Tears rappelled single-file down Ben's cheeks.

"There's no crying on Christmas!" said Mary Lou. She was not sure what to say or do. Here was a nine-year old boy who had not cried since the accident almost two years ago now. He had been the most positive of all of them. Here was a kid who would probably never walk again, whose dad was in prison, whose family was torn apart, who had somehow been bearing the weight of blame for something in which he was the victim.

"You know, Benny, you have every right to feel that way," started Mary Lou, not sure if these were the right words. "If I were you, I'd hate him, too. But unlike you, I would not be able to hide that. You are a good person! You are putting the needs of others ahead of your own feelings. And if you were this totally bad person you think you are, you wouldn't care about anyone but yourself.

"I grew up without a dad. Your grandpa died when I was only two..."

Ellie turned to the ghost, "I didn't know that. How did I not know that?"

Mary Lou continued, "... Your dad practically raised me, and he was only a few years older than me.

"He shouldn't have gotten behind the wheel in his condition, especially with you in the car. That was stupid, and I don't even know another word to describe it. I hate him for doing this to you. But I also love him. And maybe someday, you'll get to that point.

"I am sure he wishes he had died in the crash rather than live with knowing that his actions caused you hurt. And that's something he's going to have to live with the rest of his life too," continued Mary Lou. "But you don't have to forgive him. You are your own person, and you're allowed to feel how you feel. It might just help both of you if someday you can.

"And maybe Benny, maybe there's something good that will come out of all of this for you."

Benny looked at his aunt incredulously and directed her attention to his useless legs with his outstretched arms.

"I just think that sometimes even the most horrible things happen for a reason and can lead to something positive that you would have never had a chance for otherwise. So you need to keep an open mind about it and keep looking for it, 'cause if you don't, you may never see your chance."

Mary Lou's speech appeared to lift the boy's hopes a bit, and he picked his fork back up and dove into his eggs with renewed vigor.

"I didn't realize my Mary Lou was such a motivational speaker," said Ellie to the spirit, feigning sarcasm for the ghost's benefit, but also inwardly impressed with her assistant's words and the effect they had had on the boy.

"You should not underestimate the planting of a seed of encouragement in a child," scolded the ghost. "Let's hope it bears fruit."

The doorbell rang, and Mary Lou and Ben looked at each other. Obviously, neither were expecting anyone this Christmas morning.

"Well, Santa was already here," said Mary Lou, "so I don't know who this could be."

"I don't think he'd be ringing the doorbell anyway," Ben pointed out.

Mary Lou opened the door.

"Erin! What are you doing here? I thought you worked until four."

"I do! But I'm on a break, and I wanted to see my boy!" she sang.

Erin pushed past Mary Lou and entered the living room.

"Mom!" cried Ben.

Erin gave Ben a tight hug, and he gave it right back.

"Hmm. I see you're eating in the living room," observed Erin, giving a disapproving look to Mary Lou. "I don't allow that in our house, you know."

"I know," said Mary Lou patiently, "but we figured Christmas morning would be okay just this once."

"Can you stay, Mom?" asked Ben.

"No, sweetie. I have to get back to the store. But I wanted to see you and wish you merry Christmas, and I wanted to see what Santa brought you. I know he left a couple of things for you at our house too."

"Santa did? It's okay, Mom. I know."

"You don't know anything!" interjected Mary Lou and then added, "show your mom what Mr. Claus brought you."

The two women each took Ben under an arm and, with a hand under each leg, carried him to the floor in front of the tree.

Ben showed his mom his rather modest haul of presents with as much enthusiasm and gratitude as if he had received his entire Christmas list and then some. There was the Hess truck, and its accompanying speed boat, and the Iron Man. There were some other Avenger action figures and some books and a couple of bags of candy, including tree-shaped Reese's Cups and Hershey's Kisses in the seasonal, festive red and green foil wrapping.

Erin pulled Mary Lou aside. "I thought you were going to get him an Xbox?"

"No. I said I entered a drawing for an Xbox, and if I won, I would give it to Ben. As you can see, I didn't win. I can't afford an Xbox."

"Well, neither can I! This poor kid. This is a real bummer of a Christmas for him."

"I did the best I could," said Mary Lou, obviously hurt but flashing a reassuring smile over her shoulder to Ben.

"I just wish you had been more clear. I'm not sure what Ben's going to do home alone all day tomorrow," said Erin with more than a little agitation in her voice and manner.

"What do you mean?!"

"I have to work tomorrow!" replied Erin, a little louder than she intended. Then recalibrated the volume of her whisper as Ben looked over at the pair. "And so do you. So I thought if you got him the Xbox, he would be entertained for hours."

"You were just going to park him in front of a video game and go to work?" asked Mary Lou.

"I don't want to! But what choice do I have? It's time and a half! We still have legal bills, hospital bills, and my mortgage is due in a week. I don't have a choice. Can you take the day off?" pleaded Erin.

"Uh. No! I even had to work until after five last night cleaning up after my boss' tantrum. On Christmas Eve! I'm lucky I get the whole day off for Christmas. I don't want to push it!"

"I'll be fine at home on my own for a day," Ben interjected. "I can get around on my own fine." This comment settled the argument for the moment because the sisters-in-law had not realized they were being overheard and because Ben then scooted over to the couch and lifted himself onto the sofa on his own.

Both women broke into applause and heaped praise on Ben.

"I've been practicing," he explained.

Erin looked at her watch anxiously and said, "I've got to get going. I'm going to be late getting back."

She gave Ben a kiss and wished him Merry Christmas again.

"I'll be back a little after four to pick you up!" she reiterated and gave him another hug.

"Why do people have to work on Christmas Day?" asked Ben.

"I don't know," said Erin, "When I was your age, nothing was open on Christmas Day."

"I wish nothing was open for three straight days," replied Ben. "Christmas Eve, Christmas Day, and the next day."

"Oh, my God! That would be great!" exclaimed Erin. "Ask your Aunt Mary Lou to work on that for us…"

Erin was at the door and gave a look at Ben and then at Mary Lou. She ran over and gave Mary Lou a hug and said, "Thank you for everything! Merry Christmas!"

Then she ran back to the door, turned around, and said to Ben, "See you at four, buddy!" and headed back to work.

"A pity that so many families are pulled apart at a time they could be enjoying each other the most," mused the spirit to Ellie.

"What are you suggesting? That businesses shut down for two days because of the Christmas holiday?"

"No," replied the ghost, "I think what Ben suggested was that businesses close for three days for the Christmas holiday."

"Well, that's absurd! That could not happen! It's one thing to pay a day's wages for no work, but quite another to pay three days wages for no work! A business can't afford to do that."

"The boy is only talking about three days so he can enjoy Christmastime with his family, not three months. I hardly think…"

"Do you have an MBA?" Ellie cut in. "I didn't realize! A degree from Wharton, perhaps? Should I be calling you Dr. Ghost of Christmas Present?

"Let people manage their vacation time better!" Ellie demanded.

"There's an idea!" she continued, stabbing at the spirit with her pointed words.

"I'm only echoing Ben's sentiment," said the spirit, aware of Ellie's rising agitation, relegating her verbal darts to stage knives, retracting harmlessly on impact.

"He's a child," dismissed Ellie.

"Huh, you say that like it is a bad thing," returned the spirit.

Ellie's face was now flush. She felt a rare wave of self-reproach for speaking to this fatherly specter in the manner she had.

She pulled in a deep breath and held it. "Puh," was the delayed syllable she released with a lungful of carbon dioxide.

"Shall we go?" she said composedly and, at least for her, sweetly.

The spirit looked at her.

"Please?" Ellie added.

As Ellie and the Ghost of Christmas Present had been having this brief conversation, Mary Lou had retrieved the *Christmas Carol* book and settled in next to Ben on the couch. She removed the bookmark and picked up the story from where they had left off the night before.

They could hear Mary Lou reading about Christmas Day at the Cratchitt house as they turned to leave.

... All this time the chestnuts and the jug went round and round; and by-and-bye they had a song, about a lost child traveling in the snow, from Tiny Tim, who had a plaintive little voice, and sang it very well indeed.

As they approached the door, the spirit halted and reached into his coat pocket, this time appearing to struggle a bit to extricate the torch from it. Ellie had no choice but to listen to Mary Lou's cloying yet commendable rendition.

There was nothing of high mark in this. They were not a handsome family; they were not well dressed; their shoes were far from being water-proof; their clothes were scanty...

Finally, the Ghost of Christmas Present freed the torch. He gave a sheepish, apologetic smile at Ellie, who was not paying attention to him anyway but rather was intently absorbed in Mary Lou's reading.

... But, they were happy, grateful, pleased with one another, and contented with the time...

The spirit lifted the torch and waved it in the direction of Mary Lou and Ben, creating bright gold sparkles of light...

... and when they faded, and looked happier yet in the bright sprinklings of the spirit's torch at parting, Scrooge had his eye upon them, and especially on Tiny Tim, until the last.

... into which the entire scene faded, leaving Ellie and the ghost standing once again on the outside of the humble home in a tired and dull part of town.

The sun was a tick or two higher in the eastern sky and gave all appearances that it intended to illuminate the planet as gloriously as it could for the entirety of its shift.

The spirit placed the torch back in his pocket, effortlessly.

Ellie took a deep breath of cold air into her lungs, held it there for a moment, and released it, warmed, with an emphatic, "Puh!" which escaped her lips along with a wispy gray mist that soon dissipated like the images she had just observed.

"Let's be off," said the ghost. Ellie looked up at the spirit, who had moved out of the shadows and into the light. His hair, which had been jet black, was now streaked with silver. His face, still open and friendly, showed signs of wear; wrinkles had appeared where previously there were none. His eyes. His eyes, as Ellie took a deeper look, were unchanged, still bright and kind. Whereas Ellie had initially pegged him for much younger than herself, she would now estimate that he and she were close in age.

Ellie felt a twang of concern for the spirit. She did not recognize that feeling, but after some consideration, she came to that conclusion. She suppressed the urge to ask him if he was all right.

"Yes. Let's go," was her only reply.

The ghost held out his sleeve, and Ellie took it unhesitatingly. Even before they took a step, the world started moving beneath their feet. It was like standing on a phonograph's arm piece just as the needle is placed on the spinning record.

They were now walking, but the spirit's gait was more measured

and his stride more deliberate, and the world was moving noticeably slower than it had on their way to Mary Lou's house.

Ellie wondered if the reduced velocity had anything to do with
the spirit's aging. She glanced over at her companion. The look on
his face was one she had seen before, but not since she was a little
girl.

One late night — it was shortly after her mom had left them —
when she was supposed to be long asleep, she heard a strange
clicking sound coming from downstairs and could see lights were
on despite the lateness of the hour.

After checking her dad's room and finding his bed empty, she
crept down the stairs to have a look around. There, at the kitchen
table, she saw her careworn father sitting in front of a cluttered pile
of opened mail. He was hunched over his checkbook, and his
fingers were clacking away on an adding machine.

In his other hand was his head. When he lifted it, the expression
of despair on his face, that upon her observing, pierced her frail
heart, was the same countenance she now recognized on the ghost.
As if he had a line of creditors to pay but not the means to meet
their demands. She had not thought of that night until this moment.

As that little girl, she had gone to her dad and put her arm
around him, and he had looked at her and smiled and said, "As long
as we have each other, Princess, everything is going to be just fine."

As the world came to a stop, Ellie's vision was at first distorted
by tears that had welled up in her eyes from the remembrance.
Lowering her head to avoid the bright sunshine and blinking away
the watery haze, her focus came to rest first on her shoes and then
on a familiar piece of sidewalk. She did not know why it was familiar. There was nothing remarkable in it.

As she lifted her head and began to turn around, she was
surprised and somewhat irritated to discover where the journey had
led her. She slowly raised her eyes to the three loosely-set stone
steps rising from the sidewalk, then to a short, cracking, concrete
path spanning a small front yard, leading to a set of wooden stairs to
which was fastened rusty wrought iron railings. At the top of these

steps was a gray-painted, plank porch. Beyond that was the entrance to a dull brick home, the inhabitants of which included a woman Ellie often referred to as Mrs. Fielder-the-Lesser, the Lessor. The very Mrs. Fielder who was in her office earlier that day. The Mrs. Fielder who had, as Ellie now thought about it, started the ball rolling. After all, it had been an uneventful Christmas Eve until she came along.

"I don't know if you know this, though I imagine you do," started Ellie to the ghost, "but I own this property."

"I know. I am aware of that fun fact," replied the spirit, wryly.

"I wish I had known we were coming here," said Ellie while starting up the stone slabs set into the small hill, "I would have brought the eviction letter, saved myself a stamp."

Ellie could not see activity in the house, but she could feel it. She held the image in her mind of rats in a maze. She could just picture Mrs. Fielder and her children and the can't-hold-down-a-job husband, running around in there, smelling for cheese and not finding any, turning around and running off in some other random direction to sniff out a different area, and so on, all day long. Unorganized, unkempt, unproductive.

They got to the front door and stopped. Ellie turned to the ghost expectantly.

"Well, we're not going to knock, are we? Work your magic."

The spirit put out a finger, imploring her to wait a moment. He reached into his pocket for the torch.

"Oh, no!" protested Ellie. "You are not going to bless these people, are you? They are no-accounts. Bless me for not putting them out on the streets on Christmas Eve."

"My, my. We have a way to go with you, don't we?" tsk-tsked the ghost.

His assessment struck Ellie hard. She was aware that her comment was petty and selfish. She was aware that she had disappointed the spirit. She was surprised to realize she had disappointed herself. She was suddenly conscious of the fact that she was trying. On some level, despite strict orders not to cooperate with these spirits, there were parts of her that were conspiring against her.

The ghost waved the torch over the doorway, but though the bright sparkles left their source enthusiastically, they faded quickly upon entering the Fielder's airspace.

The ghost shrugged and returned the torch to his pocket and extended his arm to Ellie.

She reached to take it but pulled back her hand.

The spirit glanced her way, raising an eyebrow.

"I'm… I'm sorry. That was rude to say. Certainly, you can bless anyone you like." It was a bravely timid declaration for such a brazen soul.

The spirit gave her a soft smile and urged her with his eyes to take his arm, which this time she did.

Upon the instant, they were standing in what could have been mistaken for the aftermath of an explosion at a wrapping paper factory. But in fact, it was the living room of Martha and Arthur Fielder.

There was not a soul in sight, but faint sounds in the air gave clues to these "first responders" that suggested there were survivors.

Seeing no one, Ellie and the spirit listened again for any signs of life. There was a high-pitched whine like a grumbling fly, perhaps griping about its life to no one in particular. But flies in Pennsylvania in December are rare, and those that have managed to survive into winter should have no complaints.

There was a distant rumble of cheers and some muffled voices, maybe coming from the basement.

There was also an intermittent, weak, but distinct whistle, fairly rhythmic, like an old tea kettle trying to puff out a stubborn candle.

Ellie and the spirit heard a crackling and popping sound, but as that clue was accompanied by an unmistakable, wafting scent, there was no mystery. Someone was frying bacon in the kitchen.

Investigating the scene quickly and efficiently, Ellie and the spirit discovered the bellyaching fly noise emanating from a pair of AirPods firmly inserted in the ears of a teenage girl stretched out in an oversized chair in the family room down the hall. The volume was set very high, for as Ellie and the ghost got closer, it sounded as if the complaining fly had gotten together with its buddies and formed a garage band, and they were rocking out the neighborhood.

Leaving the family room and following the crowd noise that would lead them to other survivors, the pair descended the basement stairs to find two young boys playing a video basketball game on a large-screen television. The gaming system had been connected just that morning, judging by the Xbox packaging strewn in front of the TV. There was also an NBA 2K-something box on the coffee table in front of the boys.

"I pressed the A button, but it didn't work!" said the one boy.

"No, you didn't. You must have pressed B!" said the other.

"I did not! You gave me a broken controller!" cried the first boy.

"Oh, brother, let's get out of here," said Ellie.

The spirit led her back up the stairs and into the living room, away from the ongoing bickering.

"Okay, we just need to figure out where that whistling is coming from and who's in the kitchen." summarized Ellie. Before the ghost could respond, Martha Fielder answered both questions with one word.

"Artha!" cried Mrs. Fielder, standing in the doorway between the living room and kitchen holding two mugs of coffee.

"Uh, er, uh... I'm right here, Marthur," replied Mr. Fielder, startling Ellie as he sat bolt-up on the couch where he had apparently been napping, concealed by wads and torn sheets of discarded wrapping paper. He had been whistling through his nose on exhales. He was up on his feet and following his wife into the kitchen before you could say Jack Robinson.

"Why are you making breakfast?" he asked after a quick scan of the room. "Where's Claire?"

"Sleeping, I suppose."

A look of anger overtook Mr. Fielder. "I'll go into her room and shake her out of bed!"

"You'll do no such thing," said Mrs. Fielder grabbing her

husband's arm. "I am letting her sleep. She was up late wrapping presents, and I have a busy day planned for her. I don't want her getting cranky and ruining our day.

"Sit down here," she continued, leading her husband toward a chair at the kitchen table. "There's your coffee." She grabbed the pan in which she was frying eggs in bacon grease, turned back to the table, and doled out a generous amount onto his plate next to half a dozen strips of bacon and some cold toast. "And heeeere's your eggs!" she announced dramatically.

Mr. Fielder unfolded a paper napkin and tucked it into the neck of his tee-shirt.

"You know, Artha, about Claire," Martha resumed, now with her back to him as she buttered her Pop-Tarts, which had just sprung up from the toaster, "you probably shouldn't be going into her room, anyway, for any reason."

"What are you saying, Marthur?" He was glaring at his wife in a way she could feel without even turning around.

"You know... a girl like that? She could make up things just to get you in trouble. She's getting to that age when they figure that stuff out," replied Mrs. Fielder with trepidation, hoping to snuff out a fuse she had inadvertently lit.

"All she has to do is tell someone that you look at her in a way that makes her uncomfterble or, God-forbid, that you touch her somewheres, and goodbye monthly stipend and goodbye cook, maid and chief bottle washer! Just sayin' don't put yourself, or us, in that position."

As she set down her plate of eggs and bacon and strawberry toaster pastries and pulled up her chair, Mr. Fielder rose and threw his half-eaten breakfast, plate and all, in the sink. He swung around and put his whole head, sunny side up, in between his wife's face and her impending breakfast.

"This is my house!" he bellowed. [Ellie raised an eyebrow at that point of contention] "I will go into any room I want, whenever I want. And if that little orphan, or whatever, makes up stories about me, I will sue her for slander!"

He stood again, holding his back. It had been an awkward stance he had undertaken to position his face between his wife's gaping, vacant maw and the food intended for its imminent occupancy.

In fact, the whole time he was literally in her face, that was all Mrs. Fielder could think about: "How is a man of his age and girth able to maintain this pose?"

Unfazed, she countered, "You're going to sue a nine-year old girl for slander, genius? You can't sue a nine-year old foster child whose mother is dead and whose father died serving his country. What judge or jury would take you at your word? Look at ya! On a good day, you look like a mug shot. A court ain't gonna take your word against a little girl."

"Aaah!" he said, waving her off, "If you recall, I am the one who was studying to be a lawyer."

"You mean, paralegal. And I do recall. Online courses. That was before you were studying to be an X-ray technician and before you were studying to be a computer programmer, which was before you were studying to be a medical secretary, which was before you just gave up and bought the motorcycle."

Mr. Fielder looked on in some mixture of wonder and disgust as debris from Pop-Tarts and eggs and bacon escorted his wife's recounting of his intellectual pursuits right out of her mouth.

Unbeknownst to the two bickerers, a young girl in a gray flannel nightgown, rubbing the remnants of sleep from her eyes, wandered into the kitchen, and upon seeing the lady of the house engaged in her best wood-chipper impersonation — in that most of the tree was going in and staying down, but sawdust was in the air and on the ground around her — looked on in silent revulsion until Mrs. Fielder had finished her sentence.

She knew better than to interrupt Mrs. Fielder when she was talking or eating, and especially when she was talking and eating, a tandem in which she was a notoriously efficient multi-tasker.

"Claire, my dear!" chirped Mr. Fielder, spying the girl when he had averted his eyes from the human shredder. "Merry Christmas!"

"Why didn't you wake me?" was the girl's only response as she ducked under Mr. Fielder's arm, which was trying to make its way around her shoulder.

"Claire. Oh, good, you're up. I was going to let you sleep for another hour. Busy day ahead," said Mrs. Fielder. She spoke to Claire as if she were a day laborer who had just shown up to find out if there was any work to be had.

"I have something for you," continued Martha, but not before she tossed the last quarter of the buttered Pop-Tart in her mouth.

She picked up her plate and mug and walked them over to the sink, and tossed them in on top of Mr. Fielder's dirty dishes and the frying pan. Then she continued to a drawer from which she pulled a piece of paper and handed it to Claire.

"Here."

Claire took it and gave it a look.

"That's for you, young lady. It's your to-do list for today. My brother and his family are coming to spend Christmas with us. They'll arrive around noon. I want this house spic and span. You can start with the kitchen. The living room and family room need picked up and dusted and vacuumed.

"We will eat at three. We'll use the dining room, but you will need to bring up the card table from the basement. You'll need to set the table. There are nine of us, ten if you want to join us. Or you can eat in here. That's up to you. I splurged for the Chinet, so make sure you use those. The red Solo cups are in the pantry. But we will break out my mom's silver since it's the holiday and all. When their cousins get here, I expect the boys will be in the basement playing the new Xbox, so have a look down there and make sure it is presentable.

"You'll want to start dinner in an hour or so. The menu is right there." She leaned over Claire and pointed to the place on the list to which she was referring. That produced a grease-stained spot in the shape of a chubby finger.

"I don't know how to make all of these things!" protested Claire.

"Figure it out!" interjected Mr. Fielder, whose switch had been flipped since Claire had jilted him at the altar of his attempted grope.

"It's Christmas Day!" yelled Mr. Fielder getting into the little girl's face. "My dear Marthur deserves a day off!" In case there was any confusion as to whom he was referring, he pointed at his wife as he spoke the words.

"She worked all week!" he added vociferously.

His nose was practically touching hers. Claire could feel the heat coming off his cheeks. They were eye to eye. He paused, waiting for her to shrink.

"Well, you didn't," replied Claire, holding every inch of her ground without so much as blinking.

It was Mr. Fielder who flinched and then rocked backward, losing his balance and falling on his posterior.

"Good for her!" said Ellie to the ghost, who replied with an approving nod.

"Artha!" cried Martha. "Are you all right?" She was already helping him up.

Arthur, now on his feet, glared at Claire. "Come with me!" he demanded. "In there!" he said, gesturing toward the wrapping-paper-strewn living room.

"Artha! No!" pleaded Martha without even knowing what was in her husband's mind.

Claire calmly followed him into the living room. He directed her to a small stack of items on a chair near the Christmas tree.

"Hand me one of those," said Mr. Fielder, referring to the pile.

"Which one?" inquired the girl.

"You pick! It don't matter."

"Artha, what are you do…?" began Mrs. Fielder.

"Quiet Marthur!"

Mrs. Fielder rolled her eyes.

The short stack on the chair consisted of a six-pack of Champion athletic socks, a package of Hanes Her Way cotton panties for girls, a pair of Wrangler blue jeans, a bottle of Suave Professionals two-in-one shampoo and conditioner, a bottle of Up & Up

Everyday Moisturizing Body Wash from Target, and theater size boxes of Good & Plenty, Raisinets, and Milk Duds.

Claire grabbed what was on top and tossed it to Mr. Fielder.

"There! You just lost one of your Christmas gifts! I'm keeping this!" he said, glowering.

"Artha!" interjected Martha, walking over and ripping the present out of her husband's hands. "You are not keeping a package of girls' underwear!"

She put them back with Claire's gifts and took the Good & Plenty and threw them to Arthur.

"Here… take the Good & Plenty and go see what the boys are doing. It's too quiet. Make sure they haven't killed each other over a bad call or somethin'."

To Mrs. Fielder's relief, Arthur seemed pleased with the gift exchange, and off he trotted to the basement with his pink and white candy.

Claire turned her attention to Mrs. Fielder. "These are my Christmas presents?" she asked.

"Yes."

"I wouldn't know that because, well, even though I was up past midnight wrapping all of the presents for you and Mr. Fielder, and Kitty, and Gomer and Goober… "

"Their names are Artie and Wade! And I'm grounding from the Andy Griffith Show reruns for that comment. That's the thanks I get for giving you cable access."

"Whatever. I don't care. The tiny TV in my *closet* only gets a few channels."

"Closet! Why you ungrateful, little… we went to the trouble of fixing up Kitty's walk-in closet so you would have your privacy. We can move that cot out into her room if you can't be thankful for what you have."

"You didn't even take her clothes out of it!" argued Claire, then thought better of her tone. "I don't care. Yes! I appreciate my own space. I don't know what I would do without it. Anyway… that's not what I am talking about right now. I am trying to say, I must have wrapped close to a hundred presents for you and your family. But my few presents are just sitting there like you just returned from a Target run?"

"Claire! Really! What kind of person do you think I am? Do you really think I would ask you to wrap your own Christmas presents? That would be very insensitive. And that is not who I am." Mrs. Fielder responded in all seriousness. "Claire — you like going to your school, right?"

"Yeah."

"And you have friends in the neighborhood, yes?"

"Yeah," Claire replied, not quite sure where this was going.

"I don't approve of some of those friends, especially those older ones, but I stay out of it. That's your business. But we let you see them as often as you like, and you appreciate that, right?"

"It gets me out of this house, so yeah."

"So if our arrangement here didn't work out, it'd be a real shame if you had to go to another foster home where they didn't give you the freedom you enjoy here. I hear many are even into home-schooling!"

Claire said nothing. Mrs. Fielder was tapping the girl's fear vein, injecting anxiety laced with despair, which was now coursing through her body.

"If we sent you away, you'd get a reputation of being a problem child, and none of the good foster families would want to deal with that. You know? So you'd probably end up moving from home to home, school to school. It's awful being the new kid in school, isn't it? Or maybe you'd have to go to an orphanage. That's no life for a child."

Claire did not know how those things worked, and Mrs. Fielder knew that, so the poor girl listened with increasing dread.

Mrs. Fielder continued. "Well, I need help around here. My kids aren't gonna do anything. I got no, what we grown-ups call 'lever-age' over them. I can't threaten them. 'Sides, they know I love 'em too much to follow through on anything I might threaten 'em with. So, I got you.

"And here's our arrangement. You do as you're told, and you can come and go from here as you please so long as all your work is done."

Mrs. Fielder paused before going on haltingly. "And, well, uh, I know Mr. Fielder makes you, uh, well, uncomfterble, so, I'll, you know, I'll keep an eye on him for ya."

With that bit of unpleasant business out of the way, she continued in her more aggressive manner.

"But so help me, if you act up or cause any problems for me, I just don't need or want any parts of that, and you will have to be shipped off to a new foster family somewhere else, and then probably another and maybe another before you're done. You might not like it here, but compared to what I've heard about other situations, you've got it pretty good," Mrs. Fielder lied.

She let that last statement sink in with Claire and then continued. "You're old enough now to understand the ways of the world, and I think you're one of the most practical people I've ever met, at your age or any age for that matter. So, hopefully, we will never have to have this conversation again, because if we do, that's strike two, and under my rules, that means 'you're out.'"

Mrs. Fielder made this speech with her hands on Claire's shoulders and looking straight down at her. Claire retained eye contact throughout the monologue. Her face did not betray what was going on behind it.

But when Martha Fielder had finished, Claire began to cry.

She cried for what her life had been. She cried for what she knew her life would be. She cried because there was no escape.

Her mother, dead of an overdose almost two years ago now. A father she never knew, killed in a war somewhere, but her mother had offered no further details. What war?

When Claire was old enough to google her father's name, there were just too many James Smiths to narrow it down, and she wasn't sure if she really wanted to know where the search would end up, or if that was really his name, or if she really cared.

She was not aware of any other relatives, and searches by the authorities came up empty.

Like it or not, the Fielders were the only family she would ever know. And that was the thought that made her cry the hardest.

Ellie could feel Claire's hopelessness and added her own silent tears to the girl's sobs.

"Pull yourself together, child!" demanded Mrs. Fielder. "It's Christmas morning! The holiest morning of the year! What do you think Jesus would say if he saw you crying like this on His birthday? He would not be happy; I'll tell you that!

"I'm going upstairs to get my shower," continued Mrs. Fielder, retreating. "You have your list. I'd start in this room and get all this wrapping paper picked up."

When she reached the steps, she turned to see Claire still standing in the same spot, weeping. "Let's go!! Chop chop!" she commanded, and then ascended the stairs.

Claire threw herself on the couch and buried her head under a pillow to muffle her wails from reaching indifferent ears.

"It is time to go," said the spirit to Ellie, who was lost in the little girl's grief and did not respond.

The spirit took the torch from his pocket and waved it in Claire's direction. Bright, shining, gold sparkles flew from the head of the torch, collecting like a benevolent storm cloud over the girl's heaving body and then rained down softly on her until completely dissipated.

"One more?" asked the spirit of Ellie.

Ellie did not acknowledge the question. She stared off as if in a trance, moved by this demonstration of grief that she herself, as a little girl of a similar age and similar circumstances, could never express.

The spirit waved the torch again, this time in a circular motion over his head as if he was fixing to lasso something with it. Glorious, golden glitter poured out from the lantern in every direction, filling the entire room with tiny, twinkling stars. Neither the spirit nor Ellie could see anything through the whirling, gilded blizzard, and Ellie needed to shield her eyes from the brilliance of the storm.

When the girl finally came back into view, she was up and gathering discarded wrapping paper and placing it in neat piles while softly singing a Christmas tune.

As gold flurries still floated in the air, the ghost led a fixated Ellie away. He had to gently lay hold of her arm a second time before his touch registered. She began to move off with him, and in the bright sprinklings of the spirit's torch at parting, Ellie had her eye upon this scene, and especially on Claire, until the last.

Once outside, Ellie was restored and fuming. "Those people are worse than I could have ever imagined," she said to the spirit, heatedly. She paused and took in a deep breath and held it longer than usual before expelling it with an emphatic "Puh!"

She continued, "I intended to give them the two weeks to pay their back rent, but I think I will send my man here tomorrow and demand payment on the spot. Mrs. Fielder may need to rethink the Chinet."

Then turning to the ghost, Ellie asked, "What is Chinet?"

The spirit dismissed the question and replaced it with one of his own.

"But if you throw them out on the street, what of the girl?" he asked. "You'd be throwing her out too."

"I can't really throw them out tomorrow," explained Ellie, now composed. "Though that would be delicious. I'll just make them feel some of the despair and embarrassment they have driven that child to feel. And to do it on Christmas Day in front of Mrs. Fielder's brother will be even more satisfying."

"You know," said the spirit, visibly perturbed, "there are over a million versions of over a thousand Christmas songs, and I know all of them. And I can tell you, not one of them contains the word 'revenge.' And do you know why?" The agitated Ghost of Christmas Present shook his finger at Ellie and did not give her a space to reply. "Because Christmas is about forgiveness, charity, forbearance! It is not about retaliation!"

"Spirit," replied Ellie, ignoring the scolding, "During this visit and especially since we exited this house, you have aged noticeably. Is that supposed to happen? I don't want to alarm you. I ask out of… Well, I just thought you should know."

"I don't know if it is supposed to happen," said the ghost, collecting himself. "I suppose it's normal. I only have the day in this role. But my decline does seem to be accelerating, and there are still a few places we must go."

"Well, it is understandable. That was exhausting," said Ellie, tilting her head back toward her house, which was, for the time being, occupied by the Fielders.

"I think my decline has more to do with you than with them. I'm not here for the Fielder family," replied the spirit, pointedly. "And frankly, I don't sense we are making the progress we should be making. At least, I do not see it."

Though Ellie had been aware of being a letdown time after time to her mother, she had never disappointed her dad. She could not have, and she would not have, for anything in the world.

Because of the paternal qualities she had assigned to this specter, his reproach had stung and disquieted her, but she was not about to give him the satisfaction of showing it. Her stomach tossed and turned like an insomniac.

Ellie could only wonder if this was what a real father-daughter relationship felt like. If her dad had lived, would there have been confrontations like this? How would they have worked them out? How do any two people resolve hurt feelings between them? That was not something she knew or had ever needed to know.

Ellie's mind quickly set aside the questions as immaterial. She had been stung not only by the spirit's sharp tone but also by his assessment. She had been toying with the thought that there might be some small modifications to her manner she could make that would allow her to continue to have the life she had while rounding some of her sharp edges these spirits had pointed out and be more… tolerable…at least for certain people who could earn and keep her trust.

In any event, she was still thinking of some compromises she might be willing to make to appease the spirit world and give them a win, so to speak, if anyone was keeping score. But based on this spirit's judgment, they were still far apart on any negotiated settlement. So, as far as she was concerned, they were right back at square one.

The spirit had walked ahead. Ellie had not noticed while she was deep in thought. When she became aware that he was not with her, she made no effort to join him. There was an awkwardness now that made her uncomfortable. She had no practice at navigating that feeling.

She thought if she were a teenager and this had been an argument with her dad, she would have probably run to her room and slammed the door. Maybe after an hour or so, her dad would come and knock and ask if he could come in. He'd sit on the edge of the bed and say something like, "Listen, Ellie, I'm sorry I snapped at you, okay? You didn't deserve it. I had a bad day. I'm under a lot of pressure at work, and I, well, like I said, you didn't deserve that. So, whattya say, Princess? Friends?" Then they would go for ice cream. And that is how she imagined they would have gotten past something like what had transpired.

But the spirit was not her dad, nor, as she understood, did she have him wrapped around her finger as she had had her dad. She was not the ghost's, nor anyone else's, little princess.

"Hey, wait up!" she heard herself say as she moved quickly to catch up. "Were you just going to leave me here?"

"Of course not," replied the spirit with no aggravation whatever now present in his voice. "But my time is drawing short. And there is much to show you." And then, extending his arm, he asked, "shall we?"

They smiled at each other.

Ellie took his arm, but this time instead of walking, they were flying, much to her horror. They went straight up at first and looked down upon the Earth as if it were a globe in an elementary school classroom. Ellie observed the ghost making a motion with his hand that gave the illusion (at least she assumed it was an illusion) of causing the Earth to rotate until he saw the location he was looking for and at the hour he was looking for.

"Oh ho, there it is," he said, then without further explanation or warning, the two of them were descending rapidly to the spot as quickly as they had ascended.

On three separate occasions in Ellie's life, she had been required to go to Denver for business. Qualifying any trip by Ellie with "for business" is superfluous. Business was the only reason she traveled. Taxi drivers all over the country who started to ask, "So, are you in town for business or..." never got the word "pleasure" out of their mouths.

"Yes!" Ellie would reply hastily, emphatically, and finally, before hearing the other option.

Each time she flew to Denver, travel time from Philadelphia airport was about four hours. But with Ghost of Christmas Present Airlines, the entire flight was over before you could say, "Please place seat backs and tray tables in their full upright positions." No cocktails. No in-flight movies.

Unfortunately, also no airsick bags. Both the ascent and the descent had made Ellie feel queasy, like being in the back seat of her dad's car when he took hills too fast. Her dad had told her it was her stomach floating to the top of her throat. She had never believed him until now.

This time, instead of arriving outside the destination and having a few moments to gather herself before moving inside, they approached a tall apartment building and glided right through the brick wall and into a small, cluttered, noisy living room.

Ellie was a bit bewildered by the ghost's decision to throw her right into the scene. She reasoned it was due to the location of the residence. What were they going to do, float a hundred feet in the air while the spirit fumbled for his torch? Not likely. Nor were they going to set down in the lobby and take the elevator up.

Regardless of the rationale, the direct entrance was a shock to Ellie's senses. There was loud yelling and a crash as they passed through the wall. At first, Ellie could not see well. The curtains were drawn, and only a lone floor lamp and the lights from the Christmas tree illuminated the room. The apartment smelled like cigarettes and stale coffee.

To her ears and nose, it was as if she had walked in on not only a crime in progress but also the ensuing police investigation and all-night stakeout all rolled into one.

She wanted to leave immediately and instinctively turned to do so. Having released her grip on the spirit's forearm, she face planted into the wall.

"You can't go anywhere without me," said the spirit with a delighted air.

"I forgot," replied Ellie.

"Where are we? Who are these people?" asked Ellie, scanning the room.

The ghost only gestured with the wave of an arm, as if to say, "Watch and see."

Ellie saw and heard two shrieking children; she did not know how old but guessed five or six. They were small, hostile, angry creatures who were losing their minds over a stuffed dog playing the unfortunate role of the rope in their ferocious game of tug-of-war. The boys were taking turns screaming, "It's mine!" at each other.

They had knocked over a ceramic picture frame (the crash Ellie had heard when they first arrived), which now lay shattered on the floor. Though they had paused to survey the damage, neither child relinquished his grip on the dog, and the yelling and yanking resumed with full vigor.

The boys' parents came running into the room and pulled them apart, and rescued the dog just as its seams were about to become early victims of the burgeoning sibling rivalry. The mother was carrying another stuffed dog, identical to the one she and her husband had just saved.

"Boys!" snapped their father, grasping each boy by the arm and shaking them as if he had just pulled them out of the dryer. "You can't behave like this at Grandma's. She has bad nerves, and you're making them worse!

"Look, she got each of you the same dog so you wouldn't fight over them. Jason — your name is on this dog's tag. And Mason..."

"I know, I know. My name is on this one," he said, grabbing the stuffed dog they had been fighting over and then running off into another room. Jason grabbed his from his mom and followed his brother, yelling, "You wanna trade?" on his way out.

"What happened in here?" said a woman, making a late appearance on the scene. She was thin and pale, aged beyond her years. She was using a walker and shuffling her feet as slowly as Tim Conway on *The Carol Burnett Show*, but without any comic effect.

The man rushed over to her and helped her into the easy chair. Next to the recliner was a table upon which sat a landline telephone, the TV listings from the newspaper, an adult "sippy" cup (the kind they give you in hospital), three medicine bottles, the TV remote control, a pair of glasses, a book of word-find puzzles, a pen, a pack of Newport cigarettes with a lighter stuck into the cellophane wrapper around it, and a "World's Best Grandma" coffee mug with dark stains that indicated she took her coffee black and often.

Judging from the table contents, the long sigh of relief upon her reunion with the chair, and the positioning of the television in relation to the La-Z-Boy, this woman's universe over time had shrunk to the six-foot circle inscribed by the light of the floor lamp on the other side of the chair. She lived in this spotlight.

The younger woman was on her hands and knees, cleaning up fragments of the fractured frame.

"Hey, mom? Did you know there is another picture in here behind the photo of the boys?" asked the woman.

"What did she say?" the older woman asked the man.

"There is another picture in the frame. Behind the boys' picture!" the younger woman returned, but this time at a volume approximating a fire station's alarm whistle.

The woman held up the photo for the old lady to see.

"Oh my God!" cried Ellie. "That's me!" she said to the ghost. "That's a picture of me from the second grade."

It only took a moment for her mind to come to a conclusion. "Oh my... is this... is that my mother?" she asked the ghost while moving closer to examine the old woman.

The ghost only held up his hand, signaling for her to wait and listen.

The old woman put on her glasses and took the picture from her daughter-in-law.

"Oh, this. It was in that frame when I got it." she wheezed.

Ellie stopped her advance.

"When I bought the bedroom furniture from an estate sale last year, the movers shrink-wrapped that pixture frame up with the nightstand," the woman explained.

Ellie froze. The pendulum of emotions had swung so swiftly and violently, it had knocked the wind out of her.

"That's what happened. And there was something about that sad little girl's face. So I kept it in there and just put the kids' photo in front of it."

"I'll throw it out with the frame," said the daughter-in-law, taking it from the old woman.

"You know, just give it here with the kids' photo. I'll deal with it. Such heartsickness in that little face. Can't bear to part with it. Don't you see it?"

The daughter-in-law re-examined the photo and shrugged. "I guess. Maybe."

"My mother is dead?" Ellie asked the ghost, not bothering to turn around to face him. "My mother is dead. Now I really am all alone in the world," she said to herself.

"Had you planned on reaching out to her?"

"No, I just thought..." Ellie trailed off.

"Our time together is almost done. We must go now," the spirit said abruptly.

Ellie gathered herself and said, "Of course. It feels like it is getting late."

The spirit quickly took out his torch and blessed the family and then just as quickly returned it to his jacket pocket. There was not the heart in this effort that had been present on their previous stops. Ellie took his arm, and they again were up high over the planet. The ghost set his new destination, which, Ellie could tell by the positioning of the phantom's forefinger, looked to be somewhere in western Pennsylvania, which would place them near her hometown.

Ellie had a notion from the onset that the place she suspected lay ahead would be one of the stops this evening. And now, as she recognized Pittsburgh's cityscape below, thanks to the unmistakable visual of the confluence of the Allegheny, Monongahela, and Ohio rivers, and as they sped northward, Ellie's conjecture had all but been confirmed. They were going to pay a visit to Patty Poole.

Ellie lived a life in which she had perfected the ability to sift all emotion out of her being, to suppress any feelings that might try to make their way out of her craw. She set up defenses, so she would never need to deal with sentiment or affection, and she forbade them from speaking to her or making eye contact.

On this day, because of that "Bernice woman," those passions had broken down her door and demanded to be heard. But they were talking in a language Ellie had never learned. Their words were unrecognizable and uninterpretable. Though it was all gibberish to her, she was at least making some effort to comprehend for the first time.

One sensation that did manage to get past Ellie's security detail was trepidation. There was a palpability of dread associated with the prospect of seeing the only person, aside from her father, with whom she had made any real emotional connection.

It had been almost forty-five years since they had seen each other. "It's been, what, forty years since I stopped writing or taking her calls," guessed Ellie. It had only been two years though since Ellie received her last letter from Patty Poole Daniels.

When Mary Lou delivered the letter with the rest of Ellie's mail, she had placed it first on the stack. It was Mary Lou's job to prioritize the incoming correspondence.

"Why is this on top?" Ellie had asked, grabbing up what looked to be a personal letter, hand-written in Catholic school cursive.

"It appears to be a note from a friend," Mary Lou had replied. "And my mother always said 'What's unique is precious,' so…"

"What nonsense." Ellie had interjected, adding, "and you can tell your mother I said so. In fact, I can give her several examples that contradict that statement."

"My mother and I don't speak, unfortunately," replied Mary Lou with apparent regret in her voice and a pained expression on her face. "You see,…"

"Well, if those are the kinds of things she said when you did converse, I think you are much better off for the estrangement," Ellie had replied while reaching for the letter.

Mary Lou had stood for a moment, dumbfounded.

"You can go," Ellie told her without looking up.

When Mary Lou had closed the door, Ellie turned the envelope around in her hand. The return address on the upper left side of the front read: Patty Daniels, 131 Garden Court Road, Sharpsville, Pennsylvania.

"Guess she never left her hometown," Ellie had thought.

Ellie had removed the letter and perused it without reading. She turned it over and saw it was signed, "Miss you and love you, Patty."

She turned it back over and read the note. She learned that Patty was very sad that they had not maintained their friendship over the years, after having formed what was a "special bond" in their youths. She learned that Patty and Will Daniels would be cele-brating their twenty-fifth wedding anniversary later that year, that Patty had sent her an invitation to their wedding and it had come back marked "return to sender" (of course, Ellie knew that because she was the one who had scrawled the words, two and a half decades earlier), that she and Will had four children, that she thought of Ellie often, and hoped they could catch up and maybe even see each other soon.

Then the note went on to say that her son, Theodore, was looking for an internship that summer and would be staying with friends in the Philadelphia area, and she had thought, why not reach out and see if her "sister from another mister" would have any openings and if she could have Theodore give her a call.

"There it is," Ellie had said out loud, then finished the rest of the thought in her head: "Everybody wants something from me. If Theodore was not in need of a position, would I be receiving a letter? Of course not. She's just like everyone else."

She had tucked the note back into its envelope and placed it in one of the three wire bins on her desk — the one marked "To Shred."

Ellie and the Ghost of Christmas Present touched down in a snowy upper middle class neighborhood of large look-alike residences and postage-stamp yards. When the homes were built, everyone, except those who lived in them, likely referred to the houses as McMansions.

A black, ornate, wrought iron sign hanging from the lamppost next to which Ellie and the ghost were standing read "The Daniels" in white lettering, and beneath that hung a matching cut-out of a Scottie dog. According to that shingle, the family dog's name was Max.

The early winter sun had already set on this Christmas Day and, judging from the number of cars in the driveway, the family's Christmas night tradition, which had begun long before Ellie's experience with it at the DeCiminero homestead, had carried on at this new venue.

Though the Daniels' lived in what was clearly a wealthy neighborhood, it lacked the charm of the street on which Ellie remembered attending — though she didn't know it at the time — her one and only Christmas party with the Poole's. Here, on this street, there was an anonymous uniformity to every property.

It would be easy to imagine how an upstanding resident of this neighborhood returning home after a night out with the boys, and having trouble getting his key into the front door lock, might discover, at the peak of his frustration, that he was trying to enter the wrong house. It would not require much of a stretch of that imagination to see the same man sleeping in his car for the night after having tried several unsatisfactory fits for his house key.

One might think that the holidays would afford neighbors here the opportunity to differentiate their houses from others on the block through creative lighting and decorating. That was not the case. Every home utilized non-blinking clear LED lights, cut greens, and wide, red ribbons and bows—every home except one.

Patty's house was tastefully adorned, but it stood out compared to the other homes up and down the street. For one, she had strung multi-color lights, similar to the ones Ellie's father had used on her childhood home. And, as Ellie remembered, the same as Patty's dad had used to decorate the Poole house.

There was no plastic reindeer or snowmen, but there was a ten feet tall inflated Santa, illuminated from within, with one raised arm topped with a green mitten. The lamppost was wrapped in green garland, but again, Patty had eschewed the clear LED lights for the old-fashioned multi-color bulbs.

"Have your eyes had their fill?" asked the ghost. Ellie was unaware that she had been surveying her surroundings so carefully.

"Quite. Quite." She said, breaking from her reverie.

During this brief exchange, a dark blue SUV pulled into the long, curved driveway. Ellie and the ghost turned to observe a well-heeled woman, slightly older than Ellie, with her husband, and two who appeared to be their young adult daughters hurrying up the shoveled and salted path of the macadam. The woman was carrying a reusable grocery bag filled with wrapped gifts.

Her husband was clutching two bottles of wine close to his chest, in such a manner that if his feet were to slip out from under him, he would be able to manage his fall so that, no matter how he landed, though a vertebra or his coccyx might fracture, the wine would not be a casualty of the mishap.

Had he ever carried his daughters that deliberately, the woman wondered?

"You promise she's not going to collect cell phones at the door this year?" confirmed one daughter.

"I told her we would not come if she did that again this year," assured the mother, who Ellie now recognized as Paula Poole, Patty's older sister.

"Well, if she does, I'm out of here!" said the other daughter.

"Me too!" said Paula's husband. "I'm on call, anyway..."

"Snagged herself a doctor," remarked Ellie out loud.

"Don't worry about it! She's not collecting the cell phones this year," repeated Paula, emphatically. "And Sid, when's the last time there was an accounting emergency on Christmas night?"

"Or not," Ellie amended.

Ellie had a very distinct memory, which only resurfaced earlier that evening, of the raucous, boisterous explosion of sound that coincided with the opening of the front door to the DeCiminero's house that Christmas night of her childhood. Despite the number of cars in the driveway and on the street in front of the house, the opening of the front door to the Daniels' made no audible disturbance to what was a silent night in the neighborhood.

"Time to go in," said the ghost. He raised his torch, blessed the house and all inside, returned the lamp to his coat pocket, and gave Ellie his arm, who took it immediately. Their time was nearly done, she knew.

They entered a large foyer with hardwood floors and a chandelier hanging from a cathedral ceiling overhead. There were rooms to the left and to the right. The kitchen was straight ahead down a hallway, next to stairs that rose to the second floor and presumably a third, given the home's size.

The room to the right was a small den. There were four teenage kids in that room. One was sitting in the desk chair and spinning while playing on his phone. The other three were sitting quietly on a luxurious reclining leather couch. All of them had extended the footrests so they could be more comfortable while on their phones as well. The television was turned on, but no one was paying any attention to it.

The room on the other side of the hall was a formal living room. As Ellie and the ghost peeked in, Ellie spotted Mrs. Poole, Pea as she was known to her friends and family. She was low and 'lorn, sitting by herself in one of two easy chairs placed in front of the fireplace.

There was no sign of Mr. Poole, and from Mrs. Poole's constant dabbing of her eyes, Ellie deduced that Pea's husband had, more than likely within the recent past, exercised the out clause in his marriage vows, and upon his death, they did part.

Mrs. Poole had either wandered away from the others to self-quarantine with her grief, or she had been placed here, out of the way, so as not to be a Mrs. Grummidge to the other Christmas revelers. In any event, she was all alone with her thoughts, memories, and grief in this large room.

Under most circumstances, Ellie would have paused to admire the Christmas tree placed in the far corner of the room, but an urgency, like an undertow, seemed to be pulling her along.

The only sign that a holiday party was taking place were voices coming from down the hall in the kitchen area. Ellie and the ghost made their way to the sound.

They emerged from the hallway into a cavernous area that was a kitchen yes, but one that was open to a dining room to the left and to a large family room to the right. There were folding room dividers on tracks like one might see in gymnasiums or banquet halls. They could turn the great room into three separate spaces if desired, but they were concealed on this night.

The family room's overwhelming feature was a television, the size of which Ellie had never seen before. The audaciousness evoked a "Puh!" when she first eyed it.

There were fifteen or twenty children of a wide range of ages there, but instead of running through the house in high spirits, or playing school with a wadded-up piece of paper, or chatting in cliques, they sat, eyes on the jumbotron, mouths agape, as animated, colorful, mustachioed characters raced their cars around a track. Ellie observed that four of the brood had controllers in their hands that were operating the race cars.

"That must be a video game," she said out loud, never having seen one in action.

The rest of the kids were watching, shouting instructions or encouragement, or groaning when one of the animated creatures hit a banana peel or a turtle shell and spun out of control or was blown sky high.

On the right side of the kitchen, closest to the family room, was a vast oak farm table, around which all the adults stood or sat or leaned. Ellie scanned the faces searching for the Poole siblings. There was Paula, cheeks still ruddy from having just come in from the cold. The twins, Peter and Penny, still looking nothing alike. Preston had only been three years old when last Ellie saw him. But here was a fellow that seemed to have the same large, round eyes she remembered. "That's got to be Preston," thought Ellie.

Ellie wondered where the other one was, the one she had never met, the SIXTH child, the overkill of Mr. and Mrs. Poole's passion, or the miscalculation in the rhythm method. What was his name? Paxton? Pluto? Peabody?

The rest of the people around the table she did not recognize. There were some cousins and aunts or uncles, but she had no interest in trying to figure out who was who or match up the significant others with their corresponding Poole.

Ellie had accounted for everyone in her once and short-lived family, except for Patty.

"Who wants some cookies?" came a cheerful cry from the darkened dining room area. Lights came on over another long table covered, end to end, with dozens of varieties of cookies just like at the DeCiminero's house all those years ago.

Immediately upon hearing Patty's voice, something stirred in Ellie. It was the imprisoned child who, recognizing her old friend, raced to her cell bars with renewed energy and hope.

To most people, a brief friendship from long ago may have been long forgotten with the passage of so much time. But Ellie had made no other connections throughout her life, so being in the presence of this childhood companion moved Ellie in a way that she had not expected, but at the same time feared.

At that moment, Ellie realized that this middle-aged woman

with the at-home dye job and "Happy Birthday Jesus" ugly Christmas sweater was the only living tether to her childhood and to life on the outside of the walls she had erected.

"Oh my God, Pat!" said Penny. "Did you bake all of those?"

"I did."

"I thought we were just going to all chip in and buy cookies this year," said Paula.

"Well," replied Patty, "I just couldn't. I… I just couldn't. It's such a part of our Christmas tradition. I was off from work. I had the time. So,… enjoy!"

"You also made grandma's sauce. I smelled it the minute I walked in the door," added Paula.

"We get jarred sauce and frozen meatballs at home," chipped in Sid, the indispensable accountant.

Paula shot him a look, which prompted him to check his phone for any urgent message from work. There not being any, he nonetheless said, "I've got to take this," and walked into the family room.

"When would I have had the time, Sid?" Paula yelled to her retreating husband.

Then she explained to everyone else, "I worked until noon yesterday and then wrapped presents and made dinner for his family. That ungrateful apple didn't fall far from the ungrateful apple orchard, let me tell you."

Ellie's focus remained on her old friend. In ways Ellie could not comprehend, Patty was more a ghost to her than the phantom who had brought her there. And why not? Ellie had all but buried her. But here she was… alive again! Recognizable. Yes, more wrinkles. A little heavier. Bad dye job. Horrendous fashion choices. But Ellie could see that same nine-year old companion shining through that middle-aged-woman exterior. That was still Patty.

Patty gave the nod to her husband. That was his cue to head over to the bar area.

"Okay, everyone!" yelled Patty over the din of voices and video game music and sound effects. It's time for the annual toast! Wine's on the table, but if you want anything stronger, Will is standing by!"

Will Daniels raised his ice tongs like lobster claws to let everyone know he was ready, willing, and able.

And then to her brother Peter, she said, "Can you go see if Mom wants to join us for this? And can you tell the kids in the den that it's time?"

He dutifully obliged.

Some of the youngsters in the family room lined up at the bar. Uncle Will fixed them a mixed drink of Sprite and grenadine with maraschino cherry garnish. It looked very fancy. After one or two dramatic sips, these kids started acting tipsy, much to the amusement and delight of the entire family.

Peter escorted his mother to the kitchen table. All stood, filling the room, drinks in hand. The video game was paused. A fork clinked against a glass, and the celebrants quieted.

Patty started by toasting her mother. "To mom, Aunt Pea, Pea-ma. Thanks for your love and for showing us all how to persevere during the saddest of times. We love you, mom!"

There were a few shouts of "Love you, Mom," and "Love you, Aunt Pea," and "Yay, Pea-ma!" and everyone took a small drink from their glasses. A little girl in a party dress toddled over to "Pea-ma" and gave her a tight hug that Mrs. Poole returned with as much vigor as she could muster.

Tears welled up in Patty's eyes, and her upper lip stiffened as she prepared to deliver her next toast. She was holding a piece of paper but tucked it back in her pocket. Perhaps she had been planning a long speech, but what came next was poignant in its brevity.

"Here's to you, Dad," she said, lifting her glass. "We miss you! Thank you for everything."

Everyone took a subdued and solemn sip in honor of the fallen family patriarch.

No one made a sound, but in this moment, the grief was audible and heavy and laid on the room like a dentist's lead blanket.

"Okay, okay," said Patty, waving away the sadness like she was trying to dispel the smoke from cookies left too long in the oven.

"Now, for a tradition I started back when I was only ten. Everyone have their glasses? Raise 'em!"

She raised hers.

"To Ellie!" she shouted.

Ellie was startled to hear her own name and looked around to see if there was another Ellie in the room to whom Patty was saluting.

"*Cin cin*, Ellie!" yelled the family in unison, and then they took a drink.

"*Cin cin a tutti!*" Patty toasted back loudly.

"*Salud!*" came the raucous response, after which all congregants tossed their heads back, pointed the bottoms of their glasses to the sky, and let gravity do its thing.

Over the years this tradition, to most, became more about getting a quick buzz than honoring the poor orphan girl who lived with the family for just a short time decades ago. To Patty, it was a sincere and emotional gesture. And for that fact, so it was for her siblings, none of whom ever thought of Ellie other than during this annual toast.

"Well, Patty," said Paula, "now that you have perpetuated your annual tradition, I'll continue mine and ask, 'What do you hear from Ellie?'"

Patty just smiled. She knew what was coming next, but she had hoped that her subtle, demure expression would suffice.

"Oh, no." followed up Paula, not perceiving Patty's weariness of the subject. "This is where you always say, 'I haven't heard from her, but this is going to be the year.'" Mom and Dad should have named you Pollyanna."

"And this is where you say," replied Patty, in her best Paula impersonation, "'What is it about Ellie? You only knew her for a few months.' And then I say, 'I know, but we formed a special bond.'"

"Right! There you go," said Paula sarcastically. "Now, you remember your lines. But seriously, after all these years, give us all a straight answer. What is this connection you have with Ellie despite her blowing you off for forty years?"

Patty relented. "Really? You want to know?" she said. "Okay, I'll tell you."

Though the kids had raced back to their video game immediately after the toast, the adults, who had been engaged in side conversations, all became silent so they could hear Patty's explanation.

"She was the sister I never had."

The room erupted in laughter, even some applause. Paula smiled and rolled her eyes while Penny feigned protest but also cracked up.

Then, perhaps because on this day, of all days of the year, the pain of loss is felt most keenly, or maybe because of the burden of the diagnosis she'd received the past week but was carrying all by herself for now, through eyes still moist from the toast to her recently deceased dad, Patty explained, "Honestly, I love her like a sister. I thought she was going to be our sister forever. I think she thought that too. And then we, like, rejected her. And I can't imagine how awful that felt, especially after... you know... what happened to her dad."

Patty moved quickly to the dining room because whatever muscles she had been using to keep the tears from flowing had fatigued beyond their limits, and she was about to ugly cry and did not want to subject her family to that. She could not remember a family Christmas party where any tears had ever been shed. That was unthinkable. Depending on the severity of her diagnosis, this was not how she wanted to be remembered at future get-togethers.

Her sisters quickly pursued her to comfort her.

"I'm fine. I'm fine. You know how I get when I drink," Patty deflected.

"You've done your part to try to keep in contact with her, Pat," said Penny. "You have nothing to feel bad about. She's the one who rejected you... us. Not the other way around."

"She was hurt and alone," protested Patty. "And I just have this feeling that she still is. And maybe I'm the only one who can help."

"Clearly, she doesn't want your help," said Paula sternly. "So, I don't think you should be beating yourself up over this. You've put yourself out there, and that's that."

"I know. I know," replied Patty, mindlessly rearranging cookies on the table.

"I have an idea!" offered Paula. "Why don't you send a Christmas present? Yeah. Surprise her... with a puppy!"

Paula burst out in loud guffaws while Patty and Penny looked on in stunned disbelief.

"Am I the only one who thinks that's funny?" asked Paula.

"Yes," Penny and Patty replied in unison and hastily walked back to the party, leaving their sister in the dining room to consort with the snickerdoodles and the gingerbread men.

Ellie had stood silent as the entire scene played out before her. Her face remained stony and stoic, but her impassiveness was betrayed more than a few times by tears of her own. They rolled only a little way down her cheeks before being quickly swatted away by diligent fingers that were as quick and nimble as the ball retrievers at tennis matches.

Ellie's complete attention had been on Patty and on the genuine emotion expressed in her words and on her bearing. She was reminded of what had drawn her to Patty from the start — she was so real and honest and open. And that was so contrary to herself in those days after her dad's death, and ever since.

So mesmerized was Ellie by Patty's articulate and impassioned expression of genuine warmth and devotion, she had lost all awareness of why she was there, how she was there, and who she was with. She took a few halting steps toward Patty before the ghost placed his hand on her forearm.

The touch brought her immediately back.

"Are we done here?" she asked him vacantly.

"We are," came a weak and hoarse reply.

Ellie turned to look at the ghost and was inwardly horrified to see that he had deteriorated precipitously in the short time they had been at Patty's.

"You will take me home now?" Ellie asked, "Can I just go home?"

"Not quite yet. Soon."

"I want to go home!" Ellie demanded, her agitation making itself evident.

"Listen, you're angry with yourself, not with me," observed the spirit.

"Puh!" replied Ellie indignantly. "Mad at myself?! What do I have to be mad at myself for?!"

"You now know Patty made the effort in earnest, and you know you have missed out on a life-long friend..."

"She has a real family! She... she didn't need. . . It was all out of pity, I mean..." Ellie looked back over her shoulder at Patty sitting at the table with the others, laughing and sipping on her red wine. "... I mean, I thought it was... Now, I don't know. I don't know!"

"Because she wasn't miserable like you, she didn't care like you did? Her letters were happy and cheerful and hopeful, so you did not trust her when she said she missed you and wanted to continue your close friendship?"

Ellie was at a loss. Yes. The spirit was right. Though Patty had continued to keep in touch, her notes were about her friends and family, where they were going, what they were doing, how much fun *this* was, and how interesting *that* was. Of course, they included the obligatory 'you would have loved it' or 'wish you were with us' and always signed 'miss you and love you,' but that was just how Patty was. She probably sent notes like that to all of her girlfriends. There was nothing special about that. It didn't make Ellie special to anyone on the planet. And ever since her father died, that was really all she wanted... to be special to someone.

The ghost, recognizing that Ellie had finished her thought, brought her back with the simple word, "Child."

As softly as it was said, Ellie was still startled. She was not given to letting her mind wander and much less to following it on its rare diversions.

"There's still time to reconnect with your dear friend." said the spirit.

"I don't know. I'm not sure if I can or even know how. I will need to give that some consideration. Though, it might just be best after all these years to... "

"She's sick," interrupted the ghost.

For a brief moment, everything vanished. Ellie was nowhere. The world went dark. When she felt her legs starting to give way, she had already regained enough presence of mind to reach for the spirit, who grabbed her around the waist to steady her.

Ellie stepped back and straightened her sweater and her spine. She wanted to turn and leave the room, the house, the town, the night, the world. She took a hesitant look at her old friend.

"Is she dying?" Ellie asked the spirit.

The ghost was now also watching Patty. There she was, laughing with her sisters, pouring herself some more wine, stealing a meatball from her husband's full plate, just before being dragged to the middle of the kitchen by a couple of small kids who were pleading with her to show them how to dance the tarantella.

"I'd say it looks like she's living, Ellie. Whereas you've been dying practically your whole life.

"It's time to go."

The Ghost of Christmas Present was, at this time, much altered in his physical appearance. He was short and frail. His hair was thin and white. His shoulder blades protruded beneath a blazer that was two sizes too large. Ellie noticed, he must have been tightening his belt around his waist because his pants were bunched up at the waist, and there seemed enough belt to loop around a second time.

The spirit took out the torch and waved it, this time requiring both arms to lift it, and offered his blessings for good health and happiness.

Now, they were off. High up into a navy-blue sky and heading home, as far as Ellie could tell.

She was almost correct. When her feet again touched the ground, she and the ghost were about three blocks from her house. They were at Chestnut Hill Hospital.

Ellie wondered if the spirit's navigational faculties were perhaps similarly diminished by the aging process as his outward appearance had been evidenced.

They were in the waiting room of the ER, which was practically empty as one might expect, as it was approaching midnight on Christmas night.

"Is this where you intended us to be?" Ellie asked in a concerned tone.

"Huh? What's that you say?" replied the spirit. Then he looked around and said, "That's odd. This doesn't look to be your living room. Where's the fireplace? Hmmm. I must be losing it."

Ellie wasn't sure if he was being sarcastic or if he was truly confused.

She glared at the ghost with a feeling close to sympathy but even closer to agitation. It was late. She was tired.

"Mom! We came as soon as we got the message!"

Ellie turned to observe a man and woman rushing toward an elderly woman who had fallen asleep with a magazine in her hands.

Ellie recognized the couple.

"Oh my, it's Bucky Jr. and Ugly Hat." Ellie was proud of herself for remembering the nicknames she had instantly labeled these two with earlier in the evening at McNally's.

Though Ellie could only see the back of the old woman's head, she knew it was Bucky Jr.'s mom, the very mom who, along with her husband, had been demoted from Christmas Day to Christmas Eve dinner.

"How is he? Did they tell you anything? My God, how long have you been here? How many times do I have to tell you, don't call our landline? Thank God I noticed the answering machine blinking before I turned in for the night. Do they know what happened?"

"Probably a heart attack," the tired and sad old woman said.

"Oh my God!" cried Bucky, Jr.

"Can I get you anything, Mom?" asked Ugly Hat, sweetly. Ugly Hat was not wearing a hat, and Ellie pondered whether she needed to develop a new moniker but decided against it.

The old woman just shook her head, "No."

"This is my fault," said Bucky Jr. "It's all my fault!" Then he pointed to Ugly Hat and said, "I should not have listened to you! There is plenty of room in our house for two more people! What was I thinking listening to you?!"

"Ralph! I would think very long and hard before you say another word to me on this subject! Very long and hard, indeed! I am going to find some coffee! I expect your attitude to have improved when I get back." With those words, Ugly Hat was off in search of caffeine.

"Mom, what happened?"

"We were having supper, and Dad said he wasn't feeling well and was going to lie down for a while. I went upstairs to check on him a couple of hours later, and he was very pale and very weak and having trouble getting a deep breath, so I called 911. The ambulance came. There's really not more to tell. I called you before we left the house and I've been here since. I'll need a ride home when this is all over."

"Of course. When's the last time you had an update on Dad's condition? Oh, this is all my fault! Why does this have to happen? Why did you wait two hours to check on him? Does he usually nap that long after dinner? That seems odd. Oh, why did I listen to Evelyn?!"

"Would you just shut up!" bawled the old woman. "For Christ's sake, Ralph!

"You think I'm going to let you off the hook? Well, I'm not! It probably is your fault. You broke that man's heart. Though even if he does survive this, he'll never admit that. He worships you. He's lived his life for you. You used to be his best friend. Remember?

"You live ten minutes away, and you only visit every couple of weeks, if that. Every time a car goes by, he looks out to see if maybe it's you popping in to say hello and sit and chat.

"We know you have your own life. We raised you to have your own life. But I know, even though he has never said a word about it — he doesn't have to — he misses that young Ralphie who used to laugh at all of his corny jokes and play H-O-R-S-E with him in the driveway and, well, just everything. He doesn't deserve to die

166

with a broken heart, after all he has done for you — and with you."

Ralph's mom was crying now. He pulled out a tissue from his coat pocket, but she waved him off and pointed to her purse. When he handed it to her, she took out her own pack of tissues, dried her eyes, and blew her nose. Sufficiently recovered, she continued.

"And you know how special Christmas is to him and how he always made sure to make Christmas special for you. My God, the Christmases! Lately, his whole Christmas was about being able to be with you and your family. He would put on a shirt and tie like he used to when he worked. It was the only day all year he put on a shirt and tie.

"Oh, Ralph, you took Christmas from him, and it was too much."

"Mom... I'm..."

"What's going on here?" asked Ugly Hat as she returned with vending machine coffee and a packet of Twinkies. Then observing that they were both crying, she said, "Oh my God, did Dad pass?"

"Pass what?" said the old woman, agitated. "A tractor-trailer? Yes. He passed a tractor-trailer on the highway to heaven, Evelyn!"

Bucky Jr. shook his head "No" to his wife, who harrumphed, but held her tongue, and took a seat.

Ellie was uncertain what any of this had to do with her and was pondering that subject when she heard a familiar voice coming from the far side of the room. She recognized it as that of David Burke, her vanquished business rival, now hapless, part-time barkeep at McNally's.

"Please, help! It's my son. He cut himself. Please, hurry."

"All right, all right. That doesn't look too bad," said the check-in person at the desk.

"Well, it did about twenty minutes ago," replied David.

"Am I going to lose my finger?" asked the boy. My sister said you'd probably have to cut it all the way off."

"I told you, Jason, she was just playing with you," David said in a we-went-over-all-this-on-the-way-here tone.

"If it's not completely off now, I don't see why they would take it off, and even if it was, they'd just sew it back on," the woman reassured the boy.

Then she turned to David, "May I see the insurance card, hon?"

David squinted to look at the check-in person's name badge. "Uh. Listen, Shelly. I don't have that. He's on his mother's plan. I don't currently have insurance, I'm afraid."

"First of all, it's Sherry, and second..."

"I'm very sorry. I need new contacts, but like I said, I don't have insurance, so excuse me.

"My wife is on her way with his insurance card. I was just hoping that, in the meantime, you would get him seen and we can get out of here... preferably before she even gets here."

"We are going to take good care of him no matter what," said Sherry. "Don't you worry about that, young man," she assured Jason. Then shifting her eyes back to David, she said, "I'll need his name and date of b..."

"Oh, my God! Oh, my God! Jason! Are you all right, honey?" Making a shrill and dramatic entrance was David's bleary-eyed, high-heeled, soon-to-be-ex-wife with a friend of hers who would later be awkwardly introduced around as Jack.

In nature, there exist certain displeasing assaults to the human senses. The porcupine's quill to the touch. The skunk's spray to the nose. The sun's brilliant glare to the eyes. The brussels sprout's bitterness to the taste. Perhaps the most offensive of all naturally occurring attacks on the human faculties is Lara Burke's voice to the ears.

Lara had often been described as a "loud talker." Here, in the empty and cavernous waiting room of the ER, her words came out of her mouth like Bouncy Balls released from a cargo net above — bounding and springing and leaping and hopping, ricocheting off walls and floors and ceilings and chairs and desks and each other, then coming to rest on agitated ears.

"Hello, Lara. Who's your driver?" inquired David.

"David. This is my friend, Dr. Jack Spence." Her emphasis was on "doctor." "Jack... this is... David. And this is my son, Jason!"

"Pleased to make your acquaintances," said Jack, unbuttoning his coat, revealing a tee-shirt that read: "'Tis a Ren Faire thing, thou wouldst ne'er understand."

David managed half a nod. Jason just stared.

"Okay, insurance card?" Sherry had been eating up the situation, but her shift was nearly over, and she wanted to keep things moving.

Lara handed over the card, and Sherry took information from her as the men made small talk.

"So, what kind of doctor are you?"

"My Ph.D. is in stratigraphy and sedimentation. But I'm really stoked about mineralogy. I like to say that stratigraphy is my first wife, and mineralogy will be my trophy bride."

"Why?" asked Jason flatly.

"Let's go, Jason," said Sherry. "I'll take you back to the exam room. Would you like one of your parents to come with you?"

"Want me to come with you, buddy?" offered David.

"Nah. I got this."

"So brave!" yelled Lara. "You've got this!" she continued, starting to follow him down the hall. "You're going to beat this!"

"Far enough," said an aggravated Sherry, turning the boy's mom back toward the waiting area.

"Jack, why don't you go to the vending area and get a Coke or something?" prodded Lara.

"Uh. Duh. You know I can't have caffeine this late."

She glowered at him.

"Maybe they'll have 7-UP. Where is it?" he asked while walking a few steps in every possible direction.

"I'll show you, dear. Was headed back there, myself," said Ugly Hat, who had wandered over for closer reconnoitering when she heard the drama unfolding.

"So, you're the boyfriend?" asked Ugly Hat as the two of them departed for the vending area.

When they were out of sight, Lara started in on David.

"First of all, why are the kids up so late? They have a bedtime!"

"It's Christmas night. I told you on the phone. We were up playing games and having snacks. You know, having fun," replied David.

"I think you were purposely keeping them up so they would be tired and cranky when I have them tomorrow."

"Nonsense! That never crossed my mind. You only think that because that's something you would do. I'm not like that!"

"You're right. You know, I take it back. You're not like that. But maybe if you were a little more like that, you would not have lost your company. That lady was right about you. What did she say to you that day? 'You're too good. You're too trusting. And it may be noble to be that way, but it's bad business.' Right? Something like that?"

"And why was an eleven-year old boy slicing his own pepperoni, unsupervised?"

"He said you let him do it all the time when he's with you."

"First of all, I would never let him or Sara eat that, that disgusting stuff. You know that! Do you know what's in pepperoni?

"Second, you also know I would never let him use anything sharper than a butter knife. But, here again, he said something, and you just believed him. You believed an eleven-year old boy because he said so. If he told you I let him clean my pistols, you'd probably believe that too. You don't lie, so no one else lies. That kind of thinking cost you your livelihood, and it ruined everything. You ruined everything! Wake up, David!"

Lara's voice had risen again, and her dressing down of David had captivated the attention of Bucky, Jr., and his mom.

The old woman leaned over to her son and whispered, "Evelyn chose wrong. She took that guy to the vending machines to pry, but she is missing the good stuff."

David bowed his head and started to reply in a weak whisper. "You're right. It's all my fault. I trusted my business partners — big mistake. I trusted Ellie Printh. I should have known better. I trusted my lawyer — bad move. But the worse thing I've done in all my life..." he continued as his voice grew louder and stronger, "... was to trust you! For richer or poorer?! You were out the door and at Tim's condo before Ellie Printh's signature dried.

"Does Dr. (he emphasized the title, as Lara had done when she introduced him) Jack Spence know about Tim? Does he know the guy had to move to Texas to get away from you?!"

"David, you blame everyone else for breaking up our family. You blame Ellie Printh. You blame your partners. You blame me.

"I know this sounds strange, but if you just had one ounce of guile, one bit of deceit, not only would we still be together... never mind. I'm not doing this. It doesn't matter. You'll never change. You're who you are. Someone is going to love you for who you are. It just isn't going to be me."

"Wow," said Ugly Hat out of the corner of her mouth to Dr. Jack. The two had returned from the vending machines but milled around nearby so as not to interrupt.

"I'm going to see if I can check on Jason," said David, seeing Dr. Jack waiting in the wings, sipping ginger ale out of the can with a paper straw.

Ellie shrugged. "This is entertaining, but I don't see what connection it has to me." She turned to gauge the spirit's reaction but was surprised to see that he was no longer there.

She looked over to where Bucky Jr., Ugly Hat, and the old woman were sitting, staring off in disparate directions. No ghost.

She scanned the entire waiting room. No ghost.

"How will I get out of here if he has abandoned me?" she wondered.

Then she saw him through a bank of large windows. He was outside of the building leaning against one of the panes. He was motioning for her to come.

As she approached, he reached his arm through the glass, and she touched his sleeve and stepped through.

"What are you doing out here?" she asked.

"Even a spirit can need some air."

"Do you want to sit down on the bench? You are very weak. I... I suppose I could help you." This was a fresh grouping of words for Ellie. When had she ever offered help?

"No. My time is nigh," the specter rasped, hunched over, eyes fixed on the ground and reaching out to take Ellie's hand.

Ellie was moved beyond her capacity to deal with such feelings.

"I guess this is where we say goodbye?" she asked.

Her mind conjured up the image of her dad in the street and the car sliding out of control. In shaking the thought out of her head before seeing it through to its tragic end, she shuddered.

"I feel like I should, you know, voice my appreciation. You've indeed shown me a great deal, given me a lot to think about."

"Ellie," said the ghost, now grabbing her tightly by the forearm, "there's no more time to think. You are going to need to act. Your chance is running out, and you have far to go. Perhaps too far, I fear."

"I think you should conserve your energy," she warned as she sat him down on the bench.

"Do spirits die? Are you dying?" Ellie asked softly.

"I'm moving on. There is no death.

"That's why you must figure this out! This is the life that determines the rest of your life! And one life affects other lives!" said the spirit urgently.

The Ghost of Christmas Present clutched further up on Ellie's arm and squeezed even tighter. Ellie was surprised he still had this much strength.

She looked at him. His eyes were wild, and his face contorted in terror.

"Look out!" he cried. "She's here!"

Ellie spun her head around to see who he was referring to and felt the spirit release his grip. She quickly turned back. The ghost was gone.

The bench was gone.

The hospital was gone.

Everything was gone.

STAVE 4: THE LAST OF THE SPIRITS

*E*llie felt nothing. She had often been accused of having no feelings, but this was different. Her world had gone black. Not just dark. Black. There was no waiting for her eyes to adjust, for her pupils to find the right aperture, for things to come into view. This was blackness. And Ellie knew it wasn't blindness. She had not suddenly lost her vision. She was sure it was something else altogether.

Her certainty came from her other senses: Her ears detected not a hint of noise. The absence of sound is markedly different from silence. Her nose was dumbfounded by the lack of even a latent scent to discover that it might send some information about her situation to her brain.

But it was her absent sense of touch that was most convincing. There are always subtle vibrations or disturbances in our surroundings, a slight weight to the air that presses on our skin, and a reassuring firmness of the ground under our feet that go undetected, unnoticed, unappreciated, until and unless their presence is unfelt.

Ellie concluded was that she was, quite literally, in the middle of actual Nowhere. That was terrifying enough, though now she recalled the fright on the Ghost of Christmas Present's face and his last words: "She's here!"

"She's out there!" thought Ellie, not even knowing who, but assuming the spirit was referring to the last of the ghosts. The image of his tormented visage with the recollection of those final words was steel, striking the flinty nothingness into which she had been cast, sparking a raging terror within her.

"Dad!" she cried instinctively, from the depths of her soul, like a child who's been startled awake from a bad dream.

"Dad," she repeated, this time more softly, and through sobs.

A word came galloping out of the darkness. Ellie could feel it tingling up her spine like little hooves of a charging stallion, racing up her neck, into her ear, breaking the silence: "Princess."

Whether it was a message from beyond or a device of Ellie's invention, the effect on her had no prejudice to either. She was emboldened.

She yelled out in defiance, "Show yourself! I will not be played with!"

Upon the instant, Ellie felt her feet pulled upward as if she had been lassoed around her ankles. She was now hanging, heels over head as if from a meat hook. The blood was rushing to her brain.

She's here.

Some sparks flew off in the distance which, in the midst of absolute blackness, looked like shooting stars in an otherwise starless, moonless night sky.

She's here.

The display was followed by an orange glow as if an ember from an errant spark had found a willing partner with which to create combustion. At first to Ellie, it looked like a sunrise that had gone horribly wrong, and instead of rising and lighting a new day, this sun had snagged its rays on a jagged protrusion and was spinning just above the horizon, trying to loosen itself from the crag, but to no avail. It was a frenetic, twirling, brilliant orb of orange and scarlet and gold and pumpkin and amber and red. Now Ellie determined it was more like a blazing ball of fiery yarn, frantically unspooling as it sped toward her.

She's here.

The pressure in Ellie's brain and in her face and ears had grown almost unbearable. She writhed and wriggled and lurched, trying to grab her legs and ankles to pull herself up and raise her head, but with no success whatsoever. She chastised herself for fast-forwarding through the core exercises in her workout videos. The sense of panic was beginning to set in again.

She's here.

Her eyes were trying to roll to the back of her head. Her lids begged her to let them close. Her consciousness had grabbed its coat off the bed and was ready to slip out early from this disaster of a party.

She's here.

She was adrift on that narrow sea of ambiguity that exists between the warring states of awareness and oblivion. She was fighting hard against letting go of all sensibility when a rush of sound and light and cognizance washed over and around her, filling her sails and propelling her to one of those shores.

She's here.

Ellie opened her eyes wide to take in her surroundings, only to find all vantages blocked by a face in her face. It was a woman's face. Since she was still suspended from her feet by some invisible force, the face appeared upside down to her, yet she and this being were eye to eye.

She's here.

"I am the Ghost of Christmas Yet to Come," spoke the female phantom in a triumphant and fierce voice.

Ellie knew instantly that this spirit was not like the others. There had been some quality of kindness and humanity in both of the night's previous guides. The wisdom of the Ghost of Christmas Past had impressed her. And the warmth of the Ghost of Christmas Present had touched her.

Ellie instantly read this specter as cold and detached.

"Would you let me down?" asked Ellie.

"Are you uncomfortable?" asked the spirit nonchalantly.

"It's just that I feel that I may pass out."

"You won't pass out," assured the ghost, without regard. "I can see to that."

"Let me down!" Ellie demanded.

"My, my. You are very haughty for someone so powerless," said the ghost. "And that will not do."

"I'm going to be sick."

"Tell you what. If you ask me nicely, I may consider it. You created a little realm for yourself in your small world where you run everything and control everything. But here, in my time, you're not in charge of anything, girl."

Ellie was momentarily shocked. Somewhat by the ghost's harsh tone, but moreover, no one had ever called her "girl" before.

"All right. Please, let me down," beseeched Ellie in the sweetest tone she could manage that would simultaneously pass as sincere.

"That's better. So be it."

On the instant, Ellie and Ghost of Christmas Yet to Come were standing outside of Ellie's house. Ellie was completely restored with no effects of having been dangling upside down for she could not determine how long. No dizziness nor headache.

"We are making just a quick stop before moving on," informed the spirit.

This was the first opportunity Ellie had had to look at the Ghost of Christmas Yet to Come. She was tall, thin, attractive, and athletically built. She had a dark face and dark eyes and pitch-black, long, wavy hair. It looked like she had just come from the salon.

She was dressed as if she might be going to a cocktail party after she was done with Ellie. Her sequined onyx party dress was cut a little too low at the v-neck, a little too tight around the waist, and a little too short overall for Ellie's approval. The black leggings and heels, on the other hand, Ellie felt were appropriately stylish. If Ellie had known anything about sports, she might have mistaken the ghost for a WNBA player on her way to the ESPY Awards.

The ghost gave off a distracted air of someone who was effortlessly great at, but no longer interested in, what she does for a living after years and years of doing it.

Having eyed up the specter, Ellie turned her attention to her house. She had always kept a neat and tidy homestead. The lawn was always well-manicured in the summers, fresh coats of paint applied to trim and shutters in the spring, leaves raked up promptly in the fall, and snow removed from the driveway and walkways without delay in the winter.

Ellie quickly noticed that there was at least a foot of snow in the driveway except where two grooves had been worn where a car had come and gone enough times to create icy, shiny tread marks there. The walks, likewise, had not been shoveled, but the snow was disturbed by multiple footprints.

Judging by the number of boot indentations and tire grooves, the snow must have been there for a while without being cleared away.

Upon closer inspection, Ellie also saw other signs of disrepair and neglect. The paint had peeled from a few of the shutters, and the lion's head on the gate had adopted a curious pose, with its head now leaning to one side, as if to ask, "Don't I know you?"

Ellie knew she had been transported to a time in the future, and though some aging of her home would be understandable, given the annual transitions from bitter winters to roasting summers, what she could not fathom was what circumstances would have had to conspire that would have prevented the maintenance of the property and the upkeep of the grounds commensurate to her fastidious demands and expectations.

Her panoramic survey of the scene brought her back around to the fearsome specter. Their eyes locked. A shiver slithered like a cold snake along Ellie's spine, sidewinding across her hips and continuing down her legs all the way to her toes. The sun-melted puddle Ellie had been standing in refroze.

Ellie's rigid bearing had always worked in her favor to ward off would-be predators or sycophants. It had the same effect as a porcupine showing its quills or a skunk lifting its tail. Now though, as Ellie tried to stiffen her back to demonstrate her resolve to the spirit, she was suddenly scoliotic and could barely lift her head off her shoulder. She appeared to cower in supplication, looking all the part of a Uriah Heep, but 'umbled only by the betrayal of her backbone.

It was not that the ghost was unpleasant to look upon, but in her eyes and in her nature, there bespoke a quiet disinterest that Ellie found unnerving.

The Ghost of Christmas Past and Ghost of Christmas Present were demonstrative in their empathy and supportiveness. This ghost, however, was more like, well, Ellie Printh.

Ellie's mind had been busy reconciling the images she had just observed of her house with the situation she now found herself in and had arrived at a chilling postulation, which required some nerve on her part to present.

"Am I dead in there?" asked Ellie, not able to stop the shaking in her voice and cowering even lower in anticipation of the answer.

"Before I answer that question — and I will answer it for you in short order — let me ask you, what have you observed that leads you to that conclusion?"

The ghost posed the question without even looking at Ellie. She was playing with a string of twine, pulling and twisting it through and around her fingers.

Ellie began, "The tire marks... I see what looks like three sets of them. So, an ambulance, a police car, and the coroner's... I don't know what the actual term is, but I'll say meat wagon."

"Meat wagon!" roared the ghost. "Ha ha! I love it! I must remember that," and then she repeated, "Meat wagon. Huh. Go on."

"The footprints leading in and out of the house. That would be EMTs, police officers, and the coroner," her voice still quivering and ready to ask her follow-up question, "When?", upon the affirmation of her hypothesis.

"What about gurney marks?" questioned the spirit, like an attending challenging a resident's diagnosis. "Why wouldn't there be little grooves in the snow where its little gray wheels pressed down under the weight of your cadaver?"

"They carried me out in a body bag?" Ellie conjectured.

The spirit looked Ellie up and down. "Hmmm. Honey, you have an okay figure for someone your age, but it's not like anyone is going to say, 'You know what, forget the gurney... I got this,' and fling your lifeless body over his shoulder and carry you to the... meat wagon."

Ellie's hopes were raised a bit by this hole that was shot in her theory.

"No. You're not dead in there. I can take you to any point forward in time. I could take you to a time in the future when you are dead. I can take you to the very end of this piece of string," the Ghost said, showing Ellie what she had been playing with in her hands and then putting it away... in her cleavage, for safekeeping.

"But why would I start with that?" the ghost continued. "No suspense there. That's everyone's future in your existence. And really, what would you learn? That nobody missed you? That no one went to your funeral? That your whole life had come and gone without ever having brought any pleasure to anyone other than upon their receiving the good news of your passing?

"I mean, you know that, right? If you were a benevolent, saintly-hearted, and generous soul, you and I would not have ever made this acquaintance. If I just, right off the bat, took you to a time after your death, our time together would be over before it even got started."

"I couldn't bear that," the spirit finished sarcastically.

The ghost was sashaying back and forth in front of Ellie as she spoke, like a prison warden indoctrinating a new inmate on how things were going to be around here.

"I cannot take you in the house, per se, to observe," resumed the spirit, after a pause. "Not in the same manner the other ghosts have. For you cannot see your future self the way you can see your former self. It would mess you up pretty bad. You know, up here." she said, while poking Ellie in the head.

"Besides humans, for the most part, do not age well. They really ought to take better care of themselves. My guess is that if men and women were able to see their future selves, most would make a more robust effort at self-preservation, or maybe your street corners would be occupied by more cosmetic surgeons than those Starbucks with which your race is so fascinated.

"Let me see, have you had any work done?"

"No!" replied Ellie, "but I have considered it."

The spirit got closer to inspect Ellie.

"Your eyes?"

"Yes."

"Do it! I'd strongly, and I mean *strongly*, advise that."

Though Ellie had been up all night and had cried several times over the past few hours, and though she was sure her eyes were puffy and dark, the criticism stung. She had often offered such "advice" on attire and appearance to others but had never been on the receiving end.

"As I was saying, I am not going to take you inside the house to observe 'Future Ellie.' Instead, you're going to stay right here, but you are going to see and feel everything Future Ellie is seeing and feeling. It will be as if you are inside her body and her mind."

Ellie opened her mouth to say, "I'd rather not," but before she uttered a sound, the ghost said, "Now go." and blew warm, moist breath into her face.

Ellie instinctively drew back and squeezed her eyes shut. When she righted herself and opened her eyes, she was looking down at a lap, covered by a plaid wool blanket on which rested a pair of wrinkled hands. Hers.

Ellie was consumed with feelings of bitterness, anger, helplessness. She recognized these emotions but knew they were not her own. These affections she had known since their infancy, that she had raised and fed and nurtured, had grown stronger over the years and overthrown the regime. They were clearly in charge now.

Though she was only a visitor in her own body, she found that she had some power of suggestion over it, for upon thinking of moving her head to have a look around, Future Ellie did exactly that.

She lifted her head, though Ellie could feel that it required great concentration and care to do so.

The living room was furnished in the same way it had been the last time Ellie had seen it, only there was a much larger television than Ellie had previously owned. She found that curious. The room was cluttered too. There were some clothes strewn on the couch and on the floor. Some newspapers were piled up on the coffee table — stacked but undisturbed. Some glasses without coasters — whose? — left on each of the two end tables.

Ellie tried to suggest turning her head further to the right to see more of the room but could not get her future self to comply. She also tried to get the old girl to stand up and walk into other rooms, but she could not do so.

As each of these suggestions failed, Ellie became uncharacteristically overwhelmed with frustration and despondency. She could not understand why her feelings were so pronounced until she remembered she was sensing her future self's emotions on top of her own.

Ellie compelled Future Ellie to look at her hands again, and she acquiesced. She focused on her left hand and encouraged her to raise it. The hand went up. Now she focused on the right hand and "told" her to raise it. The hand remained on her lap, and a wave of indescribable grief and loss washed over the two of them.

Tears formed in the older Ellie's eyes and rolled down her cheeks, though the right side of her face was oblivious to them.

"Oh, my God! No!" screamed Ellie, who, after a few more small but unsuccessful tests, came to the realization that she was paralyzed on her right side.

"Get me out of here!" Ellie screamed to the Ghost of Christmas Yet to Come.

There was no reply. But an image appeared in Ellie's mind of the specter running a billy club across jail cell bars, mocking her with exaggerated cries of "Get me out of here! Get me out of here!"

Ellie shivered, and so did the left side of her future self.

Now, Ellie heard the sound of a couple of people talking, and she felt her older self drop her head and close her eyes, and Ellie knew she was feigning being asleep.

"Hey, she's still asleep. Come on out." Ellie could tell those words were spoken by a young man.

"This is the best gig I've ever had," he continued.

"Tell me about it!" said a young woman enthusiastically. "Working on Christmas, under any other circumstances, would be just awful. But I get to spend the whole day alone with you!"

Ellie couldn't know, but in her mind, she saw the woman re-buttoning her shirt.

"We're lucky," replied the young man. "Most old people would have visitors from their kids or grandkids or somebody. In my two months working here, there hasn't been one visitor — except for our pizza guy and Geek Squad guy who installed the TV. I kind of feel bad for her."

"Don't!" protested the young woman. "She was a nasty, mean lady. My family used to rent a house from her. She tried to have us evicted on Christmas Day one year. She showed up herself while we were eating and told us she wanted us out."

"Wow. You never mentioned that before."

"Not something I'm proud of. We didn't leave that day, but a couple of weeks later, we were out on our asses."

"Was that before or after that druggie foster kid ran away? What was her name?"

"You mean Claire. She ran away maybe a couple of years after we moved. She just up and disappeared one day. But, please just stop. I don't even want to think about that one. She pretty much ruined my childhood and my family. SMH!"

"Anyway, I try to forget she ever existed."

"How unromantic of you! She's how you and I met. Remember? When they brought her into the ER when she overdosed. She asked me if I knew Kitty Fielder and asked me to find you. She must have thought you were a nurse."

"She probably thought I could get her drugs. And she probably thought you were a doctor! I was a junior volunteer! Shows you how whacked out she is. I mean... Kitty Fielder, Teen Nurse, right?"

"When I went found you and brought you to the ER, I remember you taking one look at her, even though she was all scared and alone and crying, and you said... "

"Do not resuscitate!" Kitty recalled.

"Right," laughed the man, and then you walked out of there without ever acknowledging her.

"When I saw that, I thought to myself, 'Now there's a chick I need to get to know. She's a badass!"

"Chick? No. No. That ain't cool! Badass is fine. I like 'badass.'

"I hadn't seen her for months before the ER, and I have never seen her since. Except..."

Kitty recalled a hazy memory.

"One night, I heard someone go out the back door. I looked down from my bedroom window and saw my mom handing someone — I couldn't tell, the person was in the shadows, but I swear it was Claire — anyway, my mom passed her an envelope with money in it. I know 'cause the person stood there and counted it, like making sure it was all there.

"Then I heard my mom say, 'Okay? Can we finally be rid of you?' and then Claire, I mean, I know it was her, ran off.

"Wow, did you ever ask your mom about it?"

"Yeah, she said she had purchased some beeswax from a local beekeeper and that if I'd like some, she'd be happy to buy me some so I could mind my own.

"All of this talk of Claire is really putting me in a bad mood, if you know what I mean. So if I were you, I'd change the subject real fast."

Ellie could hear the couple kissing. Ellie was not a baseball fan, nor did she use sports analogies, but that was where her mind went. The thought of being trapped in the middle of the infield should this guy try to round the bases made her sick. Her disgust may have played a part in the rolling of the older Ellie's eyes and a taste of vomit in the back of her throat.

Ellie could feel the constant anxiety and dread that consumed the old woman's waking hours. "She's a prisoner," thought Ellie, "and I'm trapped in this cell within her cell."

Ellie screamed again, "Let me out of here!"

Ellie could not understand why her future self had ended up in this position. She had made provisions in her living will in the event of a catastrophic health event. Who had hired these "caregivers" for her? She assumed some management company had been assigned a budget, found cheap labor, and was pocketing the difference. She could not imagine how it could happen. But here she was, a useless captive in her home, unable to call out or flee. Even worse, she was at the mercy of Martha Fielder's daughter and some hormone in the guise of a home health associate.

"Let's get her fed and doped up again, and then we can go back to bed," said that home health associate.

"You are so smart!"

"What's the menu for today?"

"Let's see," said Kitty.

Ellie could tell she was now in the kitchen.

"In the Fancy Feast cupboard, we have Ocean Whitefish and Tuna, Chicken, or Tender Beef... and in the Friskies cupboard, we're down to just Turkey and Giblets."

Ellie was enraged, but what she felt from her older self was resignation. This was her life now.

"She had chicken yesterday, so we'll go with fish today."

"You have a mean streak I hope I never see turned in my direction," said the man.

"Just don't cross my family or me!" warned Kitty.

"Ms. Printh?" The young man was now close by, and Ellie felt him touch the old woman's left arm and could detect his unpleasant body odor.

"It's time for some nourishment and some meds. Can you wake up and give me your crooked little smile?"

The older Ellie opened her eyes slowly, pretending to be coming out of deep sleep. Ellie appreciated the guile of her future self.

The man was standing over her, and from a name tag on his white uniform, she read his name was Justin.

"Oh great," thought Ellie, "I'm in the hands of a millennial named Justin."

"Waaad-der," said the old woman slowly and with some struggle.

"Water? Coming right up. I turned the TV on for you. We're going to watch some basketball later. Right now, we're going to get you your lunch, and then you can take a longer rest, okay?"

He looked over at Kitty, who nodded her approval demonstratively.

Then, unexpectedly, the doorbell rang.

The two caregivers looked at each other quizzically.

Ellie felt a jolt of adrenaline surge through much of her host's body and could sense the curiosity and hopefulness it left in its wake.

"Did you order pizza?" Justin asked Kitty.

"No — ah!"

"Neither did I. Who else could it possibly be?"

"We better answer it, or someone might call the police to check, and that will get back to the service. Could just be a delivery."

"On Christmas Day?"

To this point, Ellie did not realize that the chair in which her future self was sitting was a wheelchair. But she sensed the old woman reach down with her left hand and turn the wheel slowly and slightly, so the front door was now in view.

Ding dong.

"You better get that," said Kitty. "I'll stay in the kitchen. I'm heating up her Fancy Feast."

Justin shook his head and went to the door, took a deep breath, and opened it to a stranger carrying a two feet high Christmas tree.

"Hi. Merry Christmas! My name is Mary Lou Haggerty. I used to work for Ms. Printh, and well, you know, I haven't seen her since the... you know... the thing."

"The burst aneurysm?" offered Justin bluntly.

"Okaaay. That," replied a somewhat shocked Mary Lou. "Any-hoo, I thought this being Christmas and all, I would stop by and visit with Ms. Printh for a little while if that's all right. And I brought her this little Christmas tree. Thought it might cheer her up."

"Well," replied Justin, "I don't think she's up to receiving guests right now."

"I won't stay long. I just want to say hello and let her know I was thinking of her. It's been a couple years."

Justin froze momentarily, considering what tone to take in dispatching this intruder, when from behind him came a slurred but discernible cry.

"Mrrrr-eee Roooo!"

"I guess you can go on in," said Justin, stepping aside, though Mary Lou had already pushed past him and was stomping the snow off her heavy-duty boots before proceeding to her former boss.

With just a shrug in the direction of Kitty, Justin communicated, "What was I supposed to do?"

Ellie felt too many emotions all at once to decipher any one in particular or whether they were hers or her host's.

"Ms. Printh? Hi. It's me. Mary Lou. Do you remember? How are you feeling?"

"You dumbass," thought Ellie, "how does it look like she's feeling." Ellie immediately felt remorse at this reaction, but it flashed an expression of exasperation across older Ellie's face that was instantly recognizable to Mary Lou. It sparked a familiarity that set the visitor at ease.

"It's been a long time, Mrs. Printh, and I feel bad that I have not visited sooner."

"Help me!" screamed the old woman urgently. Ellie heard it clear as day, but it came out of her mouth as a feeble and strangulated, "huppp — ee."

Mary Lou looked into Ms. Printh's eyes, searching for a meaning to the indistinguishable syllables. Finding none, she turned to Justin.

"Huuupp — ee," cried Ms. Printh again desperately, and even more slowly and deliberately. Ellie now understood the problem, and it sunk her, causing her older self's head to droop, which she quickly raised again with no small amount of directed thought and effort.

"I can't... I don't... " started Mary Lou to her former boss, looking confused and helpless. She then turned to Justin again for an interpretation.

"Um, I think she is saying 'happy,' you know, like she's happy to see you."

"Oh!" said a pleasantly surprised Mary Lou. She had gone there against the advice of her sister-in-law, her nephew, her friends, her therapist, a barista, and a couple of bystanders who happened to be in earshot of her announcement of her intention to pay a visit to Ellie Printh.

She had gone, knowing full well that she would likely be made to feel unwelcome and told by Ms. Printh that the Christmas tree was too small for such a large room. Then she would be summarily dismissed and told to close the door behind her swiftly to mitigate the escape of heat from the house.

But here was Ms. Printh telling her she was happy to see her!

Mary Lou quickly suspected something was not right.

"I'm happy to see you too!" said Mary Lou with a knowing nod to the lady. "Well, I didn't want to overstay. Just wanted to check on you and wish you a merry... well, you know... a merry day."

Mary Lou leaned over and kissed old Ms. Printh on the cheek and whispered, "I'll stop back from time to time to check in on you."

Ellie felt an odd mixture of hope and disappointment from the old woman. Hope that maybe, over time, her torment would be discovered. Disappointment that today would not be that day.

"Hey, Justin, is it?" said Mary Lou as they walked to the door. "Is she getting physical therapy and speech therapy on a regular basis?"

"Uh, from what I heard, she called and canceled her PT and her speech therapy. I've only been here a few months."

"She called and canceled them herself?"

"I'll bet I had a little help from Kitty," thought Ellie.

"Like I said, that was before me. I don't know the details. Katherine is busy in the kitchen, or I'd ask her. She's worked here longer.

"But you should go… we're on a schedule, and it's time for Ms. Printh to eat and take her pills. She gets real agitated when her routine is disrupted. But you said you worked with her, so you probably already know that."

Mary Lou and Justin were now at the door, and he had opened it for her prematurely. She took a step to leave and then turned back.

"The Ellie Printh I know is too vain to cancel her physical and speech therapies. And from what I heard out of her, I don't even think that's possible. She would happily put in the work to function and look and speak as she used to. And she would never allow her house to be in such disarray, inside and out.

"So I'll tell you what, Justin, I'm going to stop back here in a week or two to check in again. If the walks aren't cleared, and the driveway's not plowed, and this living room isn't neat as a pin, I'm going to make some calls.

"I was her personal assistant up until the, you know, what-you-called-it. I know what was provided for in her papers. Tell whoever you need to, but just know that I am watching now, and I'll be back."

At that, Mary Lou took her leave of Justin and Kitty, walked to her car, put a reminder in her calendar to check back in two weeks, and then drove off.

Ellie was overcome with gratitude for this spunky Mary Lou, remorse for how she had treated her most times, and regret about having missed this quality in her assistant.

"I'm going to let her keep that book she borrowed," thought Ellie.

"Now what?" Kitty asked Justin.

"I'm not worried. I've been telling them they should have someone clear the snow anyway. Then we wouldn't have to park on the street! We can just do a better job of picking up after ourselves in here. She still has no visitors. No one cares about her. This was that lady's first visit, probably her last. How will she know if our old gal is getting therapy?

"Trust me... I'm not going to let anyone ruin this for us."

The new expectation of reprieve drained out of the older Ellie, and dreadful resignation filled its void.

As the old woman lifted her head and stared vacantly at the television, Ellie observed that A Christmas Carol was playing. A ghastly creature shrouded in black was pointing at Scrooge, who was prostrate in terror. Ellie closed her eyes to the images.

When she re-opened them, she found herself once more in the presence of the Ghost of Christmas Yet to Come, and again in the middle of nowhere.

Already, Ellie's memory of what she had seen was fading, but the emotions remained: fear, hopelessness, anxiety, depression, regret. A palpable sadness clung to her as she physically struggled to shake it off.

"Spirit," she cried, "Have mercy! Please take me home. I am not up to this. It is more than I can bear."

"Mercy? More than you can bear?" replied the ghost incredulously. "Do not look for mercy from me. That is not a quality I possess. You can quit if you want. I really don't care. This rarely works anyway. If you want to give up, just say it. I won't show you anything else, and I can mark your fate as sealed and move on."

Ellie was trying to recall all that had passed while she was observing from within her future self. However, key elements were evaporating into a fog in her mind, even though she was consciously but fruitlessly endeavoring to retain it all.

"That scene will sit with you forever, but you'll remember little or nothing of it. You'll only feel it all. But your memory of yourself in the future will soon be lost to you." The spirit had not so much read Ellie's thoughts as anticipated them, and had responded accordingly.

"I won't remember any of this?" confirmed Ellie. "What's the point?!"

"That was the only part of our time together that I feel compelled to blur because if you remain unaltered, what you saw is your future. No one on Earth can know their future. As for the rest of our time together, you will remember it all. Except…"

Ellie, who had been standing hands on knees, taking deep breaths and holding them briefly and then pronouncing each exhalation with a "Puh," looked up at the ghost who had paused until her eyes were raised to meet hers.

"Except," the spirit continued, "you will not remember anything I say or that I ever spoke to you. My words may come to you from time to time throughout the rest of your life in the form of intuition or inspiration — depending on how receptive you are to them. I am far too influential to be completely erased."

Ellie felt the torturous drip of each of the spirit's words fall with condescension on the top of her head. Although there was nothing menacing in their denotation, the tone of the voice that spoke them was the same as an impatient parent to a child.

"You think ill of me," declared Ellie.

"Not at all."

"Oh? Surely you don't think well of me." Ellie scoffed.

"No," explained the spirit, "I don't think anything of you. I don't think of you at all. You don't matter to me in the least. I could leave you here, in this crevice of time forever, and no one would care, least of all me."

Ellie had some brief notion that Mary Lou would, but she quickly dismissed it as nonsense.

"Now, I'm not going to do that, of course. For one reason, it might mean my running into you again every now and then throughout eternity. And that would be unpleasant for you and me. More for me than for you, but nonetheless…"

The spirit pulled at her dress and at her leggings, mindlessly straightening out some wrinkles that had formed, while Ellie shivered and shook at the thought of being left alone in nothingness for infinity.

"Is that what death is like?" asked Ellie fearfully.

"Oh, darling, death is far worse for someone like you. Well, enough of this chit chat. We girls, when we get together, we do go on, don't we?" said the spirit derisively, glaring at Ellie.

"Spirit," entreated Ellie, "why do you look at me and speak to me with such contempt? I can only reason it is because you think I am weak? I assure you I am not..."

"Maybe I just don't like you and don't want to waste my time," interjected the ghost. "I've been through this enough times to form an accurate assessment and probable outcome."

The phantom paused a moment and looked Ellie up and down. Then she continued, "You know, Ellie Printh, the future is a dark and frightening place for humanity. But it would not have to be if it weren't for people such as you. We had never met until now, of course, but I have known a couple of thousand people just like you. Humankind consists of countless men and women more despicable than you. There is nothing especially awful about you. You're not here because you're the worst person on Earth this year. You alone aren't driving the misery to come. It's the sheer volume of people like you in your world. If each person would just focus on making their little corner of the world a little better for everyone else in it, the future would be a brighter and more promising time for your race."

"If there are so many like me, why me? Why am I the one here tonight?"

"I don't know these things. Though there must be some opportunity, some possible purpose associated with you. I don't see a reason to go through all of this just for you. I don't see why we three spirits would suffer through this time investment with you, just for you. I don't see a quality in you, but someone must."

"And girl, I can count on one hand the number of times any of this was even remotely effective. I don't know who orders it. I don't know why. I just show up at the time and place appointed. And I let people see glimpses of what is going to happen. And I watch them observe. Some with indifference. Some with temporary remorse. And some with resolve.

But in a world such as yours, resolve is a ship at sea. When a storm comes, if that ship isn't moored, it is swiftly abandoned. People like you are adrift without tethers or anchors. Your destinations are quickly dashed to pieces in favor of your escape to the familiar shore. The few people who make a sincere effort to reform settle back into their darker selves as soon as they are challenged or feel uncomfortable because they are attached to nothing and to no one.

"I digress. If you want to be done, I'll gladly take you home and put you back in your bed and tuck you in and kiss you and your hereafter good night. You didn't ask, but if I were you, I'd just call it quits," the specter goaded, and then placed her hands on her hips and growled at Ellie, "Well? What's it going to be? Speak up!"

Ellie took a moment. She was a little girl again, and her mother was standing over her, displeased and disappointed with her diluted daughter.

"Don't be mad, mom. I'll do better. I promise." Ellie heard those little girl replies of retreat, always retreat, in her head, and was filled with that same fear and anxiety she had felt in those moments. It was as though instead of being in her future self, she had gone back in time for a moment and inhabited her former self, and she wanted out of that skin as well.

Ellie had made up her mind. She needed to go home. She wanted to be left alone. She longed for this all to be over. She was fine with her life as it had been. It was decided.

So, the words that came out of her mouth were surprising, if not to the Ghost of Christmas Yet to Come, at least to her own ears.

"Press on, girl!" declared Ellie. The words were awkward in their vernacular yet graceful in their earnestness. "I have come this far. I will at least finish this. I must go on."

"Interesting," was the response from the ghost. "Let's, as you so eloquently put it, press on, girl. Follow me. We are just going a couple of years further on."

Though the world around them was completely black, the spot where they had talked was illuminated from above, as if they were standing on a stage lit expressly for a solemn soliloquy.

When the ghost moved off, the light did not follow; she moved into the darkness, and Ellie, with more than a little reluctance, followed her into the blinding gloom.

"Stay near," came the words of the spirit from someplace up ahead. "And don't turn around."

Ellie took a few halting steps toward the ghost's voice before her curiosity, and her contrariness usurped her reason. She took a quick half peek over her shoulder and immediately turned right back to the darkness. What she thought she had seen was a brightly lit tunnel, but incredibly, it was throwing no light into the blackness.

She had not been turned to stone any more than her emotional properties had already hardened toward that disposition. So, she turned fully around to take a closer look.

The cave-like opening was brilliant, and the walls of the tunnel were illuminated with scenes of Ellie's past, starting with the most recent, from just earlier in the evening before this nonsense began. There she was at McNally's. There was Mary Lou asking to borrow that infernal book. There was Mrs. Fielder sweating and wringing her hands in her office. The furthest back she could discern from where she stood were images, though blurred, of a check-up she had had at the cardiologist's office the week before. But she was aware that this portal would lead her back through her entire life.

"Go ahead," said the spirit from behind her, startling Ellie.

The ghost must have read Ellie's thoughts as she was considering whether to go inside.

"Impossible to resist, isn't it? That's why I told you NOT to turn around. But, of course, I knew you would."

"What is this?" asked Ellie, her gaze still fixed on the tunnel.

"Ultimately, it is oblivion, but technically, it's your life up to now."

"Can I go in?"

"If you go in, you will never come out. But it is your choice."

"If I go in, can I alter events, fix things?"

"No. You can't change things in the past. Just like you can't alter the future until you get there. The only time you can change your life is in your present, in each moment. That's it."

The Ghost spoke a graveness and fervency that was inconsistent with Ellie's experience with this spirit. Whether it was what she said or how she said it, her words broke through Ellie's trance.

"It's safe in there for sure," said the Ghost of Christmas Yet to Come, her biting attitude returning, "but if you go in, you'll never find your way out. It's true what they say, 'You cannot live in the past.' But, whatever!" added the specter before walking off again into the darkness.

Ellie took one last look at the bright tunnel, then turned her back to it and followed in the direction of the ghost.

"This way," said the spirit from far ahead.

Ellie took several slow, careful steps toward the sound of the voice.

Though there were no walls nor ceiling nor, impossibly, floor boxing her in, she was again feeling a panic like claustrophobia. Her skin crawled from the inside, and she wanted desperately to claw and scratch at the darkness that she might peel some of it away and see just a fragment of light or feel a brief wisp of fresh air.

The anxiety caused this interlude to feel like minutes, but in reality, it was only a couple of seconds until lights came up around her. A carpeted floor was under her feet, and walls materialized, as did a couch and a fireplace and matching recliners and a coffee table and a television and… Martha and Arthur Fielder.

"Oh, great!" Ellie started to say as she turned to the ghost. Only, the spirit was nowhere to be found. "Puh!"

Judging by the Fielders' aged appearance, Ellie estimated she was probably close to ten years beyond the present. Mrs. Fielder's roots revealed her hair had gone mostly gray. She had clearly lost weight, but her skin hung on her like a damp cotton sweater.

If Mrs. Fielder's weight had been lost, Mr. Fielder was the unfortunate finder and keeper of it. Broad-headed, narrow-shouldered, skinny-limbed, and pale as paste, he was. His girth was contained in his round middle. His shape reminded Ellie of a Lindor truffle in its wrapper.

His hair on top had thinned to a countable number of strands, though he inexplicably stained those stragglers the same color as his wingtips.

"Another Christmas morning in the books, Marthur!" he said, laying back in his recliner, sounding quite self-satisfied.

"Yep. Another one gone, Artha," replied Mrs. Fielder, then letting out a long and weighty sigh.

"What's the matter, my dear?"

"I was just thinking, it's just not the same as when they were little."

"This time next year, we will have a tiny tot running around," said Arthur, trying to cheer up his bride.

Martha rolled her eyes. "Oh, right! It will be great to hear the pitter-patter of the little bastard's feet in the house."

"Marthur! She's just upstairs. She'll hear ya!"

"I don't care! How could she be so careless! And to think our future grandchild was conceived in that Printh woman's bed! That's what really gets me!"

"Now, we don't know that. It could have happened anywhere."

"Okay. Sure, Artha, you're right. Maybe it happened at church. Or at the grocery store."

"Oh, you're just being dramatic there, Grandma!"

Mrs. Fielder burst into tears but stopped instantly when there was a light rap at the front door.

"Who could that be?" said Arthur.

"Well, it can't be Ellie Printh this Christmas!" said Martha blotting her eyes with the sleeves of her robe. "Sit still, Artha. I'll see who it is."

The polite thumping had now turned into an impatient pounding.

"Hold your housecoats," yelled Martha, ambling toward the door.

Martha took a quick look through the peephole and shrieked.

"Artha! Artha!" she cried, looking back into the living room at her husband. "It's the guy!"

"What guy?" asked Artha, annoyed by the assumption he would instantly know who she was talking about from that description. But on some level, he did.

"The guy who came that night with Claire."

"Well, pretend we're not home."

Again, there was more beating on the door, this time even harder.

"I'm going to let him in. I don't want the kids coming back downstairs and have to explain any of this to them."

Artha rolled back and forth in his chair like a beetle on its back, trying to get himself out of it.

"Just sit there. Let me handle this," Martha commanded.

As she turned the doorknob, the man pushed his way in, nearly knocking Martha off her feet.

"Stop! Hold on there!" Martha cried in a hushed and hoarse shout.

When the man turned to face her, Martha didn't like what she saw. She did not know what most concerned her, the desperate look in his eyes or the hunting knife in his hand. Ironically, the glint of the Christmas tree lights could be seen in both.

"I, I mean we, need money! If you give me some, I'll leave, and you'll never see me again."

Mr. Fielder had now loosed himself from the grip of the recliner and was on his feet.

"That's what she said last time!" he barked angrily.

The intruder, who had not previously been aware of Mr. Fielder's presence, now turned and trained his attention on the master of the house.

"Arthur! Sit down and let me handle this," scolded Martha sternly.

"You're him," said the guy with the knife, advancing a few steps in the portly man's direction.

"What? What are you talking about?" asked Arthur retreating.

"You disgusting piece of... How could you do those things to a little... "

Martha cut him off.

"Listen! This has been settled, right? We gave Claire ten thousand dollars that night. You know. You was there. I saw you in the shadows."

"We spent all of that a long time ago!" said the man.

"Well, that was everything we had. That was our life savings and more," said Arthur.

"Artha! Would ya keep your mouth shut!"

"I'd listen to her, pops. I've skinned rabbits and squirrels with this knife, and I've just been looking for the opportunity to work my way up to sex offenders."

"Now, see here!" yelled Arthur. "She was always a little flirt, but I never..."

The man charged at Arthur with the knife.

"Stop, Sam!" The tired and weary voice cut through the mayhem.

The three of them turned to see a pale and emaciated woman standing in the open doorway. Her clothes were ripped, worn, dirty, loose, and not at all suitable for the winter climate in Pennsylvania. Dark circles under her eyes had bled into her pronounced cheekbones. Her lips were barely thick enough to cover and conceal what remained of the teeth in her mouth.

The man she had just called Sam instantly stopped and turned.

"Claire — I told you to stay outside."

Ellie gasped.

Mrs. Fielder took a second look at the girl in the doorway.

"Claire?" she asked in disbelief.

The girl looked at her.

"Claire!" cried Mrs. Fielder upon recognizing the unrecognizable. She was genuinely moved and horrified at the sight of the waifish creature. "My God child, what's happened?"

Mr. Fielder, who had run behind the recliner for protection and to hide the evidence of a skittish bladder when Sam had charged him, stood expressionless.

"Let's go, Sam," said Claire, weakly. Then she turned to Martha Fielder, "I'm sorry to have disrupted your Christmas. This was stupid."

Sam slid the knife into his belt and moved slowly toward the door, turning once to snarl at Mr. Fielder.

"Wait," said Martha, grabbing her purse from the hall table.

She grabbed a wad of bills from her billfold. "Here. It's not much, but it's all I got. I only want ya to use this for food and nourishment for the two of ya," she insisted, handing the money to Sam. "Nothing else. Do ya hear me! You're killing yourselves with that stuff. Nothing else!"

Sam pocketed the cash.

"And one more thing… Artha, throw me that winter coat ya got me for Christmas."

"I'd rather not," he replied from behind his chair.

"Oh, for crying out loud!"

Martha fetched it herself and placed it on the girl.

"It's huge on you, but pull it tight."

Martha gave Claire an awkward hug.

"Claire, I never meant…" she whispered. "I didn't know… I'm so sorry…"

Claire lifted one arm around her former foster mother's back and patted it a couple of times before letting it fall back to her side.

"My God, there's nothing to you. My God! Take care of yourself, child," Mrs. Fielder said with tears in her eyes and on her cheeks. "Take care of her," she repeated to Sam.

"But don't come back here looking for any more money!" cried Arthur from behind the recliner. "You wouldn't have gotten a nickel from me!"

Martha watched the two huddled young people until they disappeared into a gray and bitter Christmas chill before closing the door.

Before heading upstairs, she paused at the entrance to the living room where her husband had finally braved his way out from behind the recliner.

"Artha…"

"Yes, Marthur?"

"I don't think you should live here anymore. Clean yourself up and go."

And with that, she headed upstairs for a bath.

The walls dissolved. Much of the scene faded. Arthur, along with the urine that had soaked his pajama bottoms, evaporated. And yet, Ellie barely noticed. For, still in her eyes was the young woman's face, drained of all its color and life and hope, devoid of the spunk, fight, and potential Ellie was sure the younger Claire possessed. Ellie had been confident Claire would be fine. Now there was no doubt that Claire was lost to whatever demon had overtaken her and to those who led her into its grasp.

As Ellie again became aware of her surroundings, she was alone on what was like the set of a play after the theater had been abandoned for the night. Sparse lighting barely illuminated the area. She felt the presence of the Ghost of Christmas Yet to Come but could not see her until she entered from stage right.

"You have felt some strong emotion from what you have seen?" asked the spirit.

"The girl," replied Ellie. "I had previously felt some kinship with her, but I see we are very different. I thought she was headstrong and determined. I thought she would take command of her circumstances and make something of her life, but now I see she has allowed herself to be controlled by whatever addiction has her, and influenced by those 'friends' who got her involved with it. It is lamentable to see. I hope that I… I hope there is something I can do. Maybe, warn her somehow."

"I see. Yes. Because people often listen to those kinds of admonitions. Good plan!" chided the ghost. "What will you tell her? 'Don't do drugs?' 'Just say no?' 'Don't give in to peer pressure?' Maybe you could have some buttons made with those happy little slogans for her to wear and hand out to her friends."

"I am surprised to see that this drug crisis persists so many years in the future," said Ellie, trying to move past the ghost's taunting.

"Oh, ho! That is rich! Political parties know that there is no power in solving a problem. The power is in promising to solve a problem. You couldn't possibly imagine the number of times the same cans get kicked down the road. Some for generations! From my vantage point, I see them all. To me, it is comical. It's a laugh riot. But I can't fathom why humans keep falling for it. It's your own fault you end up with such terrible leaders. Of course, it's not your fault. You don't vote."

The ghost had grown more and more agitated during her brief tirade.

"Yes, well," started Ellie, in the unfamiliar position of trying to steer a conversation to a more positive subject. "I was caught off guard by the Fielder woman's generosity. Giving the young girl the coat was very kind of her."

"I will tell you that within an hour of receiving that coat, which Mr. Fielder purchased on sale for $150, the girl, Claire, at the strong persuasion and advice of her boyfriend, sold it for $20. It may have been 'kind,' as you say, but it was also stupid. The two are not mutually exclusive. It was the least Martha Fielder could do. It was the LEAST she could do. She knows what's going on there. If she wanted to, she could have seen all of this coming. Believe me, the cash and the coat did more for herself than they did for that poor creature. Mrs. Fielder used them to wash her hands."

Ellie had been standing in front of the fading Christmas tree, wandering with her thoughts through its pale, twinkling lights. She was also now aware that the whole scene had almost completely dissipated. The tree was barely visible, and Ellie could look through it into the darkness without.

"Spirit," said Ellie, turning to the Ghost of Christmas Yet to Come, "There is a family. The Daniels. Patty Daniels is a friend... rather, an acquaintance of mine. The Ghost of Christmas Present took me to her house. To a family Christmas party there. She was ill. I was curious about how she and her family may have fared over time. I was wondering if you might make their home one of our destinations."

"I don't see the point."

"Oh?"

"I see a death associated with the family and their house now occupied by people who are strangers to you."

"Oh, of course. Of course," replied Ellie as stoically as she could manage.

"Also," said the spirit with rising anger. "I thought it would be obvious to you, but apparently it isn't. I am the Ghost of Christmas Yet to Come, not a wedding DJ. I don't take requests. Understand?"

"Uh-huh," replied Ellie mindlessly. The tree and her surroundings were now merely a mist. Ellie feared that if she were to let out a heavy sigh, the whole scene would blow away, so fragile it seemed. She didn't dare, though, because she wasn't sure if that would leave her once more entirely in the dark.

Ellie reached out to see if she could place her hand through the murky tree. When she came into contact with the nebula, all of the scene's remaining particles began to purposefully dart off in different directions. They were like members of a marching band, dutifully making their way to their assigned positions in a new formation.

The existing molecules were joined by others, and now new walls were forming around Ellie. Different features, colors, and furniture now comprised the room. When everything was in place, two people took shape at a card table that served as the dinner table for a middle-aged man and an older woman Ellie assumed was his mother.

Ellie recognized the man as David Burke — the man whose company she had maneuvered out from under him. The same man who she last saw in real life tending bar at McNally's. And the same man she most recently observed in whatever dream or other-worldly experience this was, in the emergency room with his son, being pilloried by his soon-to-be ex-wife while her new lover looked on.

The apartment was a small efficiency. With knowledge of such properties, Ellie quickly discerned there was only one room serving as a combination living room, kitchen, and bedroom. Ellie also spied a door that she likewise knew had a bathroom hiding behind it. After surveying the place, Ellie again noticed the Ghost of Christmas Yet to Come had vanished. The spirit's disappearing act simultaneously pleased and annoyed Ellie.

David and his mother were having Christmas dinner. On the small, fold-up table was carved turkey, canned cranberry sauce, mashed potatoes in a black plastic tub, Heinz turkey gravy that had been microwaved in its jar (steam was still rising from it) and set on the table to be poured out of directly, a bag of King's Hawaiian rolls, a stick of butter, and an oven mitt, presumably for the application of the gravy.

"Davey, I am worried about you," said the old woman, touching her son's arm. "Are you getting enough sleep?"

"Why did you ask that? Do I look tired?" replied David, picking up a butter knife and looking at his reflection.

"No. You look fine, dear. Very handsome as always. It's just I couldn't help notice the sleeping pills in your medicine cabinet."

"My God, mom, the medicine cabinet door sticks. I can barely open it. Anyway, yeah, they were prescribed for me, but I don't take them. You probably couldn't help notice the bottle is full. Didn't you count them?"

"Davey! Stop! I'm your mother. I can tell when my child is unhappy. I'm just concerned about you."

"No need, Mom. I'm fine. Right as rain, as they say," David answered back in a tone that walked a line between reassurance and sarcasm.

"Well, I think it's terrible those kids chose to go to Saint John with their mother and what's-his-name instead of spending Christmas with their dad."

"Mom, can you drop it? Please. I don't blame them. They're adults."

"Huh!" scoffed David's mother. "Adults do the responsible thing."

"I'm fine with it. I'd do the same thing if I were them. Look around. Where would they sleep anyway? This place is a pit."

David's mother looked around. "Your father and I lived in a similar place when we were just starting out."

"Mom, I'm not sure if you are aware, but I'm not just starting out."

"Well, if you hadn't scrimped and saved to put those two through college…"

David dropped his fork and threw his napkin on the table. He stood up to march off in a huff, but either decided against a dramatic exit or else realized his only sanctuary was the john.

"I haven't paid a cent toward their college, okay?! Lara and… 'Thing Three' paid for everything. I told them I'd pay them back my share, but that's just never going to happen. I'll never have that kind of money."

"Oh," said David's mother, surprised. "Still, they are your son and daughter, and they should be spending Christmas with their father. I'm disappointed in their choices."

"I have to work later, anyway. That's why we're eating dinner at 11:30 in the morning! I'll see them when they get home."

"I don't understand why you need to go in to Best Buy on a day they're closed."

"They are open tomorrow, and someone needs to get the store ready. It's time and a half! That's good money."

"It's not good money, Davey. You used to make good money. Great money. Ever since you lost your company, you just can't get your act together. You're still that same guy who built a successful business. You've still got a lot going for you! You're smart and good looking, and that alone should get you somewhere. But, more than that, you're decent and nice and honest. And you don't find those qualities in most people these days. I'm proud of you. And I know your dad would be proud of you as well."

David's mother teared up on the memory of her late husband.

David picked up his napkin and sat back down at the table.

"You know, Mom, it's 'decent, nice and honest' that's the reason I'm in this crap-hole and not in the Caribbean with Lara and the kids."

"No, David."

"Yes. Lara was right. A person needs some deceit and some guile to succeed. Otherwise, you get eaten alive."

"Don't talk like that, Davey."

"It's true. I have only myself to blame for all of this. But the sick and sad thing is that I don't even know how to go about being underhanded. You and Dad could have maybe taught me the ways of the world. That might have helped."

"Your reward will be in heaven, David," his mother said sternly.

"Well, I hope I get there soon."

"David!"

"No, it's true. I don't have a purpose here. I have no friends. My kids think I'm a loser compared to Carlos — and you can't tell me the guy's name isn't really Carl. He's not Hispanic. He's Jewish. Carlos, my ass!"

"David Charles Burke! On Christmas Day!"

"What? Mary rode into Bethlehem on one, but I can't mention mine?"

"David! Forgive him, Blessed Mother!"

"Lara despises me and blames me for our break-up," David continued. "I mean, seriously. If I died, it'd be at least a week until anyone even noticed."

"Oh, I would notice, son, but to be sure, you should call me more often.

"I'd be destroyed. Don't talk like that. It worries me to hear you say those things. You don't own a gun, do you?"

"Of course not. Let's just change the subject."

"One last thing. That lady who stole your company from you... she got hers, didn't she? Serves her right. Is she still alive?"

Ellie had some vague sense of what the woman meant by 'she got hers,' but the memory darted away from her before she could grab it and shake it down for answers.

"I don't know, mom. I can't even afford a newspaper subscription, and I certainly don't keep track of Ellie Printh's status."

"Anyway, don't let her win! Go make a success of yourself again. If you don't, and if you give up, you're letting her win. She took one thing from you, don't let her take everything."

David's mom reached across the table and placed her hand on his.

"Promise me you won't hurt yourself!"

"I am not making any promises to anyone about anything. I'm tired of letting people down.

"If it makes you feel any better, I doubt I would even have the nerve to go through with anything like that."

"It doesn't," said the weepy woman. "It just makes me so sad that you are this unhappy."

"I'm sure it will be fine. Just fine," said David as the old woman dabbed her eyes with the napkin.

"Let's just put this nonsense aside and enjoy this... feast... before it gets cold, Mom."

"I love you, Davey. We're all that's left of our little family. We had some great times, didn't we?"

They continued to chat and reminisce, but Ellie could no longer hear what they were saying as the mother and son began to fade, as did the room around them.

"That's hardly the same David Burke I know," said Ellie softly. "He seems very down. I do hope he does not take matters into his own hands. You know... the sleeping pills."

"Spirit, tell me, will..." Ellie had turned to her right to ask the ghost about David's fate, but the specter was not there.

"You've certainly impacted a lot of lives," uttered the ghost, suddenly appearing at Ellie's left, confounding her, though Ellie made no outward expression of surprise.

"It was just business..."

"Ha! That is what you all say! I hope somehow this thought sticks with you — it is never just business. It is never just business!

"Are you doing what you love to do?" the spirit paused her tirade to inquire.

"I don't know. I guess. I don't see how that…"

"Most people hate their jobs. Makes them miserable their whole lives. They can't do what they love. So they do something else. Like go to work for the likes of you. Mostly you get employees who can't do what they love, but that doesn't mean you can't make it easy for them to love what they do.

"By all accounts, this man was such a boss. His company was doing well. His employees were happy and productive. You changed all that when you stole his business out from under him."

"If I hadn't done it, some other shrewd entrepreneur would have. You don't understand. He'd still be in this situation, only by someone else's hand. Though I must say, I could not have foreseen his losing his family, his house, and his confidence. David is a smart man. I assumed he would land on his feet."

"Did you assume that?" asked the spirit somewhat angrily. "Did you assume anything? Did you consider anything? Or did you just see the opportunity and take it without weighing ramifications? You people who say it is just business… well, I meet a lot of you."

"That is not fair! I certainly did not intend for that man to lose his family!" Ellie protested. Then, pausing for a moment and trying to suppress a strong surge of emotion rising up within her, she continued. "I know about losing your family. And I would not do that to someone.

"Spirit, I know you know my future, but do you know my past?"

Ellie had now begun to cry. The Ghost of Christmas Yet to Come looked at her curiously.

"I never had a family. I… I think if I had, maybe I wouldn't be like I am, like I have been."

Ellie was embarrassed to have lost control of her emotions in front of this spirit but thought she could perhaps play it to her advantage. She lowered her head and stared down at her feet, awaiting some word of comfort from the ghost. When none came, Ellie raised her eyes and met the specter's gaze.

"Waaa! Waaa! Waaa!" mocked the ghost. "I told you not to look for mercy from me. '*I never had a family, boo hoo,*'" jeered the phantom, to Ellie's disbelief and horror.

"I don't want your mercy!" insisted Ellie. "But I am trying to tell you that I know the way I am, and back when I used to think about things — very long ago until tonight — I often wondered maybe if I had had a family, I wouldn't be this way."

"All right! Enough!" yelled the ghost, briefly covering her ears to block Ellie's whiny excuses. "I'm not your therapist! You did not have a family. Blah, blah, blah. So, make your own family!"

"Make your own family," the ghost repeated.

"Well, I hardly think…" began Ellie. "It's too late for that for me."

"How do you know that? Have you been given some divine guidance about how long your earthly existence will span? And even if you had only one day to live, if you could better yourself and improve your state without hurting anyone else, why wouldn't you do it?

"You are among the most frustrating creatures I have ever encountered! And I am done with you," said the ghost emphatically. Then she turned to walk away.

"Wait. What? You can't leave me here. The room is practically gone, and I'll be alone in the dark. At least send me home!" Ellie implored frantically.

"I didn't say you were done," replied the specter, turning back toward Ellie. "I said I am done with you!"

"What does that mean?" asked Ellie incredulously.

"Walk ahead a little way. You will come to a place that is one year later than the scenes I have just shown you."

"How will I know it?"

"You'll know it."

"And then?"

"It depends. A light may appear off in the distance, and you will just need to walk to it, and you will find your way back to your time, to your house, to your bed, where you will wake up in the morning, and this will all seem like a dream.

"But it is also possible that you will stumble around in this blackness for what could feel like years, but will be only minutes in your world. No one will know you're gone.

Or something else altogether. It's always different, really."

The thought of wandering in the dark for years horrified Ellie. She was unsure if there were some criteria she would need to meet to find the light, but she was determined to enlist all the powers of observation she had developed over the years. She would try to let down the defenses she had spent a lifetime erecting so that she might absorb the lessons the three spirits had intended for her. Lessons which, she had to admit to herself, up to now had eluded her comprehension.

The Ghost of Christmas Yet to Come reached out her sinewy arm and pointed. Though the spirit said not a word, Ellie understood that she was to move forward in that direction. As the last of the glow from the tiny cinders that comprised the apartment faded to blackness, the spirit vanished into it.

The same could be said of Ellie. She put her hand in front of her face but could not see it. She had to touch her nose and lips just to assure herself that she was still there. That she was still flesh and bones.

Ellie took only a few steps before she sensed a change to the surface on which she was traversing. She had literally been walking on air but could now feel something uneven and spongy under her feet.

She also felt something else. A chill. Until this moment, she had not been conscious of any climate at all while she was in this place. She interpreted the temperature fluctuation as evidence that the Ghost of Christmas Yet to Come had indeed abandoned her. The specter was not observing her from the wings, ready to swoop in and deliver a surprise reproach. She had said she was done with her, and now Ellie knew she had meant that.

The air now became even colder as Ellie was walking into frigid gusts. She could feel icy, wet drops hitting her face and hands. "Sleet?" she asked out loud to no one. She still could not see anything, but having lived in Pennsylvania all of her life, she was familiar enough with the sensation of being pelted with icy shards to know sleet when it hit her.

Similarly, she knew the feel of snow under her feet. She squatted and reached down with her hand. She could tell that a dusting had fallen because her fingertips first brushed the tips of blades of grass rising out of the accumulation. She was like a giant reaching down into the fog, but first encountering skyscrapers and church steeples.

As Ellie walked on, the precipitation subsided, but a bitter gale whipped around her. A cardigan served as Ellie's only protection from the elements, and it proved to be woefully insufficient. Her eyes watered and formed crystals on her lashes, which she had to wipe away repeatedly. Her blue lips concealed teeth that were like rows of masons who had inadvertently set their feet in cement and were now wriggling side by side to free themselves, knocking into each other in the futile process.

Her cheeks burned, the tops of her bright red ears felt as if they were pinched in binder clips, like the ones she used in the office to keep all of her eviction notices together. Ellie kept her head down, pulled her cardigan around her as tight as she could, and crossed her arms in front of her chest as additional, yet ineffective, efforts to fend off the blustery blast.

Ellie could hear the crunching of her shoes upon the snowy, frozen turf and could see her own trudging footsteps making lasting impressions on its frosty canvas. She noticed a wet, glistening gold and red heart-shaped leaf that had attached itself to her shoe. As she instinctively bent down to pluck it and toss it aside, it dawned on her. Light! She could see! There was light!

Ellie had been so lost in her thoughts and in trying not to freeze to death that she had not been conscious of the murky, milky irides-cence, courtesy of faint moonlight from behind thick clouds over-head. Under normal circumstances, Ellie would have nonetheless removed that leaf from her shoe before continuing on, but at this moment, it was a beacon of hope, her good luck charm, and she hoped it would stay with her for the duration of this journey. "That little leaf is my only worldly companion," Ellie thought. She decided to leave it where it had attached itself, and it would be her barometer. When it was gone, she'd know her luck had run out.

The moon glow had confirmed what she had deduced in the darkness; she was walking on snow-covered grass. She could also now make out that there were large trees around her, spaced far apart, and there were benches under several of them. Was she in a park? she asked herself. She looked around for other clues to her whereabouts or for any familiar landmarks. The scant lunar illumination had a filmy, foggy quality that made it difficult to distinguish objects. The blur reminded her of when she would sit in her little chair in front of the steamed-up window waiting for her dad to get home from work. She wished she could just wipe this haziness away to behold his car headlights turning up the driveway.

But she knew that was not going to happen.

Ellie remembered the spirit's words: *"No. You can't change things in the past. Just like you can't alter the future until you get there. The only time you can change your life is in your present, in each moment. That's it."*

"That's it," said Ellie out loud.

She looked up, as to the heavens, just as the clouds parted enough to let a moonbeam slip through and shine down on a small patch of earth just ahead of her. Ellie walked apprehensively toward the area. Despair rose up in her as she saw that the brighter spot resembled a recently filled grave. There was a small mound still visible rising out of the otherwise flat ground.

Despair had turned to dread, which was now pushing up at the back of Ellie's throat, trying to force its way out as a scream. It was driven there by her increasing certainty that she was approaching a place where a dead person had been not long ago laid to rest.

Ellie hadn't attended her father's burial service. She had never visited a funeral home. Not once in her life had she been present at, or even invited to, a memorial service. She had never seen a dead body, nor ever been in the same room as one. Ellie had never stepped foot, "Oh God, no," in a cemetery.

So, the thought of being alone, here, under the weird and watchful lunar eye, with a solitary grave, petrified Ellie to the core. She had already been shivering because of the chill. Now she was trembling from fright. She looked up again, appealing for the courage to move her terrorized limbs, this time witnessing the clouds pull apart completely, acquiescing to the moon to light the whole scene.

Ellie heard ferocious rumbling, like rocks being knocked together and crushed, as the earth quaked violently under her feet. She screamed as gravestones and tombstones and monuments shot out of the ground all around her. Ellie tried to run, but as she turned to do so, a large headstone sprung up just behind her, knocking her forward, causing her to lose her balance and fall onto the fresh grave to which the moon ray had been directing her. Ellie rolled over quickly, off the mound and onto the snowy grass.

She lay there for a brief while, screaming on the inside, trying to will herself to get up. In the brief moment she had been on the hump of displaced dirt, she had noticed a small marker set in the ground at the head of the grave. It was covered with the fallen snow. She intuitively knew that if this night was ever going to end, if she were going to avoid wandering around wherever she was for what would feel like years, this moment would have to culminate with her coming face-to-face with the name on that plaque.

She also knew there was a strong likelihood that the name would be her own: Eleanora Printh. She knew that coming to grips with one's own mortality could be a life-changing experience, and wasn't that why she was there in the first place, for just that kind of trans-formation? All else had failed. This was going to be the ghosts' last-ditch effort.

As certain as Ellie was, she knew nothing could prepare a person for seeing her own name on a grave marker, so she did not discount the ploy. The trepidation and palpable anxiety that were causing her to shudder violently were proof that Ellie had no idea, even though she was sure what was about to happen, the effect it would have on her.

Ellie got to her knees and grabbed the headstone of the grave onto which she had rolled and pulled herself up. She had never touched a headstone before. It was smooth on its front and rough on its side, but it was cold all over. Just like death, Ellie imagined.

Frozen, depleted, tormented, and terrified, Ellie shuffled toward the head of the muddy mound. She placed her toe at the edge of the tiny marker. She intended to clear the snow away by sliding her foot across it. She slipped on the slick, wet grass and nearly fell with her first pass, missing the marker altogether. Ellie righted herself and repositioned her foot. She looked away and scraped the sole of her shoe deliberately across the stone, clearing the obscuring rime.

Standing just over the marker, she stared off over the sea of graves. She was shaking so uncontrollably, the many headstones looked like hundreds of buoys bobbing up and down on a turbulent black sea. Her heart — Bernice's heart — was pounding its fists inside Ellie's chest, screaming for her to let it out! Ellie took a deep breath. She held it for as long as she could and released it. "Puh!" Then she turned her head back toward the mound and looked down at the name on the icy stone.

"Oh, no!" Ellie cried. "No! No! No! No!" she screamed from someplace deep inside. Her wails went up, up with the wind into the frosted branches of the mourning trees, compelling them to bow and weep upon the plaintive sight.

Ellie, stricken, backed away from the grave in grief and horror, while her eyes remained fixed on the name on the marker. As she continued to withdraw, both her hands over her open mouth, she slipped again. This time there was no chance of righting herself. Her feet sailed out from under, propelling her backward, high into the air with great force. Ellie twisted and contorted, trying to manage her fall, but the back of her head struck first against the solid, coarse leg of a concrete bench.

Ellie was stunned. Her eyes opened and closed and opened again, involuntarily. She stared up at the moon, then out over what she could see of the cemetery. The black sea was now calm. She felt the sickly sensation of being tugged and pulled into the frozen earth. In her mind, she was frantically searching and reaching for anything, or anyone, to grab onto to keep her from being engulfed by dirt and rocks and roots and worms.

Finding nothing, feeling nothing, she decided to let go.

Ellie Printh closed her eyes and disappeared into the blackness.

STAVE 5: THE END OF IT

The light first appeared as a slight and bleary sliver. Then came a burst of intolerable brightness. Then the light disappeared altogether, and then it returned again, flickering in a gossamer beyond. This succession continued for several moments as Ellie struggled to comprehend it and compel her beaten and battered being to move toward it.

Meanwhile, she could hear a muffled murmur, like from an old loudspeaker off in the distance. It sounded as if someone was saying, "Help me. Help me."

The voice grew closer and more discernible, "Ellie, help me."

And then more intelligible still, "Ellie. Ellie?"

"Ellie, can you hear me? Ms. Printh?"

Ellie, who had started crawling her way toward the glow, into consciousness, had been finding it difficult to lift the garage doors that had evidently been installed in place of her eyelids. But now, hearing her name and discerning it spoken in what at least sounded like a regular, mortal voice, Ellie threw them open and stared up at pure, clean, clear light from above.

"Ah, there she is," said someone, still unseen. "Do you know where you are?" asked the pleasant, and more importantly to Ellie, earthly voice.

"No," she replied, still somewhat disoriented. "Where am I?"

"You're in Chestnut Hill Hospital. One of our doctors found you unconscious just outside, in front of the building. Apparently, you had a rather nasty fall and banged your head against the bench. You're lucky he went outside when he did. You could have frozen to death."

"Yes. Yes. I guess I was lucky," repeated Ellie, feeling the back of her head for blood or a bump.

"Is there anyone you would like us to call?" the nurse inquired.

"No. There's no one."

The nurse flipped back a page on the clipboard, scanning it for some piece of information.

"Not Claire?" asked the nurse.

The mention of the name sliced through Ellie's daze and cleared away the fog completely. "What? Who?"

"It says here, when they brought you in, you were murmuring the name Claire over and over again. I just thought…"

Ellie closed her eyes. Suddenly, she was back in the cemetery, falling face-first on the dirt mound and espying the snow-covered grave marker. She touched the slick, coarse, cold granite of the headstone she had used to pull herself up, felt her foot slide briefly out from under her as she first tried to wipe the snow clear from the stone. She read, again, in shock and grief the poor girl's name there, and re-experienced the sensation of flying backward and upward into the moonlit night as her feet, as well as the world as she had known it, went out from under her.

Ellie grabbed at the back of her head, expecting this flashback to reprise the impact.

"Are you all right?" asked the nurse with concern, reading the discomfort and anguish on Ellie's face.

"Right as rain," replied Ellie, and she meant it.

"Do you recall what happened?" asked the Rubenesque nurse in blue scrubs, writing something on a clipboard.

"No. No, I don't," Ellie lied. Then she asked, "What's today?"

"Why," said the nurse, "it's Christmas Day. Almost anyway. It's almost four a.m. You were unconscious for over an hour."

"All well and good. I only asked for the day, but you gave me the time as well. Thank you. Now, I need to get out of here," Ellie informed the nurse.

"You're not going anywhere, Ms. Printh. We're going to keep you overnight for observation. You appear to have avoided any serious head trauma, but yours is a very curious case. When we found you, you had a bump on the back of your head the size of a softball. Now it is completely gone. There's no bruising, nothing. The hematoma had to go somewhere, but it is completely gone. The doctor is waiting for results from your CT scan."

"Well, if the doctor is waiting for them, I see no reason why I must be similarly inconvenienced and detained. I feel perfectly fine, and I will be leaving now."

"Let her go," said an older woman in a white lab coat entering the room. "I have had many dealings with Ellie Printh here — hello, Ms. Printh — and I know we would have to break both her legs to keep her here, and since that is in direct opposition to the Hippocratic oath, there's nothing we are going to say or do if she has her mind set on leaving. Just have her sign a waiver."

"Thank you, Dr. Khatri," said Ellie. "I, I do appreciate," she said haltingly, "all of the care you and this nurse, Margaret I believe, have given me tonight. It's just that I am feeling great, actually, and I have some important business to attend to."

She offered these words so earnestly and sweetly that Dr. Khatri, who had determined the injury was a routine bump on the head, and who had ordered the CT scan as a mere precaution, was now given cause for concern by Ellie's sudden change in disposition.

"That's very kind, but Ms. Printh, if the CT scan shows any major problems, I will send an ambulance and EMTs to your home with a straight jacket if necessary to retrieve you. Understood?"

Within ten minutes, Ellie had signed the waiver and was discharged with instructions to return if she experienced nausea or blurred vision. But Ellie had not been listening. She had other things on her mind.

On her way out of the hospital, Ellie walked through the waiting room where she assumed David and his son, his estranged wife, and Dr. Jack would be later that night. She looked through the window at the bench where the paternal Ghost of Christmas Present had left her, the same bench where she was quite sure she had not hit her head. This time exiting the hospital, she went through the automatic doors and stepped outside into the brisk, still, dark Christmas morning.

The hospital was a few blocks from Ellie's home. She walked the distance briskly and purposefully. On her way, she passed a residence that, despite the hour, was still lit up brightly. She recognized it as the house of the proud little girl who had beamed as brilliantly as the nose on the lawn ornament Rudolph when she told Ellie her daddy had decorated it for her. In this pre-dawn hour of a new Christmas Day, Ellie paused and looked at the display in a different light.

"Not atrocious, at all," she thought. "Why, it's quite tolerable, really. No, beautiful."

She could have admired the twinkling decorations until sun-up, but Ellie had been forming a very long to-do list while on her walk. Also, she was frozen to the core.

When Ellie got to her driveway, the gate was open, but she paused and took a look at the lion's head on the bars. She touched its mane as if she was pinching its cheek.

Ellie hurried inside the house and when the door closed behind her, what she first noticed was her home's emptiness, not in material things like furniture and electronics and art and so on. There was plenty of that. But empty like an unfulfilled promise or a broken vow.

She turned and took a quick look at herself in the mirror.

"Ugh! You look a fright!" she told herself. And she was right. She was dirty, muddy, grassy, disheveled, bleary-eyed, and weary.

She had created an agenda and itinerary in her head and a

precise order and timetable for accomplishing each item. But she had already begun wavering a bit on whether these plans were a prudent strategy or the product of a long, sleepless, emotional, preternatural night.

She went to her bedroom and sat down at her vanity, intending to rest momentarily before deciding on a course of action or inaction. As she stared at herself in the mirror, Ellie's rational reflection began a logical closing argument for inaction.

"Ladies and gentlemen of the jury... surely no one would deny the unusual series of events that my client here appears to have endured over the past several hours. Certainly, the memories that have been evoked, and the visions that have been conjured up are sufficient to inspire reckless conniving in any person. But let us not forget that what my client believes she experienced is a fantastical, extraordinary, yes, admittedly life-like, but fictional journey through time and space. In fact, the very premise of her ordeal derives from a work of fiction. One must only thumb through *A Christmas Carol*, a book referenced earlier in the night by my client's assistant, to find the inspiration for this delirious delusion, this heightened hallucination.

"Have we so soon forgotten? My client was, less than an hour ago, released from the hospital. The nurse testified that my client was found unconscious, that she had been out cold for some time, that she had had a big bump on the head, and that, inexplicably, it is now gone. Where did it go? Perhaps the blood has drained into the brain, and it is continuing to cause poor decision making and warped reality.

"I submit to the jury that what my client supposes she experienced this night was merely the result of a good old-fashioned knock on the head and an ensuing stupor. She is Dorothy in Oz. I submit that if my client is permitted to lie down and rest for a couple of hours and spend the day engaged in matters of business and gain, she will concur that her story is the stuff of dreams, bad dreams. Yes, let her go to bed and sleep away those dreams."

Ellie listened to the argument in the dual roles of defendant and jury. There was no opposing counsel, so Ellie had to judge the case on the merits presented. A strong case had been made for inaction.

On the other hand, Ellie knew what she saw, what she felt, what she experienced. Ellie believed that if she could allow herself to trust that a person she had never met, but whose heart was beating in her chest, had implored the three ghosts of Christmas to make her this year's reclamation project, and if she could honestly accept without a doubt that this sensational venture, this painful, beautiful journey, had really come to pass, and was not just a concussion-induced invention, then she could and would enthusiastically embark on the implausible, irrational, illogical machinations she developed on her way home from the hospital.

At the end of Ellie's deliberation, she determined, siding with the attorney in the mirror, that a couple of hours of uninterrupted sleep might be conducive to judging which reality she had just endured.

Resigned now to crawling into bed, Ellie bent over to take off her loafers. There, on the top of her left shoe, was a small, still wet, red and gold heart-shaped leaf. The leaf from nowhere. The leaf that had clung to her through space and time.

"Dorothy in Oz, my ass!" she cried, reaching down and carefully pealing the little leaf off her shoe. "It happened! It was all real! I've got things to do!"

Ellie pressed the leaf to her lips and placed it carefully on the vanity.

There was now urgency and deliberateness in Ellie's actions. There were a number of arrangements she would have to make, places she would need to visit, and contrivances she would need to devise. And time was of the essence.

She grabbed a quick, hot shower and threw on a new but similar outfit. She did not bother to fuss with her hair, and her locks crawled up into the softest of curls that bounced jubilantly on her head.

Ellie pulled on her coat, snatched her keys and wallet, and was out the door within minutes of kissing that leaf.

At the top of Ellie's list this pre-dawn morning was the selection of a Christmas tree and decorations to adorn it. She knew where she was going for that Douglas Fir. It would be a little more than an hour's drive to Lancaster County. Because of her love of Christmas trees, Ellie had long been aware of many places to get fresh trees, but she had never once even considered visiting any of them.

Ellie knew that because it was Christmas morning and she would arrive well before seven a.m., she would have to use some of that Ellie Printh assertiveness to get what she wanted and be back on the road as quickly as possible.

She arrived at Olivia Farms before there was even an orange hint of a sunrise. Leaving the Volvo station wagon's engine running with its lights on, she marched right up to the residence and rang the doorbell, then knocked, then rang the bell three times more. She would have continued ringing and knocking, but a light came on, and she could hear cursing from within.

Suddenly, the door flew open, and an old man and shotgun appeared.

"This better be good, lady! This ain't no dairy farm! My roosters ain't even up yet."

"Well, it's like this. I was passing by and realized I don't have a tree, and I saw your sign. And, uh, what luck, yes?"

"No!"

"Who is it, Herb? What's going on?"

Herb's wife now appeared with her own shotgun.

"This lady wants a tree," he explained.

"You must be Olivia," Ellie ventured.

"Not even close! Olivia was the daughter of the previous owner of this god-forsaken money pit."

"Oh, I see."

"They saw us comin', I'll tell ya. Two retirees wantin' to move to the country and run a quaint Christmas tree farm! Huh! This one had 'sucker' written all over him," she said, swinging her shotgun in her husband's direction as if it were a third thumb.

"We sunk our whole retirement into this place," the lady of the house continued. "This one's lifelong dream." Now she was pointing the shotgun squarely at him.

Ellie envisioned the old woman blowing her better half dead away, closing the door, turning out the porch light, and stomping back to bed. Ellie thought, "Then where would I get my tree?" And of that, she concluded, "Clearly, any transformation at work in me is not complete."

"It's a nightmare. If we lived in the city, I wouldn't be standing here at 6:15 a.m. in my nightgown talking with a crazy stranger, now would I?"

"Aww, can it, would ya, Millie. This lady isn't interested in your whining. Go back to bed, and I'll handle this."

The woman turned and trudged away without another word.

"So, I'm getting a tree?" Ellie asked excitedly.

"You're lucky you woke Millie along with me. If I go back to bed now, I'll have to listen to her go on and on again about how we'll have to be buried in this financial sinkhole. I'll get my boots."

"I will be needing tree decorations, too."

"Jee-zus, lady! Nothing like waiting 'til the last minute. I'll open the store. I hope you brought cash."

"Oh, I did."

Herb tied the tree to the top of the car for Ellie, who practically bought out what was left of the rustic but charming little Christmas store in one of the barns on the property. She paid Herb in large bills with a tip that made his eyes widen, and then she drove off into what would soon be a sunrise.

Ellie was a little behind her schedule. She had aimed to be at her next destination before dawn. She had known that was an unrealistic expectation, but the way time and space had been bent and twisted all night, she had still held out that aspiration.

She arrived at the home of David Burke slightly after sun-up, still early enough to hope that she could catch him before his children were awake. This would likely be her only window of opportunity to talk with him without interfering with his Christmas.

Ellie noticed that David had at least made some middling effort to adorn his house for the holiday. There was a wreath on the door. Silver garland was wound around the lamp post, leading to the lantern on top in which the typical white candelabra lights had been replaced with green and red bulbs. Ellie presumed this was a change made for the Christmas season and perhaps as a weak substitute for stringing lights.

The object that darkened these holiday embellishments was the "For Sale" sign on the front yard. Though only about four feet high, it cast a shadow over the entire home.

Now here was Ellie on David Burke's front porch with the sun just slightly above the horizon. She had seen lights on in the house's first-floor window when she drove up and hoped that was a sign that David was already awake and downstairs. She was dually hopeful that visions of sugar plums (or whatever that line was) were still dancing in his kids' heads.

Ellie paused momentarily while trying to decide whether to take a peek into what she assumed to be the living room window or just knock and take her chances. She chose the former. She scooted behind a cushioned love seat glider on which were displayed holi-day-themed accent pillows and a galvanized steel bucket with a Coca Cola Santa Claus painted on it. Inside the bucket were some pine branches and some red and silver Christmas balls.

As she squeezed and maneuvered herself between the house and the back of the glider, Ellie looked like Spider-Man scaling a building with her arms and legs akimbo as she stretched and leaned her torso to position herself to get a look in the window without being detected.

The first thing she saw was a decorated, unlit tree with some wrapped presents under it. It appeared that the kids must still be asleep. She observed three or four empty tree ornament boxes and one that was as yet unopened. There was a bag of silver tinsel on the floor next to it.

She extended a little further so she could see more of the room. Her eyes moved right to left across the scene. On one end of the couch was wrapping paper and ribbons in a heap on the cushion.

Next, there was a mound of empty shopping bags, Amazon boxes, and packaging.

Sprawled out next to all of that and fast asleep with a "World's Best Boss" coffee mug dangling from his hand was a man who had apparently been so exhausted that caffeine had had no inspiring effect on him.

"There's David. And he's alone," Ellie said out loud in a whisper, as if she was a police officer, letting her partner know what she had found.

Ellie quietly eased her way out from behind the love seat, brushed herself off, straightened her sweater, straightened her spine, straightened her mind, and proceeded to the front door.

She rapped lightly. Even through the hard, thick wooden door, she heard the "thunk" of a ceramic mug hitting the carpeted floor.

She heard David ask his Lord and Savior, "What time is it?"

To make sure David knew the knock was not part of a dream, she applied her knuckles to the door quickly and softly three more times, wanting to wake him and no one else in the house.

She heard David call upon the Lord again, then heard footsteps approaching.

When David opened the door and saw Ellie on the other side of it, his immediate inclination was to slam it shut it on her.

Ellie read his mind. "Don't!" she interjected. "Please. I just need a minute."

David was still disposed to close it, but he observed an uncharacteristic softness in her face and a pleading in her eyes that made him curious about his early Christmas morning visitor. And had she just said, "Please"?

"Let me guess," started David. "You just stopped by to let me know that you bought my house, and you're giving me an hour to get my things and my children off your property?"

"Right you are!" said Ellie. Then quickly placing her foot next to the door frame to thwart any effort on David's part to leave her chilling on the porch, she added with haste, "No. No. I was kidding."

She then realized that was the first time she had ever had to utter that disclosure.

"May I come in for a minute?"

David stepped aside.

Ellie entered the living room. It looked as if a freak Christmas tornado had hit after passing through Macy's Santa Land, picking up wrapping paper, bows, and ribbons along the way and depositing them all on this man's floor.

David could read what Ellie was thinking and explained, "I was working late last night, and I still hadn't put up the tree or wrapped presents. I'm pretty much done. I just need to clean up before the kids wake up. So, if you could get on with telling me why Ms. Ellie Printh is standing in my living room on Christmas morning, I would appreciate it!

"Wait, let me guess again! You're actually Santa Claus, and you came to give me back my company."

Ellie laughed heartily at this remark, and though it hardly came out as "Ho ho ho," it was a cheerful sound.

David was taken aback. He had never seen Ellie Printh smile, let alone laugh. He assumed that if he had, it would have sounded more like "Bwah ha ha ha ha!"

When Ellie composed herself, she said, placing her hand on his shoulder, "David, I can't give you your company back. I acquired it honestly and legally, though you might say ruthlessly. You lost it because you are a trusting soul who takes people at their word. And that just doesn't work in the business world, especially when there are people like me around who will make you pay dearly for your guilelessness."

Ellie turned and walked to the tree. She searched around the base, and then spying what she had been looking for, she knelt and picked up the plug and placed it in the outlet, illuminating the tree.

David was dumbstruck by the act.

She stood again and admired the twinkling lights and their reflections in the colored glass balls.

"My kids will be awake soon," said David, interrupting Ellie's reverie.

Ellie turned back toward him.

"You must be a good dad to put up this tree for your kids, I mean, given the year you've had. Looks like you were up all night decorating for their Christmas and wrapping presents."

"Thanks. Despite it all, I am trying," replied David. "What do you want? What are you doing here?"

"David, as I was saying, I can't give you your company back. It doesn't feel right to give you your company back. But what does feel right is to ask you to run mine."

David, stunned and skeptical, did not react immediately. He turned away from Ellie, not wanting her to read the consternation on his brow while considering what to think and then what to say. His head was spinning. He looked over at the couch, half expecting to see himself still sleeping there and dreaming all of this.

Knowing Ellie the way he had, he could reach only one conclusion.

"Okay, I get it. It's not enough that you have ruined me? Now you have to come here on Christmas morning to taunt me? Is that what this is?" asked David angrily, but in a hushed and hurried manner, mindful of his children asleep in their rooms. Everything he knew of Ellie Printh told him her offer was a ruse. And yet…

"David, I know I have given you no reason to believe any of this. But I am sincere in all I have said. It's time for me to step aside. I mean, I'll still own the company, but I'd like you to run it, with my guidance, of course. I have been thinking this morning, maybe I am not doing what I love. I have had success in my career because I am very good at it, not because I love it. Though I do love success!"

"Of course," interjected David if for no other reason than to assure her he was listening intently.

"I'm in the financial position to go do what I love. I imagine most of my employees are not in that same situation. So, we must make every effort to ensure that they at least love what they do. And that has not been possible under my reign of terror. You can fix that.

225

"I also fear that my staying in that role and playing that part will prevent me from being the person I want to be, which is not the same person others expect me to be. And I plan to be occupied with other interests. I promise to stay out of your hair. And I will pay you well.

"So, what do you say? Will you do this?"

Though still astonished by the offer, David saw earnestness and, moreover, humility in a woman in whom he had previously never observed an ounce of either.

"Well, I'm on the verge of being thrown out on the street, so I'm going to say yes. But I'm telling you..."

"Great!" interrupted Ellie as she began wrangling stray wrapping paper from the floor.

"Leave that. I'll get it," said David.

She handed him what she had collected and then said, "Oh, just a couple of things... we can work out the details next week, but I'd like you to start Monday — I assume you don't need to give notice to anyone, so that should not be a problem. I'm giving the whole company tomorrow off, so Monday makes sense, don't you think?"

"You're giving your employees tomorrow... paid?" asked David incredulously.

"Yes, David. Yes, I am. Won't they be thrilled? I can't tell you how wonderful it feels to do that for them. I'm delighted, really!"

"Huh. I can definitely start Monday."

"Another thing, I can't have the president of The Printh Company tending bar as a sideline. You will need to give that up posthaste."

"Not a problem."

"Third, and this is a high priority. As your first order of business, I want you to make inquiries about acquiring this business." Ellie took out a card and handed it to David.

David glanced at the card and then at Ellie. He started to open his mouth.

But Ellie, placing her hand on his forearm, just nodded, "Yes." Then she added, "It's important that we get this done as soon as possible. And I want you to overpay for it. And I want the buildings and the land and anything else that goes along with it."

"I'll have it for you by Tuesday," assured David.

"Good!" chirped Ellie. "Now, let's get this room straightened up and get me out of here before your kids come downstairs."

"May I ask you, Ms. Printh…"

"Call me, Ellie. Please."

"May I ask you… Ellie… why me?"

"Well, David, you're a smart person. Of course, I know smarter people. You're a hard worker. Of course, I know people who are more industrious."

"I guess I better stop you before you talk yourself out of it," interjected David.

"Here's what separates you from everyone else. You trust people. I have always found that people who trust others can be trusted. I don't trust people, and as you well know, I cannot be trusted. I am trying to change that. I need to start by trusting someone. I'm going to trust you. I know you will do what you think is best for the company and for my interests. You are a good person. If there were any doubts in my mind," here Ellie paused and looked wistfully at the tree and around the room, taking in all that this overwhelmed father had done to give his children a happy Christmas, "they have been erased this morning."

The two of them quickly dispensed with the boxes and paper and bows by throwing them down the basement stairs. "I'll deal with that this weekend," said David.

At the sound of feet hitting the floor upstairs, Ellie thanked David and reminded him of his assignment for Monday.

As she got to the door, she turned and said, "David, one quick thing. If you are having snacks later tonight, make sure your son takes extra care with the knife if he is slicing pepperoni. I can't get you on our group plan until Monday."

At that, she winked, turned, and headed to her car.

As David stood watching her leave, he saw her uproot his "For Sale" sign and toss it aside before getting in her car.

From David's house, Ellie drove straight home, but she was only there long enough to unpack the car, haul the tree into the house and set it in the stand. After adding water and standing back to admire it for five seconds, she was again out the door, this time on foot. Ellie wanted to make sure her head was clear, and the brisk walk in the crisp Christmas air would be just the thing. Remarkably, she was back on schedule.

In the charming urban village of Chestnut Hill were any number of shops and restaurants and boutiques owned by dedicated proprietors, many of whom lived in apartments above their businesses. Ellie's company had acquired several of these properties in its takeover of David Burke's firm, thus making Ellie the landlord to these hard-working entrepreneurs, and her shadow an unwelcome darkening of their doorsteps every first of the month.

So, when Nadine Sargsyan looked down from the window of her second-floor residence, atop her Busy Bee Toys and Electronics store, to see who was pounding on her door so eagerly and so early on Christmas morning, she was surprised and angered to discover it was her landlord.

Ellie had stepped back on the sidewalk and looked up at Nadine's window, waving and pointing for her to come downstairs and open the door.

"There had better be a gas leak!" thought Nadine.

In her pajamas and slippers and still carrying her coffee mug, Nadine opened the door to Ellie Printh.

"I'm sure I'm paid up," were the first words out of Nadine's mouth.

"I'm sure you are! I'm sure you are! And anyway, that is not a concern today. Ms. Sargsyan, um, Nadine, could I impose upon you to open your shop for me this morning, right now? I need a few things, and this is a matter of some urgency."

"It's Christmas morning," said Nadine incredulously. "You may not care what day it is, but, among other things, it's a rare day off for me."

"I understand. I apologize. I do," Ellie replied sincerely. "Wal-

Mart is open. I could go there. But I wanted to support a local business. I will make it worth your while."

And Ellie did. She purchased more in the ensuing fifteen minutes than Nadine had sold in the previous two days combined.

Ellie repeated this effort at another shop, then another, and another, and at the grocer. By the time she had left the third store, several merchants could be seen outside milling about in front of their businesses, hoping to catch the eye of Ellie Printh's platinum credit card that glimmered so brightly in the Christmas morning sun. To these dedicated shop owners, bruised and battered from their annual holiday battle with big box stores and online retailers, its brilliance was like the radiance of that star in the night sky over two thousand years ago. Several swore afterward that they could hear a choir of angels when they looked upon it.

But Ellie was on a mission, and that mission had a timetable, and although she had a desire to visit and patronize every one of the loitering merchants, she was not about to deviate from her important itinerary. So most of the proprietors returned to their residences disappointed and, for the time being, continuing to curse the name Ellie Printh.

At each establishment where Ellie had shopped, she had asked the owner to wrap up the items, telling them she would return within a few hours to pick them up, except for one purchase which she kept in her possession.

When she arrived home, she placed that package in her car and drove to a house that, at least to the inhabitant's knowledge, she had never visited before.

Placing the wrapped box under her arm, she walked to the front door. She checked the sun's position in the sky and knew she had only a few minutes to accomplish what she needed to do. She considered the preposterousness of not only this moment but of her entire plan for the day.

Her mind again ran her through all the reasons she should just abandon the whole idea and go lie down, or at the minimum, wait for the CT scan results before making such crucial decisions. But then she recalled the leaf. The heart-shaped leaf.

Ellie rang the doorbell.

Mary Lou and Ben looked at each other. Obviously, neither were expecting anyone this Christmas morning.

"Well, Santa was already here," said Mary Lou, "so I don't know who this could be."

"I don't think he'd be ringing the doorbell anyway," Ben pointed out.

"Oh, my God! Ms. Pr…" cried Mary Lou, as she opened the door to her boss.

Ellie put her fingers to her lips and then sternly motioned for Mary Lou to step outside.

"Ms. Printh!" Mary Lou admonished in a loud whisper, "This is just over the top, even for you!"

"Who is it?" yelled Ben from inside the house.

Ellie shook her head as if to say, "Don't tell him."

"It's Santa Claus! I'll be right back in," Mary Lou yelled to her nephew and partially closed the door. Then turning back to Ellie, she asked, "What's this all about?"

"Well, um, first of all, uh, of course, um, merry, uh, merry Christmas." This was the first time since she was a very little girl that Ellie had extended that greeting to anyone or even spoken those two words together out loud. She loved the way they landed so cheerfully on her ears. She loved how her lungs had especially warmed the air she used to form those words and how they felt in her mouth as she shaped them. And once they were out, she loved how they hung there as a mist in the cool air, like mistletoe suspended from an archway, inclining people to embrace. Most of all, she loved the way they softened Mary Lou's features upon her hearing them.

Ellie loved speaking the phrase so much, she could not help herself from saying it again and again, "Merry Christmas! Merry Christmas! Merry Christmas! Merry Christmas!" She had grabbed Mary Lou's hand at some point in the reprisals and was shaking it vigorously until Mary Lou was finally able to free herself from the grasp to throw her arms around her boss, confounding Ellie long enough for Mary Lou to return the felicitation.

"Merry Christmas, Ms. Printh!"

"You're to call me Ellie. I mean, please, call me Ellie."

"I'll try," said Mary Lou, doubting that would be possible for her, but willing to give it a go.

Ellie had set the package behind her and now pulled it out from behind her back and presented it to Mary Lou.

"I came into possession of this, and I have no need of it, and I thought perhaps your nephew might want it."

"How nice of you! What is it?"

"I believe they call it an Xbox."

Mary Lou's jaw dropped open, and she started to tremble as tears rolled down her cheeks.

"Oh my God! He really wanted this, and I couldn't afford one and, oh, thank you so much!"

Mary Lou hugged Ellie again.

"There's some games included and a gift card. What would I do with something like that? You mentioned when you borrowed the book that you had your nephew, so…"

"That is so kind. Listen, I was just about to make breakfast."

Ellie looked up at the position of the sun again, and then looked back at Mary Lou and said, "Yes, I know."

"Well, would you like to stay?"

"No. But, but thank you."

"I'm going to read more from that book you lent me. Are you sure you won't stay?"

"Quite sure. I have a great deal to do today. But don't tell me how it ends. I do plan to read it someday."

Then Ellie added, pointedly, "Enjoy the quality time with your nephew. Maybe don't give the Xbox to him until after breakfast."

"Well, thanks again. See you tomorrow," said Mary Lou as she turned back to the house.

"Oh, Mary Lou, I know you're frozen, but just two other things, work-related, I'm afraid."

"Yes?"

"Are you able to send a message to all employees today through the same group text we have set up in case of weather or other emergencies?"

"Yes. But, Ms. Printh, um, Ellie, I have to tell you, it's a bad idea to disturb people on Christmas Day with work messages."

"Well, they will want to know this. Please send a text telling them that they are to take tomorrow off as a paid holiday. The Printh Company will be closed tomorrow so they can extend the holiday celebration with their families. Can you do that?"

"I sure can! I most certainly will! Thank you!"

"We will be making Christmas a three-day paid holiday going forward. You don't have to tell them that. But you can mention it to your nephew if you want."

"What? Why would I… "

"Last thing, Mary Lou. Who is on call today for maintenance and emergencies?"

"Pretty sure it is Jimmy Hobbs."

"Oh, good. Widower, no kids or family as I recall. So I probably won't be putting him out today."

Ellie handed Mary Lou a slip of paper. "Could you reach out to him and ask him to meet me at this address at noon today?"

Mary Lou recognized the address. "This is the rental property where the Fielders live. Are you serving them an eviction notice today?" she asked, disappointedly.

"Let's just say that someone will be leaving that house today, and I'm expecting that I may have some trouble with the extraction. Martha Fielder won't be happy, but it is all for the best."

"But, Christmas. Christmas Day, Ms. Printh… Ellie."

"Will you or will you not take care of that for me?"

"I guess so. I'll let Jimmy know to meet you at noon."

"Thank you, now get inside before you catch your death!"

Ellie turned back and caught Mary Lou before she escaped back into the house.

"Oh, Mary Lou! I nearly forgot. Dinner. My place. Six o'clock!"

Ellie added that she could bring her nephew, but she already knew from her earlier "visit" that Mary Lou's sister-in-law would be picking him up at four.

Mary Lou hesitated only a moment and then replied, "Thank you! I'll be there. It will just be me. Thank you, Ms. Printh, I mean, Ellie."

More than four decades had passed since Ellie had walked under a threshold of a house of worship. The last time she set foot in a church was the Christmas she spent with the Poole family, the year after her dad died. Ellie had forgotten most of that day until last night when the Ghost of Christmas Past placed her in that memory from her childhood. Ellie had been of late, revising her estimation of that spirit. Perhaps it was wiser than she had given it credit.

She had sat in the pew at Saint Dunstan's patiently as Monsignor Rymar droned through his sermon. She had sung Christmas carols while crammed in the backseat of a station wagon with the other Poole children on their way home from church. And she had loved that day while living it.

The adult Ellie, though, had felt anger and guilt upon viewing her younger self disregarding the memory of her father so soon after his death — in fact, on the first anniversary of his accident — by laughing and singing in the car with other kids who still had a father.

But now, in her contemplation, a thought occurred to her. Make your own family.

And now Ellie understood that that was all her little self was trying to do. Instinctively, she was just trying to make her own family. And when the Pooles sent her away, that little girl felt so hurt and rejected, she didn't dare to believe she would ever be a part of a family again.

Other foster families Ellie had lived with over the years had invited her to church, but she always declined, and no one ever tried to force her to go. The truth was, she had no desire to go to church. When she was very young, she had attended Sunday school, or as her mother had called it, "a moment's peace." She had gone to kindergarten in the basement of a Presbyterian church. She knew who Jesus was. She knew bible stories. She had sung "Jesus Loves Me, This I Know" at an Easter pageant. Though, over the years, she had arrived at the conclusion that even Jesus didn't want her in his family.

Ellie believed that everything she had accomplished, she had achieved on her own. Why should she credit God for any of her success? In fact, any notion that Jesus was watching over her would have only limited her freedom to maneuver in many of the business dealings that had led to her triumphs against her more God-fearing rivals. She had believed that a conscience was a millstone that ineffective managers wore around their necks. So, even though Ellie had a suppressed fondness for Christmas, manifested in her fascination with the decorated trees, she had never really cared to make the connection between the holiday and its origin.

Today though, was different. As Ellie had laid out her day, with detail and precision, attending Christmas service was set into her schedule like a keystone into an arch. Today, she was thankful. Thankful for her father, even for the brief time they had had together. It was a gift. Thankful for her time with the Pooles. She learned from her short time with them what it meant to be in a family with brothers and sisters and parents and grandparents and aunts and uncles and cousins and nuns and neighbors and friends, and how perfectly imperfect growing up in a family could be.

Ellie could not think back on the Pooles without regretting the years she had let slip away that could have been filled with friendship and sisterhood with dear Patty. Ellie was unsure how to pray for Patty or if her putting in a word on her behalf would be received by the God she had ignored for decades. But it felt like the right place to start, and hopefully, one day she would get up the courage to call her sick friend.

Ellie was also thankful for Bernice, not only for the heart that was beating so strongly in her chest, but also for whatever she did, and whyever she did it, to persuade whoever made the decision to send the three spirits to her this Christmas.

It was a brief ceremony. There was a reading from the Gospel of Luke, a short sermon, a prayer, and a lot of carol singing. Ellie joined in quietly on some verses, but she just enjoyed the voices of the choir and the congregation for the most part.

To say that many of the churchgoers were surprised to see Ellie Printh in their midst would be an understatement. Even though one husband, likely expressing what was on the minds of more than a few people there, murmured to his wife, "She must want to buy the church and turn it into apartments," Ellie was greeted warmly and genuinely by those who mingled outside after the service. She wished a merry Christmas more times that morning than she had in her whole adult life.

Nervousness was starting to work at Ellie as she drove the short distance back to the shops to pick up the packages. The church service was the penultimate item of her master plan. This upcoming last step certainly would be the most significant, unpredictable, and irreversible. Everything she had done this morning up to now could be undone, she thought to herself. She could fire David Burke. She could take back the Xbox from Mary Lou and cancel tomorrow's paid holiday for staff. She could return everything she bought from the stores. She could even go back to the church and ask the pastor to return the money she placed in the collection plate. None of that would be beyond Ellie Printh.

"Well," she said to herself, parking across the street from Busy Bee Toys and Electronics, "None of that would have been beyond Ellie Printh."

Ellie collected the wrapped presents and tipped the merchants generously again, and drove home.

There wasn't time to decorate the tree before taking care of business at the Fielders. But she planned to get to it later, so she set out all of the ornaments and trimmings she had purchased at Olivia's Tree Farm. She realized that she had bought enough to decorate a dozen Christmas trees.

She also set presents under the tree. She thought back to the boxes under her first tree that fateful Christmas morning when the

Harrisons arrived with the puppy. For the first time ever, she was curious about what was in the presents she never opened.

Then she thought back to the gifts the Pooles had cobbled together for her from the other children's piles. And she smiled at the remembrance.

Ellie knew there had been a change in her. She felt at peace with everything that had happened to her in her past. She accepted that she could not change any of it. And she was excited to try to use each moment to change what lay ahead. And that would start with a showdown at the Fielders.

The only blight on her genuine joy and contentment of this Christmas morning was the occasional thought of the depraved Arthur Fielder and his unspeakable, unthinkable intentions. Now she was only about fifteen minutes away from making sure that poor little Claire would never be subjected to the atrocities of that man, not in the present or ever.

Jimmy Hobbs was already milling around outside the Fielders when Ellie pulled up in the Volvo. Given Ellie's reputation, Jimmy certainly had not wanted to be tardy for this assignment. So he set off for the address as soon as he received the text from Mary Lou.

When he saw Ellie pull up, he exited the truck and pulled his toolbox off the bed.

"You won't be needing that, James," said Ellie.

"My mother called me James," returned Jimmy, who then realized to whom he had made that casual reply. "Sorry, Ms. Printh!"

"I'm sure she was a wonderful woman to have raised such a fine son as you. If that was an invitation to call you Jimmy, then I will accept it. Please call me Ellie. And, merry Christmas!"

"Merry Christmas!"

Jimmy was confused. He had never actually met Ellie Printh, but he had indeed heard stories. Lots of stories. And none of them included pleasantries like he had just exchanged.

"I just need you for backup," said Ellie. "Stay close. And, I'm afraid, if there's any trouble, I will need you to intervene."

"No problem," said Jimmy, who fished around in the toolbox he had just placed back on the truck until he pulled out a large, heavy wrench. He held it up to show Ellie.

She nodded approvingly and said, "Let's do this."

Ellie's heart was beating fast and furiously as she walked up the steps. She stopped for a moment to take some deep breaths and give one last reconsideration of whether she really wanted to go through with this. Her head was reluctant. Her heart urged her on.

She climbed the stairs to the porch. Jimmy followed, staying a respectable three paces behind.

When Ellie got to the door, she turned to look at Jimmy, who replied with a thumbs up and a nod of assurance, even though he still had no idea what was going on.

Ellie rang the doorbell.

"You gonna get that, Marthur?"

Ellie could hear the loud but muffled voice through the door.

"It's too early to be my brother," she could hear Martha respond, more and more distinctly as she neared the door.

"So, I wonder who…"

Martha opened the door.

"Oh, my God! Ms. Printh! What are you doing here? Ack! Is this about the rent? You said in your office that my congressman gave me fifteen more days.

"You're not going to throw us out on Christmas Day with a turkey in the oven and my brother and his family coming?" cried Martha through sobs.

"The table's not even set," she added nonsensically.

"Is your husband at home, Mrs. Fielder?" asked Ellie coolly.

The sobs stopped.

"Huh? What?"

"The man you married. Is he inside this structure in which you live, and which I own and lease to you?"

"Whaddya wan' wit Artha?" asked Martha. Intoxicated with incomprehension, she was slurring her words.

"Much. Would you get him and bring him outside? I do not wish to discuss this in the house."

Arthur, who had been lying on the couch and listening to the exchange and hoping not to be pulled into it, appeared without any prompting.

"I'm right here!" said Arthur aggressively. "What do you mean by showing up at my house on Christmas morning?"

"Your house? We must discuss the definition of ownership at a later date."

"If you're here for the rent, I told you in your office yesterday, I don't got it right now," said Martha, sobbing again.

"I haven't come for the rent money, Martha."

Again, the crying stopped.

"Aw, you called me Mar…You haven't come for the rent? Then, what?"

"I've come for the girl."

"What girl?" asked Martha and Arthur simultaneously.

"Your foster child."

"Howdya know Claire?" asked Martha in drunken bewilderment.

"I do not know Claire, but I intend to take her out of this home today, now."

Mr. Fielder pushed past his wife and charged at Ellie, who stood her ground without so much as a change of expression. Jimmy, however, took two disrespectful paces forward.

"You're not taking Claire anywhere!" said Arthur Fielder, waving his finger in Ellie's face.

"I am leaving with her now. Would you please call her, Martha?" asked Ellie, ignoring Mr. Fielder.

"But she's in the middle of a list of chores I gave her. Can this wait until tomorrow?" asked Martha, still befuddled.

"I don't believe the girl is safe here, so it cannot wait another minute," insisted Ellie.

"What do you mean she's not safe here!" screamed Arthur. "She is under my protection. That means she's safe."

Ellie paid no attention to Mr. Fielder's ranting but kept her eyes locked on Mrs. Fielder.

"Martha, I have seen, rather, I should say, I believe you have decency and compassion in you. Though you do not want to accept it, you know what will happen if Claire stays in this house. I know you think you will be able to prevent the unthinkable, but you cannot be everywhere all the time. And I know with absolute certainty you do not want any harm to come to her."

Ellie saw the wave of understanding wash over the woman as if she had been awakened from a trance.

"What the devil is she talking about!" shouted Mr. Fielder, looking to Martha and Jimmy. "The girl stays here!"

"I'll get her," Martha said resignedly.

"Marthur!" screamed Arthur as his wife went back into the house.

Martha ignored him.

Arthur became enraged, making undecipherable guttural sounds and lifting both his fists as if to bring them down on Ellie. Jimmy lunged forward and raised the wrench over his head. Arthur immediately cowered, and his grunts were reduced to whimpers.

"I will be asking the authorities to keep an eye on you. I will also be talking to the foster agency about not placing any girls — or any children for that matter — in your home, 'under your protection.'"

"How dare you!" seethed Arthur through clenched teeth, but still recoiling.

"I know what you are. You may not be yet. But I know what you are if you are left alone to be it. I believe your wife knows it too."

Ellie took a step closer to the horrified man and looked him up and down, and then said, "Now, if I were you, I'd get inside, out of the cold, before your soaked pants freeze to any delicate areas you hope to protect from such indignities."

Arthur looked down and saw the evidence that his jittery bladder had betrayed him. He immediately ran into the house, muttering something that sounded like, "All over my favorite sweats."

Martha appeared at the door with Claire, who already had her coat on as well as mismatched mittens and knitted hat.

"Hello, my dear. I'm Ellie," said Ellie, extending her gloved hand. Claire placed her mittened hand into it and shook politely.

"I'm Claire."

Martha turned Claire around and placed her hands on her shoulders, and said, "You're going to go with Ms. Printh. Ellie that is. Legally, I s'pose, I could stop this. But it is for the best, child."

"I don't understand what is going on," said Claire. "So, I'm not living here anymore? Just like that?"

"I know it's confusing, but I'm sure Ellie will explain everything to you. God bless you, Claire."

At that, Martha gave Claire a hug and turned her back around to Ellie. Though Claire had lived with Martha for close to two years, there was no emotion in this parting. The only tears that were shed belonged to Jimmy, who had now connected all the dots and was moved considerably.

"Wait!" interjected Claire. "What about my stuff? I don't have much, but it's all I've got in the world."

"Well," said Ellie, "if Mrs. Fielder would be so kind as to box them up, I can send Jimmy here, back for them later."

"There's not much," confirmed Martha. "You know, the stipend doesn't stretch that far. I'll pack them up now if your man wants to wait or come back. Shouldn't take but a half hour."

"No problem!" said Jimmy, dabbing his eyes with a handkerchief. "Ms. Printh, you take this young lady on ahead to your house, and I'll drop off her stuff in a little while."

"That your car?" asked Claire, pointing at the silver Volvo wagon in the street.

Before Ellie could respond, Claire darted down the steps and the walkway toward the street. Ellie turned and followed without another word to Jimmy or Martha.

It was a short drive to Ellie's house, and Claire filled the time with rapid-fire questions and comments:

"Is your house far from here?

"I'm sorry, I forget your name?

"Do you have satellite radio in this thing?

"I like your hair. Who does it?

"How do I put this seat back?

"Do you have a hairdryer? Should we go back for mine?

"Never seen this part of town before. Niiiice.

"By the way, I'm going to need some new clothes.

"I think Mr. Fielder watered himself back there. He does that when he's surprised.

"I am so glad to be out of there."

Every time Ellie tried to answer or respond, Claire jumped back in with another observation or query. But as they approached Ellie's neighborhood and the homes became statelier and the stone and iron walls around them made them look like storybook castles, Claire could only manage two more questions during the rest of the trip:

"Are you rich?"

"If you mean, do I have money? Yes, more than enough."

"Can I have an iPhone?"

"Here we are," said Ellie, pulling into the driveway.

"Wow! You live here?"

"Yes. This is my house."

"Are you married?"

"Nope. Just me."

"You live in this big house all alone?"

"Until now."

Claire was the first out of the car and ran to the front door excitedly, like a puppy trying to tell its master it needs to go outside. She looked back for Ellie, who had been trying to keep pace, and was just now joining her on the small porch.

"This is the security panel," explained Ellie, showing Claire how to get in the house. You need to enter the access code for the door to open."

"Can I try?"

"Absolutely! Push 2-7-1-8-1-2. And say 'Open sesame.'"

Claire pushed the buttons and said, "Open sesame."

The door swung open.

"That's lit."

"You don't really need to say 'Open sesame,'" Ellie pointed out.

"Yeah, I knew that. I was just going along with you."

Claire walked in slowly as if she were waiting for the room to unfold in front of her. As she was taking it all in, there was a look of wonder on her face like she was walking into the Magic Kingdom for the first time.

"This place is on fleek!"

"Is that a good thing?"

"Uh, yeah! That means it's fire!"

"Well, good," said Ellie, assuming that meant Claire was pleased with the accommodations.

"Can I see my room?" Claire asked, hopefully. "Doesn't look like I'll have to sleep in a closet here."

"Of course, you can practically have the whole upstairs. My room is down on this floor, just down that hall. I have an office upstairs, but otherwise, you could sleep in a different bedroom every night if you want."

"Nah. I have always wanted my own room... but, well, I mean, how long will I be here?"

Ellie's nervous excitement was creating a tingling feeling in her stomach. That was a sensation she had not experienced for a very long time. In fact, she realized, she had not felt this way since her dad and the Harrisons placed that wobbling, jiggling box down in front of her on that Christmas morning.

The part of her elaborate plan that Ellie could not fully flesh out was when she would have the necessary conversation about her intentions with Claire. Nor had she been able to decide how she would start the discussion or what she would say. She had resolved that she would just recognize the moment when it presented itself and trust that the right words would come to her. She had not expected the moment to arrive so soon.

"Well, we can talk about that right now, if you'd like. Go on in. Make yourself at home."

As Claire went into the living room, she noted the untrimmed tree and the presents underneath it. "You didn't decorate your tree yet?" she asked.

"I was kind of hoping you would help me with that later. Would you?"

"Would I? Yeah! I would love to do that. I've never decorated a Christmas tree before. Mrs. Fielder made me bring the ornaments and lights up from the basement, but I wasn't allowed to put any of them on the tree. She said it was a family tradition, and I wasn't family."

"Well, that leads us right into our conversation. Why don't you sit down there on the couch, Claire. We can discuss our arrangement."

Ellie immediately chastised herself for using such a cold word as "arrangement." She had specifically wanted to avoid her natural inclination to frame every relationship as a business partnership. After that start, she thought, the poor girl probably thinks she is at a disadvantage here, having not brought along her lawyer.

Claire sat down on one end of the couch. Ellie took the other end of the sofa, leaving one cushion between them. Ellie agonized over whether she should have sat closer, but she didn't know, and repositioning herself now would be awkward. So she stayed put.

Ellie had no experience dealing with nine-year old girls. She remembered the Ghost of Christmas Past telling her that she should give the child within her a voice. After years of suppressing and ignoring her, Ellie was now hoping that her inner child would speak up and quick.

Ellie started over, "Claire, I can only imagine what you're thinking and feeling right now. A total stranger shows up at your door on Christmas morning, and the next thing you know, Mrs. Fielder is placing your coat and hat on you and rushing you out the door. You probably didn't even get a chance to say goodbye to the Fielder kids."

"Ugh, those dweebs. Doesn't matter. Am I ever going back there?"

"Do you want to go back there?" asked Ellie, needlessly nervous about the girl's reply.

"No! I hate it there. I am like Cinderella there. That's how I feel. Cinderella with no hope for a ball, no mice helping me, and no fairy godmother! Only, unlike Cinderella, I stand up for myself. Anyway, what I was trying to say is, I do all the work around there while Goober and Gomer and the little princess sit on their butts. And I know I'm never going to get out of there. Mrs. Fielder told me so."

"Had you stayed, you would have learned that a lot of things Mrs. Fielder says are… less than accurate."

"Well, I won't miss the Fielders, but I will miss my friends. Can I have my friends over sometimes?" asked Claire with some trepidation.

"I have no problem with your having friends over. This is your house too. But I will need to meet them and their parents first. Your friends can either help you be more than you were made to be or push you into being less than you were meant to be. They can greatly influence who you are and who you become, so it's crucial that I know your friends. I want to make sure you get every chance to be your own person, your best self."

"So, this is going to be my new foster home?"

For decades, Ellie had closed herself off from all physical contact and eschewed any display of affection or compassion toward any of her fellow human beings. So the fact that what came next happened without a moment's thought, without the slightest hesitation, confirmed, if she had had any doubt at all, that a transformation was working within her.

Ellie slid over onto the empty cushion and took Claire's hands in hers. Claire searched Ellie's face anxiously for some expression that might signal what she was about to say.

"No, this will not be your new foster home," replied Ellie.

The little girl's heart sank.

"I don't think it would be fair to either of us, at your age or at my age, for me to make this your foster home."

"So where will I go?" asked Claire, "How soon?"

"Claire, this won't be your foster home because I want to give you a permanent home. I want to adopt you. Raise you. But it is not just up to me. You must have a say. Would you want that? It would be much different from what you've known. There are no other kids, and there's not going to be. I've never been a parent before, so neither of us knows how that will go, but I imagine that I will run a pretty tight ship. It would just be the two of us. That may sound pretty boring to a young girl. Maybe it isn't enough for you. So what do you think?"

Looking at the confused little girl, it now seemed to Ellie that she had thrown too much at her too quickly.

"Why? Why do you want to do that?" asked Claire. "You don't even know me."

"I don't know you, that's true. But it is also true that I do know you. I was you. I know what you've been dealing with. I want to give you a home, a home like I always wanted when I was your age. You deserve a family. I deserve a family. So, we will be our own family."

"I've never been in a real family before. How would we do that? Doesn't there need to be more of us?" Claire lowered her head. She had been excited to live in this house for a while and have her own room and show the place off to her friends, and this woman seemed nice enough, but Claire also remembered what it was like when it was just her and her mom.

This woman wasn't a user like her mom was. Still, it seemed to Claire, from what she had overheard from Mrs. Fielder, that Ellie worked a lot, and no matter what the addiction, to Claire, it still meant putting herself to bed most nights, getting herself up and ready for school on days she bothered to go, and three or four nights a week of Easy Mac for dinner. As much as she detested her time with the Fielders, there was some comfort in hearing other voices in the house at any hour of the day and having to wait for a bathroom.

"More of us? There doesn't need to be." answered Ellie, "But you know, Claire, ever since I woke up this morning, a thought has been circling around in my head: 'Make your own family.'

"So, I've been thinking, the two of us will just make our own family. When we come across people we like, and who are good to us, who we find interesting, and who we enjoy, we will add them to our family. They won't live with us, of course, but we will keep them close and make them part of our lives. We will collect 'family' as we roll along. We will be like a snowball. And I left my job this morning, so we will have plenty of time to discover new family members!"

Claire's head remained down, and she did not say a word.

Ellie was heartbroken in the silence. In her haste to pull off this complex operation, she did not consider that all nine-year old girls are not the same. Whereas Ellie, all those years ago, had been delighted by the reality of a family that included just her and her dad, Claire probably wanted two parents and brothers and sisters to play with. "After all," she thought, "why would she want to live alone with a fifty-three-year old woman? What was I thinking?"

Ellie had already started forming a plan B. She would personally oversee finding Claire an excellent foster home, a family like the Pooles, where Claire could have brothers and sisters and live in a nice neighborhood with lots of kids. It was settled then, and Ellie was about to tell Claire that right now, to unburden the poor child, when she saw a drop hit the cushion of the couch, and then another.

"Claire?"

The little girl raised her head, tears now streaming down her face.

"Claire, are you..."

Claire did not let Ellie finish the question. She threw her arms around her and squeezed so hard it forced the air out Ellie's lungs. "Puh!"

Ellie squeezed back, her tears now also staining the couch.

Neither Ellie nor Claire had been really hugged in such a long time; neither was eager to release her hold on the other.

Finally, Ellie asked, "Does this mean you like the idea?"

"Very much! Very much!" declared Claire as she released her embrace and wiped her eyes.

"Funny thing is, I have no tissues in this house to offer you. I have a feeling I should probably keep a supply of Kleenex on hand from now on." Ellie was drying her eyes with the sleeve of her sweater.

"How about I give you a tour of your new home and let you pick your room, and then I'll make us some hot cocoa, and we'll get started on that tree?"

Included in Ellie's shopping spree that morning were whole milk, Hershey's syrup, mini-marshmallows, and whipped cream. And while Claire remained upstairs, trying the beds and deciding which view she preferred, Ellie got started on the hot chocolate.

After Claire had made her choice, she joined Ellie in front of the tree. The two Christmas tree decorating novices sipped their hot cocoa from big ceramic mugs, personalized with their names on them (a presumptuous Christmas morning purchase). At the same time, they wrapped the tree in thousands of lights and placed enough ornaments on it to obscure every branch.

When they were all finished, Claire asked hopefully, "Who are the presents for?"

"Oh, Santa must have known you were coming and…"

"That's okay," Claire interrupted. "You don't have to do that. Kitty Fielder told me."

"Nonsense! Santa comes to this house. They are all for you. Go ahead. Open them!"

Claire did not have to be told twice. Though she had as little experience opening a wrapped gift as she had decorating a tree, this activity came far more naturally to her.

There were some clothes and pajamas — Ellie had guessed at the sizes but had been spot on — and board games and puzzles and a Lite Brite.

"Maybe we can play with that later," suggested Ellie.

They had just finished throwing out the wrapping paper and putting away the extra ornaments when the doorbell rang. It was Jimmy. He carried in two boxes and a small suitcase, the sum total of Claire's worldly possessions.

"That's everything. Sorry it took so long. Mrs. Fielder insisted on finding a box in the basement that had been sent by the foster agency when Claire first moved in with them. She said it's just some baby pictures and stuff.

"Whoa! Your tree looks beautiful!" declared Jimmy, shielding his eyes. "That's a lot of lights and ornaments for one tree! You two have been busy!"

"Thank you!" said Claire. "It's my first time, so I may have gone a little overboard."

"I think it's perfect!" assured Jimmy. "Well, if there's nothing else, I will be going."

"That's all, Jimmy," said Ellie. "Thank you very much, and enjoy the rest of your holiday!"

Jimmy turned to leave.

"Wait!" cried Claire.

Both Jimmy and Ellie were startled by the outburst.

"Would you like to come back and have dinner with us today? You know, if you don't have any other plans," asked Claire.

Ellie looked at Claire, a bit confused at first, and then realized that the girl had already started collecting family. Jimmy was a good person who, through his tears earlier and his praise of the tree, and his manner in general, had shown that he cared about them, and he brought them joy. Ellie was proud of Claire for her astute judgment and her eagerness to invite kind and amicable souls into their family.

"What a wonderful idea!" exclaimed Ellie. "Please?"

"Well, this is unexpected. But I have no plans. I bought a turkey dinner for later. It's a Marie Callender…" The brand seemed to be momentarily weighing into his decision. "But it'll keep. I'd love to!"

"Then it's settled. Come back at six," said Ellie.

Claire helped Ellie in the kitchen as they made their first Christmas feast. Claire had developed some cooking skills from her time in servitude to the Fielders, so she was more practiced in the culinary arts than the head chef she was now assisting.

When Mary Lou arrived, she was surprised to be greeted at the door by a nine-year old girl. When Claire explained who she was and why she was there, Mary Lou cried and hugged her and then found Ellie in the kitchen and hugged her. When Jimmy arrived and told his version of the story, Mary Lou cried and hugged him. And then hugged Claire again and then Ellie too.

Throughout the dinner, Mary Lou had to dry her eyes with her napkin every time she looked at Claire.

The food was delicious, the company divine, the box of wine that Jimmy brought was… thoughtful. Around the table were laughter and goodwill and friendship. Mary Lou and Jimmy shared happy stories of Christmases past. Claire and Ellie, on the other hand, could only enjoy the happy tales and know that their good memories lay ahead.

"Oh, look at the time," said Mary Lou. "I need to be going. I'm watching my nephew again tomorrow. I'd like to practice the Madden football game on the Xbox tonight, so I have a fighting chance!"

"I'll be getting along, too," said Jimmy.

Claire handed them their coats, and Ellie walked their guest to the door.

"Oh, wait!" Mary Lou exclaimed. "I almost forgot. I have a present for you."

She removed a small, flat, wrapped box from her pocket and handed it to Ellie. "Merry Christmas! Open it."

Ellie was caught off guard by the gesture. She had not been given a Christmas present in a very long time. She unwrapped it with great anticipation, lifted the lid from the box, pulled back the tissue paper, and gazed upon an old and familiar envelope.

"Is this…?"

"Yep," confirmed Mary Lou. "You had placed it in the 'shred' basket, but I couldn't bring myself to do it. I thought I'd just hold onto it until… I don't know. It has her contact information. You should call her."

Now it was Ellie's turn to initiate an embrace.

"Thank you! I have thought about calling Patty but didn't know how I was going to find her."

"You should call her tonight just in case you wake up in a different attitude tomorrow."

Jimmy shot Mary Lou a sideways glance.

"What? It could happen," Mary Lou whispered to her new friend.

"Call her. Now," insisted Mary Lou, picking up Ellie's phone from the end table and handing it to her.

MEANWHILE, at the Poole house in Sharpsville, Pennsylvania, Patty had just finished her yearly toast to Ellie.

"Well, Patty," said her sister Paula, "now that you have perpetuated your annual tradition, I'll continue mine and ask, 'What do you hear from Ellie?'"

As Patty started to open her mouth to answer, her cell phone buzzed.

"Hello?

"Oh... my... gosh!" Patty cried excitedly into the phone. Then to Paula, "I have to take this. It's Ellie. I'll let you know what I hear from her when I'm off."

THE TWO FRIENDS could have talked for hours, but Patty had a houseful of party guests to get back to, and Ellie had a little girl who had had a long day and whom she should probably be getting ready for bed. But Ellie and Patty would talk again often and see each other soon. After all, they were family.

After some more tears and hugs, Mary Lou and Jimmy said good night. When the new housemates were alone again, Ellie said, "Let's see what's in these boxes."

She carried the cardboard containers over to the couch and set them down on the floor in front of them. The first box held some toiletries and some knickknacks Claire explained she kept near her "bed" in what the Fielders called a room. Under those items were the Christmas presents Mrs. Fielder had given her earlier in the day, minus the Good & Plenty candy.

The other box had been taped shut, but the strip was so dried and crackly that it came right off when Ellie pulled on it.

Inside this package were a couple of small stuffed chipmunks.

"Chip and Dale!" shrieked Claire. "I wondered what had happened to them." She took them from Ellie and squeezed them close to her.

There was a stack of old crayon drawings obviously created by Claire years ago. She had signed the bottom of her handiwork with the letters of her name all facing off in random directions — except the "i."

Ellie found an 8"x10" baby picture. "What an angel! So adorable!" she said, making a fuss.

"Stop," said Claire, blushing.

Ellie reached the bottom of the box and pulled out a file folder, with some yellowed newspaper extending out of the top.

"Hmmm. What's this?" Ellie asked no one in particular. "Were you ever in the newspaper?"

"Not that I know of."

Ellie pulled out the clipping and, for a moment, could not speak or even breathe.

"W-w-w-why would you have this?" she managed to ask faintly.

Claire leaned over and looked at the newspaper, at the large picture on the page.

"That's my mom!" She pointed. "And that's me when I was like two or something. But who's that holding me?" Claire looked at Ellie and back at the newspaper photograph. "Oh, my God! That's... YOU!"

"Oh, my God! That is you?" cried Ellie. "That IS you!"

"How did you know my mom?"

"I... I... didn't."

"Then why are you in a picture in the newspaper with her, holding me?" the girl asked incredulously.

"Claire. What was your grandmother's name, do you know?"

"Bernice," answered Claire. "I don't remember her, but I remember her name. It's a funny name."

"Claire. I'm in this picture with your mom because your grandmother was an organ donor, and I needed a heart. I had the surgery on Christmas Eve, seven years ago. After I recovered, this newspaper did a story about it."

Ellie then took Claire's hand and placed it on her chest.

"Do you feel that?" How could she not, thought Ellie. "That's your grandmother's heart."

Claire looked at Ellie in amazement.

Ellie thought back to Bernice's ghost's last words to her before being sucked out the door, "The reason will be clear."

"The reason is Claire," Ellie said.

"What?" asked Claire.

"Nothing. Just thinking out loud."

"This doesn't change anything, does it?" Claire asked. "I mean, you seem all weirded out. Personally, I think it's fire."

"No! It most certainly does not change anything. I think it's... fire... too! I mean, if thinking something is 'fire' is a good thing."

"Okay, good."

Claire hugged Ellie again and then said, "Thank you for a really nice Christmas! I can say it was definitely my best yet."

"Me too. The best yet, but it won't be the best ever. Those are to come."

"Is it okay if I head up to my room? Can I keep this?" asked Claire, picking up the newspaper. "I'd like to read the article."

"Sure. I'll be up in a few minutes to make sure you have everything you need."

Claire leaned over and gave Ellie a kiss on her cheek, and then ran up the stairs, excited to go to sleep in her own bed in her own room.

Ellie touched the spot on her cheek where Claire's kiss had

landed. What a difference twenty-four hours had made, if it had been only twenty-four hours. Suddenly, she was exhausted. She wondered how long she had actually gone without sleep.

Ellie looked over at the front door that had blown open the previous evening, announcing Bernice's ghost, and had swung closed on that same spirit after she departed. She recalled the urgency and desperation in her manner at parting. It all made sense now.

"Thank you, Bernice, wherever you are. I get it. None of this was about me. You just needed me in order to save Claire. You clever girl."

Ellie did not wake up with a different attitude the next day, as Mary Lou had feared, or any day after that.

The following week was an eventful one. On Monday, Ellie introduced David Burke as the new president of The Printh Company and then left him to run it. She didn't even bother to go to her office. She called a team meeting, made the announcement, and departed. She then went directly to her lawyer's office to start the adoption proceedings. Ellie would never step foot in the Printh building again.

On Tuesday, David Burke, as he had promised, acquired for Ellie the company that's name was on the card she had handed him on Christmas morning. It was a firm run by a retired couple that wanted out of their struggling Christmas tree farm business. David told Ellie that when he made the handsome offer for Olivia's Tree Farm, the old man's eyes had widened, and the old lady threw her shotgun aside and told her husband that maybe he wasn't such a dumbass after all.

That night, Ellie discussed with Claire the idea of the two of them moving to the country into a farmhouse and selling Christmas trees. Ellie was concerned the girl would not want to have to go to a new school and make new friends. To her delight, Claire responded by throwing her arms around her and saying it would be like a dream come true.

The following day, Dr. Khatri called and explained to Ellie that the fall she had in front of the hospital was a blessing in disguise. The CT scan showed a small aneurysm that, left untreated, may have ruptured at some time in the future, causing traumatic brain damage or worse. However, because they caught it so early, they would treat her with medicine and keep a close eye on it. "You're a lucky woman, Ms. Printh," Dr. Khatri concluded.

A couple of months later, with the adoption and the acquisition behind them, Ellie and Claire were residing at and running the newly-renamed Bernice's Tree Farm and Christmas Barn.

Ellie suggested the new name, and Claire clapped with approval. It was Claire's idea to add hot chocolate, cookies and sleigh rides to the Christmas tree selection experience. These embellishments made Bernice's Tree Farm a Christmas time destination and annual tradition for folks from as far away as New York, New Jersey, and Maryland.

Ellie created a program to provide free Christmas trees, stands, and decorations to families in need during the holiday season. When Ellie sent Santa and his helper to deliver the trees, Santa would ask the good girls and boys what they wanted for Christmas. And through the Ghost of Christmas Presents Foundation, which Ellie and Claire established, as many of those gifts as was reasonably possible were dropped off to the parents by Christmas Eve, so they could be placed under the tree in time to be opened on Christmas morning. Included with every delivery, just for good measure, was a Lite Brite set.

Ellie and Patty spoke on the phone almost every day after re-establishing their friendship. Then, about a year after Ellie's move, there was a sad death, just as the Ghost of Christmas Yet to Come had foretold. Patty's mother, Pea, passed away. A few months after that, Patty and Will Daniels sold their McMansion in Western Pennsylvania and moved to Lancaster County to be closer to their son Theodore and his young family, and, not so coincidentally, Ellie. Patty and Will were frequent visitors to the farmhouse and even enthusiastically helped out at the farm and shop on busy holiday weekends. And to Patty, who had made a complete recovery, Ellie did become the sister she never had. As dear and as close were they to each other as any "sisters from the same mister" could be.

The farmhouse became a second home for old friends and new acquaintances alike. Mary Lou and her nephew drove out often. Jimmy retired from The Printh Company and became the new handyman at the farm, and lived in a cottage on the grounds. He ate many of his dinners with Ellie and Claire and with other regulars and new friends who would drop in — no invitation necessary.

They were family now. As were Patty and Will Daniels, of course, and the other Poole relatives who would traverse the turnpike for a visit. David Burke, who regularly came for business meetings, would bring his new wife. Even Martha Fielder would occasionally make her way "out to the sticks" to check in.

Their home was the hangout for Claire's classmates from school, and Ellie made friends with the other parents and neighbors and Christmas Barn customers. And she and Claire, when setting the dinner table, always had room for one more, and then one more, and so on. Whoever was in the house at dinnertime had a place at the table.

They became that snowball Ellie had described, not just collecting nice people as they rolled, but attracting them. It was as if folks knew a special thing when they saw it coming and jumped in its path to be swooped up and carried along. Ellie and Claire were so selfless and welcoming that their circle grew and grew into an ever-increasing, incredible family.

Observant new visitors to the farmhouse would often inquire about a lonely picture that adorned the fireplace mantle. Ellie would explain that it was a picture of a woman named Bernice. She would tell the story of the heart transplant and the unbelievable coincidence that linked her and Claire.

Of course, dear reader, you have been made privy to much more of the story than any of Ellie's curious house guests.

But what you don't yet know is that Bernice's picture on the farmhouse mantle was the same photo and frame from Ellie's office. Ellie found it in one of the boxes she had packed herself for the move. The thing is, Ellie had no recollection of putting it in there. In fact, Ellie had never gone back to her office or to the desk in which the photo had been incarcerated. Nor had she asked for, or received, anything from her office, which had remained just as it was when she left there that Christmas Eve. It was unexplainable; yet there it was on the mantle, and Ellie was only too happy to display it because that seemed to be Bernice's wish.

Ellie lived another lifetime in her new attitude. Bernice's heart proved resilient and prolific, giving Ellie the time on this Earth to more than make up for the lost time she had imposed on herself. She had suspended her life when her dad died. In Claire, she now had someone to grow up with. And the two of them were inseparable through that string of millions of moments that make up lifetimes.

And so it was that Ellie and Claire made their own family, as real and as faithful and as tethered to each other by love and camaraderie as any blood relatives in any other family in this or any other world.

Every Christmas night, the farmhouse was lit up as brightly as Ellie's and Claire's first Christmas tree! All of their friends were invited, and they would come with their whole families. Patty would make a large pot of sauce and meatballs and enough cookies for everyone to have their fill and take a box home with them as well. Claire would teach the little kids how to play school on the stairs with a wadded-up piece of paper, just as Ellie had shown her, and just as Patty had shown Ellie all those years ago.

And invariably, it would get loud and crowded and uncomfortably warm in the house. And children would run hither and thither, and laughter would rise above the cacophony. And Ellie would love every minute of it.

On those Christmas nights when the farmhouse swelled with the burgeoning family, a particular acquaintance of Ellie's lingered outside, never announcing his arrival, only peering in windows and smiling at his friend. On those evenings, the visitor felt blessed by the Christmas cheer that radiated from the happy home, just as others had once been blessed by the bright emanations of his torch. Every Christmas, he found gathered there in convivial kindredship and wonderful unanimity, a family *"happy, grateful, pleased with one another, and contented with the time."*

May the same be truly said of us and all of us, at Christmastime and all the year round.

THE END

ABOUT THE AUTHOR

John C. Derr has waited 58 years to have an About the Author page. John is the author of *Another Christmas Carol*, which you are either holding in your hands right now or looking at online. If you have purchased this book, thank you! If you are reading this, trying to decide if the book is worth your time and money… well, it is. And, he could use the encouragement. John and his family call Lancaster, Pennsylvania home. Visit him online at www.johncderr.com or at facebook.com/johnderrauthor.

facebook.com/johnderrauthor

twitter.com/TheRealJohnDerr

instagram.com/johncderr

CPSIA information can be obtained
at www.ICGtesting.com
Printed in the USA
BVHW031423021221
623077BV00015B/783/J

9 781737 498803